LIKE IT NEVER HAPPENED

Emily Adrian

DIAL BOOKS
An Imprint of Penguin Group (USA) LLC

DIAL BOOKS
Published by the Penguin Group
Penguin Group (USA) LLC
375 Hudson Street
New York, New York 10014

Ⓟ

USA / Canada / UK / Ireland / Australia / New Zealand / India / South Africa / China

penguin.com

A Penguin Random House Company

Library of Congress Cataloging-in-Publication Data

Adrian, Emily.
Like it never happened / by Emily Adrian.   pages cm
Summary: As one of The Essential Five theater students at her alternative high
school, Rebecca Rivers is preparing to become an actress and enjoying junior year
with the perfect boyfriend until life-changing rumors threaten everything.
ISBN 978-0-525-42823-7 (hardcover)
[1. Theater—Fiction. 2. Interpersonal relations—Fiction. 3. Teacher-student
relationships—Fiction. 4. High schools—Fiction. 5. Schools—Fiction. 6. Family
life—Oregon—Fiction. 7. Portland (Or.)—Fiction.] I. Title.

PZ7.1.A27Lik 2015   [Fic]—dc23   2014019390

Manufactured in the United States of America

1 3 5 7 9 10 8 6 4 2

Designed by Mina Chung • Text set in Chapparel Pro

FOR DAN SCHILLINGER,
BEST FRIEND I'VE EVER HAD

LIKE IT

NEVER

HAPPENED

CHAPTER 1

IT WASN'T LIKE HE BEGGED ME TO SIT SHOTGUN IN HIS ancient station wagon. Mr. McFadden only offered me a ride home because I happened to be backstage looking for a taxidermied puffin. Two weeks earlier, during curtain call for *The Seagull*, Mr. McFadden had placed the puffin in my arms instead of something normal, like roses. The whole audience had laughed. It was somehow funnier for being the wrong kind of bird.

Afterward I had been so excited for the cast party, I had forgotten to take it home. But now, on the last day of tenth grade, I wanted the puffin. As a souvenir.

Mr. McFadden was crouched behind his desk packing old props into boxes. He didn't hear me push through the stage doors.

"Have you seen my puffin?" I asked.

Startled, he toppled backward, which was strangely satisfying to watch. Running his hands through his hair, he sighed. "I was about to toss it with the rest of this stuff nobody has any use for." He set aside a broken typewriter and a tambourine and produced my puffin, half crushed.

"I have a use for it," I said.

Mr. McFadden stared at me clutching the dead bird to my chest and shook his head, like he didn't even want to know. He hoisted a box into his arms. "Help me carry these to the car and I'll give you a ride."

I hesitated. I was buzzing with that feeling you get exactly once per year, on the last day of school. In an hour I had to be home for my mother's birthday dinner and I wanted to walk with my friends. We were going to get Slurpees for the first time since January, when Charlie had calculated that we had spent a collective $588 on them since the start of the school year. To combat our addiction, we had sworn off Slurpees until summer.

"Unless you have something else you have to do." Mr. McFadden raised his eyebrows.

I opened my mouth to explain the situation, but stopped. Because wondering about Mr. McFadden's personal life was one of our favorite group activities. The Essential Five might forgive me for missing Slurpee day, but they would never forgive me for missing the opportunity to see inside our director's car. They would want to know everything—whether there was garbage on the floor, music on the stereo, evidence of a girlfriend or boyfriend. I zipped the puffin into my backpack, grabbed a box, and followed Mr. McFadden to the staff parking lot.

His car was faded red, except for one brown door, and probably older than I was. Maybe even older than my sister. Flattened Starbucks cups littered the floor, and one of those tree-shaped air fresheners hung from the mirror.

I buckled my seat belt and waited for the speakers to betray him. What if they played something awful, like Barbra Streisand, or Creed? Even more startling would be something truly good. In my sister's old room I had recently discovered an acoustic Nirvana album and realized that Kurt Cobain was not just for boys with bad taste in T-shirts. If Mr. McFadden listened to something as hauntingly good as acoustic Nirvana, I wouldn't even know what to think.

Only we weren't moving. Mr. McFadden looked pained and on the cusp of confession. He stayed quiet so long, my pulse started to race.

Finally he said, "You have to lift your butt up."

My cheeks promptly burst into flames. "What?"

My director took a deep breath. "When the car was designed in 1987, it came equipped with several innovative safety features, including the ignition's refusal to turn when the passenger seat is occupied, but the seat belt unbuckled."

"My seat belt is buckled," I pointed out.

He nodded. "Sometime in the last twenty-five years, the car got confused, and now it only knows that you're here. It can no longer sense that you are safely buckled."

I stared at him, wishing I could take this sort of thing in stride. "You've had the same car for twenty-five years?"

"It was my mother's car first."

I remained planted to the seat until he released a small sigh. "Everyone has to do it," he said.

As our director, Mr. McFadden was so sarcastic and short-tempered, he was like a character himself—one that happened to dominate every rehearsal of every play. But right now, he was approximately as awkward as any of my friends.

I lifted my butt off the seat. Mr. McFadden started the engine and threw the car into gear. "I would get it fixed," he said, turning onto Hawthorne Boulevard, "but my mechanic said it would cost more than the car is worth. You can sit down now."

I sank.

We drove ten blocks in silence. No music played, which was disappointing. I searched for something to say, but my brain was now incapable of processing anything besides *You have to lift your butt up.*

"So," he said, eventually, "are you excited to attend the Shining Stars Summer Camp for Performing Arts?"

I groaned. In February, Mr. McFadden had convinced me and Charlie to apply for jobs at a theater camp in eastern Oregon. It had seemed reasonable at the time—like a good, wholesome commitment on behalf of our future selves. But now that we were our future selves, I wished we could stay in the city with the rest of the Essential Five. As long as we were all together, it was easier to ignore the way my heart hammered every time Charlie came near me.

"I'm kind of nervous," I admitted.

"It will look good on your résumé," he said for the millionth time.

"Uh-huh. Special skills: changing sheets on bunk beds, late-night kitchen raids. Broadway will be so impressed."

He rolled his eyes. "I meant for college."

"Maybe I don't want to go to college." In my head, my mother gasped, causing me to remember her birthday. We were stopped at a red light. A sign in a convenience store window said FRESH-CUT FLOWERS.

"You can let me off here," I said abruptly.

"Do you live here?" asked Mr. McFadden.

"No, but I want to buy some flowers."

"Oh." He shrugged and slid into a parking space. "I don't mind waiting."

The store sold mostly instant noodles and cat litter, but by the cash register sat a bucket of fresh lavender. I grabbed a fistful. The flowers were cheap and ordinary, but I thought my mom might appreciate the gesture. She was a big fan of gestures.

The second I got back into the car, the smell of the lavender was very strong and I was suddenly self-conscious, like I was the thing that smelled.

"It's my mother's birthday," I explained.

"How old is she?" asked Mr. McFadden.

"Fifty-six," I said.

He looked surprised. "Really? Mine too."

"How old are you?" The question just kind of slipped out. Maybe because I was practically high on last-day-of-school euphoria.

Mr. McFadden's shoulders stiffened. I remembered that he was my teacher. "Sorry," I said. "Pretend I didn't ask that."

I didn't much care, anyway. He looked about thirty, but I'm bad with age.

CHAPTER 2

AT BICKFORD PARK ALTERNATIVE SCHOOL, YOU WEREN'T
allowed to go out for the plays until you were in tenth
grade. The rumor was that Mr. McFadden decided
instantly if he liked you or not. He would cast his favor-
ites in every show until graduation. But if you messed up,
that was it. You could still join debate team, or choir, or
the international club—which was actually just a bunch
of kids who liked pad Thai a lot. Honestly, if you couldn't
be a thespian, you were better off joining nothing at all.

We had become the Essential Five in September that
year, when we had auditioned for *The Crucible*. Mr. McFadden hadn't let us audition with material from the actual
play. Having to pick our own monologues had made the
whole process especially terrifying. Tim Li had gone first

and read the chapter from *Are You There God? It's Me, Margaret* in which Margaret finally gets her period. Of course it worked. It always works when boys do things like that.

Next had been Tess Dunham, pretending very hard not to know me, even though we had spent the first half of the summer together. She delivered one of the *Vagina Monologues,* which is the kind of thing you can maybe expect to get away with at Bickford Park if you ask permission. Tess did not ask permission. Watching her pretend to have an orgasm onstage was like watching a car crash. I wanted to look away but I couldn't and I kept thinking, *I hope that never happens to me.* Mr. McFadden gave her a standing ovation before he sent her to Principal Gladstone's office.

I knew she would get in. I was trying not to think about it.

Up next were Liane Gallagher and Charlie Lamb. Like Tess and me, they had a history, only everybody knew about theirs. They had been best friends since they were little kids. Together they performed a scene between Ophelia and Hamlet. At practically six feet tall, with curly hair and a nose ring, Liane *was* Ophelia. She had clearly considered what it would feel like if your boyfriend went crazy and demanded you get yourself to a nunnery. Charlie, who was so attractive he almost wasn't, made an appealing Hamlet. It was hard to ignore his perfect bottom lip quivering as he threatened to give Liane a plague for her dowry. When they finished the scene, Mr. McFadden said, "Classic. Ambitious. You're both in."

I was so nervous I felt like I had just stepped out of a cold shower. I tended to keep a low profile at Bickford Park on account of some unflattering rumors that had flared up in seventh grade and still hadn't been completely extinguished. As I took the stage I braced myself for whispers or a single anonymous catcall. For once, only the lights buzzed.

I performed the part from *Breakfast at Tiffany's* in which Holly Golightly explains why she doesn't have any furniture. In a way, it was a risky choice. Stage directors have a tendency to roll their eyes at the entire film industry. But I knew I made a good Holly Golightly—almost as good as Audrey Hepburn, if nowhere near as gorgeous. And onstage my nervousness vanished completely. I was fifteen in September and I had already been in twenty-three plays and one commercial. There was no way Mr. McFadden was going to deny me a part in *The Crucible*.

In the final minutes of class the next day, the secretary's voice had come crackling over the intercom. "The cast list for the fall play is now posted on the bulletin board outside the auditorium."

Charlie was in my class and he didn't wait for the bell to ring before scraping his chair across the floor and racing out of the room. Our teacher feigned an exasperated sigh, but also bit down a smile. Teachers loved Charlie. Teachers did not particularly love me, but I wasn't about to stay behind. Cramming my books into my bag, I chased after him.

"Yes!" Outside the auditorium doors, Charlie clasped his hands above his head. "Fuck yes!"

Looking over Charlie's shoulder at the cast list, I followed the dotted line from *Rebecca Rivers* to *Abigail Williams*. I felt a smile stretch across my face. Mr. McFadden had given me the female lead.

Liane came running so fast she had to grab Charlie's arm as she skidded to a stop. She peered at the list as if it required some kind of translation. "Shit," she said finally. "I wanted to be Abigail."

By now the bell was ringing and Tess Dunham, moving like a newborn calf in her platform flip-flops, was shouting, "Am I in?"

My eyes flew to the list and located her name, just as Charlie shouted confirmation.

The bell stopped ringing and Tim joined our huddle. He performed an awkward victory dance, moving his hips a lot and his feet not at all. Other kids approached the list, nodded or sighed before drifting away. Charlie, Tim, Tess, Liane, and me had landed the five best parts in *The Crucible*.

None of us were total strangers to one another, but now we formed a cautious circle, acknowledging that we had devoted the next few months of our lives to the same cause.

"Great audition," said Tim to me, with a crackle of nerves. "I mean, you were really good."

Liane raised her eyebrows and Charlie crashed his hip against hers. "Why so pissed?" he asked.

"I've already memorized half of Abigail's lines," Liane admitted. She wore lace gloves with the fingers cut off. Heavy black curls framed her face and fell to her shoulders. She was the kind of person you wanted to stare at.

Charlie responded with a sly smile. "Well, Rebecca's had more experience than you."

I forced myself to keep a straight face. I did, as a matter of fact, have more experience than all of them. But Charlie wasn't talking about my twenty-three plays; he was talking about my one commercial.

Tim took the bait. "I see a donkey!" He tilted his face toward the ceiling, pretending to be watching clouds.

"I see an ice-cream cone," Liane deadpanned.

In that extra-high pitch boys use to imitate girls, Charlie delivered my infamous line: "I see overcast skies with a forty percent chance of precipitation!"

In the commercial, the camera then cut to a promotional shot of Sondra Wilson, Portland's favorite source for around-the-clock weather updates. Sondra looked approximately like I might look in thirty years, with the blessings of the Botox gods.

I splayed one hand across my face. Through the cracks between my fingers I could see Tess smiling vaguely. Months earlier she had mocked me mercilessly for that commercial, which had a tendency to appear between late-night TV programs.

"Tim's right, though." Charlie elbowed me. "You are really good. Even in that commercial it was clear you had talent."

I couldn't tell if he was being at all sincere.

"What?" Charlie smirked. "You don't believe me?"

"Is that what you want to do?" interrupted Liane. "Commercials?"

"No," I said slowly. "I did that because my dad's friend owns the station. I want to do stage."

Liane nodded kind of wistfully. "Me too."

"Rebecca has the perfect stage name," said Tim. He tested it out, bellowing, "*The Crucible* . . . starring Rebecca Rivers!"

"Look," said Liane, suddenly all business, "*The Crucible* is pretty intense. If we want this to be good, we're going to have to schedule extra rehearsal time."

Given that Mr. McFadden had already scheduled rehearsals from three to six, Monday through Friday, this seemed excessive.

"We can start by running lines at lunch," Liane continued.

"You mean like every day?" Tess frowned.

"Fine by me," said Tim. "I'm not exactly the BMOC." He rocked on the heels of his waterproof sandals.

"What?" Tess tilted her head.

"Big Man on Campus," Tim clarified. "It's not me. At this school, I am mostly reviled."

"That's because you wore the same pair of pants every day last year," said Charlie.

"It was a social experiment," said Tim.

"Yeah?" asked Charlie, intrigued. "What were you able to conclude?"

Tim paused, deep in thought. "That people don't socialize with you when you don't change your pants."

"Groundbreaking," said Liane. "So are we doing this?"

Charlie was quick to say, "Absolutely." He was no stranger to overachieving. Everyone knew he wanted to go to Harvard and then law school.

Tim stuck two thumbs in the air. Tess heaved a sigh, but mumbled her consent. Her gaze fell to the floor as everyone waited for my decision.

Technically, I didn't have anything better to do with my lunch periods. Since the first day of school, I had been eating with a group of kids I had known since junior high. My makeshift friends were nice, and had never mocked me for my misspent ten seconds of fame on the local news. They were also kind of hopelessly dull. But that wasn't really why I agreed.

The moment I looked Liane Gallagher in the eye and confirmed, "I'm in," her expression had relaxed into a look of respect. Instantly I wanted to agree with her on a hundred more things.

That was why.

CHAPTER 3

THE LAVENDER DIDN'T EXACTLY HAVE THE EFFECT I WAS hoping for. When I entered the kitchen holding the flowers by their stems, my mother looked at me like I was a cat with a mouse between my teeth. Granted, she often looked at me that way.

"Happy birthday," I said.

She resumed spraying the counter with disinfectant. "Did you pick those from Mrs. Almeida's yard?" she asked.

Mrs. Almeida was our ninety-year-old neighbor whose front yard sprouted weeds and stone cherubs in equal measure. I avoided her at all costs, partially because she was always wearing a nightie, and partially because she terrified me.

"No." I blocked my nose to avoid breathing the air,

humid with Lysol. "The guy at the Lucky Stars Mart might have, though."

Mom blinked at me. She didn't know the convenience stores by name. When she needed groceries, she drove to the Whole Foods downtown.

Suddenly it dawned on her that I was trying to be nice. Flashing me a sterile smile, she grabbed a vase from the top shelf. "Put them on the table," she said. "Your father insists on grilling chicken."

I knew it wasn't really the chicken my mother opposed—just the idea that old age was something to celebrate. In the dining room, I centered my pathetic FRESH CUT FLOWERS on the table, already set with crystal water glasses and cloth napkins. My mother would most likely decide she was allergic to lavender. Cheap things always made her break out in hives: bar soap, Hondas, et cetera.

Through the window I could see my father half shrouded in grill smoke and smiling to himself. He was wearing his KISS THE COOK apron, which my sister had given him at some point in the late nineties.

For the record, I didn't hate my parents or anything, but they were exhausting.

While we ate, Dad tried to compensate for Mom's misery by looking extra-happy as he chewed. I didn't even attempt to play along. Last year, when she turned fifty-five, I had made the mistake of listing the movie theaters and fast-food establishments where she could officially claim a senior citizen discount. It was supposed to be funny—because of how obviously she did not require a twenty-five-cent hash brown from McDonald's—but actually it caused her to burst into tears. Now I knew better.

The phone rang and Mom almost knocked over her chair trying to answer it in time. Dad lowered his chin and just barely shook his head.

"Only a telemarketer," Mom chirped, sitting back down.

My sister, Mary, lived in California and had a poor memory—at least when it came to important dates, phone numbers, and having once been born to a set of parents. Mary had been gone for most of my life, but my mother had never stopped anticipating her return.

"I don't see why they always have to bother us at dinner," said Dad, like he would have welcomed the interruption at breakfast. Briefly, my father's eyes met mine. My gaze promptly fell to the lavender leaning in all directions against the lip of the vase.

After dinner my mother served slices of gluten-free cake and Dad and I sang "Happy Birthday to You" terribly. Dad was tone-deaf. I could actually sing, but nobody performs an earnest version of "Happy Birthday" without feeling like an idiot.

My mother chewed her cake and stared glumly into the backyard, where leftover smoke distorted the view beyond the grill. With a sigh, my father let his face relax into its normal, comforting pile of wrinkles.

"How did you get home?" he asked me. Lately he had been asking all sorts of questions out of the blue. It made him seem very old. "Did you take the bus?"

My father's white eyebrows were raised in anticipation, his fork paused in midair. I sensed that telling the truth would result in more questions. Even though it hadn't felt at all wrong or daring, there was a big difference between getting into Mr. McFadden's car and telling my father about it.

"Yes," I lied. "I took the bus."

CHAPTER 4

FOR LONG STRETCHES OF THE SCHOOL YEAR, I HAD managed to forget that there was anything weird between me and Tess. Eventually some comment of hers would remind me of phase one of our friendship, and how badly it had gone, and I would feel overwhelmed by guilt. The rest of the Essential Five had no idea that Tess and I had ever spoken prior to auditions for *The Crucible*.

In truth, we had met at the end of ninth grade in health class. We had been watching an ancient film in which Richard Gere suffers from bipolar disorder. We were supposed to be keeping track of his highs and lows—like when he rides his motorcycle at top speed with his silver hair flying everywhere, versus when he says things like "I . . . I can't stop the sadness."

From across the aisle, Tess passed me a note: *Was it good?*

I looked at her warily. Normally when near-strangers passed me notes, they said something dirty.

To clarify, Tess pointed at my binder. Beneath the plastic I kept a playbill from *Grey Gardens,* which my parents had taken me to see at The Armory for my fifteenth birthday and which I absolutely loved. Eagerly, I scribbled: *It was amazing!*

And there, in the flickering light of Richard Gere's breakdown, our friendship commenced.

One thing Tess and I had in common, apart from our enthusiasm for theater, was a certain kind of reputation. Mine had been cemented in middle school, after an embarrassing incident that, to my peers, had counted as evidence of my sluthood. Tess's fame for sex was self-inflicted. She used the word *semen* more often than most people said *water* or *ChapStick.*

Naturally, it was tiring to always be hearing about the older guys Tess found loitering outside the clubs on Burnside, or the favors she granted her lab partner "just because." But her whorish tendencies could also be fun, like when we stayed up watching *Talk Sex with Sue Johanson,* a shockingly old lady who spent her hour of airtime arranging mannequins into undignified positions. I had never laughed that hard, about that kind of thing, with anyone. After enduring years of false accusations about the status of my virginity, Tess made me feel practically immune to embarrassment—like sex, in the end, was only a joke.

Our first friendship had lasted from the beginning of last June through the end of July, when her family invited me to spend a week at their house in Seaside. Afterward, I had spent the remainder of the summer trying to forget what had happened there.

The obvious thing would have been for Tess and me to never speak again, but then school started and we both got into *The Crucible*. I wasn't about to give up my part. So when Tess had pretended to meet me for the first time, I had just played along.

In September, Mr. McFadden had been prone to watching us rehearse with a half-dreamy, half-drunk look on his face. He always sat in the second row with his feet on the chair in front of him. Once, overcome with enthusiasm, he shouted, "Who are you people? Why aren't you hiding in closets weeping to The Smiths like the rest of your miserable peers?"

Broken-character grins stretched across our faces. Even though I had never really heard The Smiths, I screamed in response, "I danced for the devil!" Which happened to be my line, but which happened to feel like the truth.

Halfway through November, things changed. It had

been raining for weeks and the whole auditorium smelled like a wet dog. Mr. McFadden frowned in the middle of act two. His face stayed that way through Charlie's recitation of the first nine commandments—then he rose from his seat before Liane could deliver the tenth: adultery.

"Liane, darling."

Onstage, Liane and Charlie both froze. Mr. McFadden's tone was awful, like somebody's mother attempting to mask rage with a pet name.

"You are single-handedly rendering this production of Arthur Miller's masterpiece a farcical nightmare."

Liane, who was generally very stoic, panicked and turned to her costar. Charlie just nodded in agreement with Mr. McFadden. He had a tendency to suck up to teachers in a way that would have been completely intolerable, if he hadn't been so damn good-looking.

Liane squeaked an apology, which wasn't like her, and I winced at the sound. Backstage she tried to shrug it off, but she was clearly close to tears. She was a fantastic actress and there was likely nothing farcical about her performance. Mr. McFadden was probably just suffering from some adult problem, like divorce or migraines.

Before I could offer any comfort, Tess was taking Liane's face in her hands, saying, "Don't let that asshole piss on your fire. You are a beautiful actress and he is a bitter old homo with a two-year degree from Spokane's Premiere School of the Arts."

For the record: Mr. McFadden was not that old, not unhandsome, not necessarily gay.

Later that week, he requested Tim do something about his voice "crackling like a pubescent campfire." Tim's lips disappeared. Deep creases appeared between his eyebrows, but he bravely finished the scene. A number of uneventful rehearsals followed before Mr. McFadden cupped his hands around his mouth—this time to yell at Charlie.

"Charles Lamb! Can you loosen up? Your shoulders are as stiff as a homophobic gym teacher's."

Color spread from Charlie's cheeks to the tips of his ears. He looked like somebody experiencing humiliation for the very first time.

So many days would pass between attacks that we would wonder if we had finally won our director's approval. Of course, like any seasoned predator, that's when Mr. McFadden would strike. He described Tess's stage presence as "Courtney Love, the later years." When Liane had a cold he told her to sit out until she "ceased to sound like a chain-smoking receptionist." To Charlie he said more than once, "This is not an episode of *Seventh Heaven*!" which none of us had even seen on account of this being the twenty-first century.

In response, we developed a ritual of consoling whom-
ever Mr. McFadden had victimized that day. We assured
Tim that the cracks in his voice were barely noticeable. We
fed Liane cherry-flavored lozenges and herbal tea. Charlie
declared that Courtney Love was a "hot mess," and Tess
returned the favor by calling Charlie "the Ryan Gosling of
the thespian troupe."

I told myself they weren't flirting so much as licking
each other's wounds.

"You guys ever notice the way Mr. McFadden looks at
Rebecca when she's onstage?" Charlie posed this question
on the school steps, after our first dress rehearsal for *The
Crucible*. It was early December and the night air was all
mist.

Tim clasped his hands and blinked rapidly, like a love-
struck cartoon.

"You are weirdly exempt from Mr. McFadden's wrath,"
said Liane.

"That's not true," I protested. "The other day he told me
I sound like a chimp when I sneeze."

"Yeah, when you sneeze," said Tess, "not when you act."

"How do you know it was a real sneeze?" I argued
lamely. "Maybe it was a performed sneeze."

Charlie's laugh always made him sound older, and

always made me want to attach my mouth to his. "Face it, Rivers." Charlie grinned at me. "You're Mr. McFadden's leading lady. You can do no wrong."

"Don't worry." Tim patted my shoulder blade. "We can forgive your raw talent."

Charlie stooped to whisper in my ear, "Tim speaks for himself."

Hopefully the color had faded from my cheeks by the time we stepped into the fluorescently lit 24-Hour Hotcake and Steak House. We stood in line to order milk shakes and hotcakes—plus steak for Tim, who claimed a gluten allergy—then squeezed into the coveted half-circle booth. Liane went to the jukebox for the purpose of changing Hoobastank to David Bowie. Some bearded men in construction hats stared at her butt, causing Charlie's eyebrows to furrow protectively.

I tried not to feel so jealous.

After devouring our food, we were all kind of sleepy. Tess leaned on Tim's shoulder. Liane took long, noisy slurps of her milk shake.

"Rebecca," said Charlie.

"Yeah?" We were sitting on opposite ends of the curved wooden bench.

"Why did you start acting?"

Tim grabbed the saltshaker and held it to my lips like a

microphone. I pushed it away and groaned. "Why did you start acting?"

"College applications," said Charlie. "I have to have diverse interests."

Liane rolled her eyes. "There's no time for diverse interests."

"Wrong," he said. "Tomorrow I'm volunteering at the homeless shelter on Burnside. Monday at lunch I'm welcoming the latest additions to the German Language Honor Society."

"Impressive," said Liane.

"*Schönen dank.*" Charlie licked syrup off his lip. "Rebecca?" he pried.

"It's embarrassing," I said.

"Why?" His stare was relentless.

I sighed. "So when I was little I was really shy. Like, I wouldn't talk to anyone except my sister."

"I didn't know you had a sister." Liane sounded almost offended.

"She's ten years older than me," I explained. "She lives in California and never comes home. But when I was a kid she was practically my whole world. I didn't really have any friends."

Charlie took this information in stride. The rest of them were slumped in a hotcake-induced stupor.

"Anyway," I continued, "when my sister was in tenth grade, she was in *A Midsummer Night's Dream* at Cleveland High. They needed a few younger kids to play fairies, and my parents forced me to do it. I think they thought it would help me to, like, break out of my shell."

"And?" Charlie asked.

I returned his stare. "I loved every minute of it."

His eyes went all crinkly. "Of course you did."

Liane was studying Charlie very intensely. "That's bullshit about your college applications," she announced. Her tone, as usual, was hard to read.

"Oh?" said Charlie.

To the rest of us, Liane explained, "When Charlie and I were little, we lived in the same apartment complex, and I used to write plays."

"Really?" I asked. "What about?"

Liane waved her hand. "Dumb stuff. The Oregon trail, Christmas miracles. But I used to hold auditions for the neighborhood kids, and since Charlie was my best friend—"

"*Was* your best friend?" Charlie interrupted.

Liane ignored him. "He took his auditions extraseriously. He didn't want anyone to accuse me of nepotism."

Embarrassingly, I had never actually had a best friend. Theater had taught me to love an audience—but ending up alone with another person could still make me nervous.

"Aw," said Tim. "You guys go so far back, you're practically related."

Charlie took a long drink of water. Liane appeared to be waiting for a cramp to pass.

Finally, Liane asked, "Tim, why did you start acting?" She was sitting perfectly straight in the wooden booth. Her flat-ironed hair was beginning to protest, curling near her temples. I was jealous of the bangles on her wrists and the metal rings on her fingers. I could never pull off stuff like that.

"Well!" said Tim brightly. "Last year in English, Ms. Kramer told me I have the best reading voice she has ever heard." He paused to let us grasp the magnitude of this compliment. "She made me read aloud from *The Odyssey* for like three days straight, then told me I probably have the stamina to record audiobooks if I want. Sounds awesome, right? I thought theater would be good practice."

"Awesome," Liane confirmed.

When it was Tess's turn to answer the question, she drawled, "I don't know if you guys have noticed, but I *really* enjoy being looked at."

I laughed with everybody else, because there was something about Tess and her deliberate sexiness that still appealed to me.

Then Charlie said, "Attention whore."

And Tess said, "I'm not the only whore among us."

She waggled her eyebrows at me. Of the five of us, only Tess ever joked about my old reputation, and I never knew how to react.

Charlie stood up from the table, tapping a fresh pack of American Spirits against his palm. "Anyone want a smoke?" he asked, nodding toward the parking lot.

Tess and Tim shook their heads. Biting her thumbnail, Liane stared at the syrup congealing on her plate.

"Rivers?" Charlie raised his eyebrows at me. Trying not to appear too eager, I followed him outside.

A cigarette was the last thing I wanted after so much food, but I took one anyway. At first we smoked in silence, exhaling toward Powell Boulevard. Charlie had that boyish, self-sufficient way of standing that made me feel unnecessary—until his lips curled into a smile.

"So if your parents hadn't forced you onstage, would you have discovered theater on your own?"

"Yes," I said immediately, no doubt in my mind. "Maybe it would have taken a couple more years, but yes. I love it more than anything."

Charlie stuck out his jaw and blew smoke at the sky. "I wish I felt that way."

"About theater?"

"About something."

"But you like acting," I said, as if to convince him. He gave me a funny look. "I mean, you don't really do it just for your college applications, do you?" I made myself look him in the eye.

A grin stretched across Charlie's face. He ground the remainder of his cigarette against the diner's brick exterior. "No, Rivers. Not *just* for my college applications."

I blushed, acknowledging what he meant—or what I thought he meant. Charlie was already holding open the door, letting damp air invade the hotcake house.

"Ready?" He cocked his head. I dropped my cigarette and followed him back to the half-circle booth, where our friends were inventing details about our director's personal life.

"Probably he lives in a fancy Pearl District condo," Tim speculated. "With a French bulldog named, like, Nicholas."

Charlie and I slid into place, eager to harp on a favorite subject.

I guess we were all fairly obsessed with Mr. McFadden, maybe because we knew nothing about him, while he knew practically everything about us. Backstage we never censored ourselves like we would have for a regular teacher. Our director was privy to Tess's sex obsession, to Charlie's constant bragging, and to Tim's tendency to sing in a high falsetto whenever he was bored. But Mr. McFadden never joined in, never offered any commentary of his own.

It hardly seemed fair of him, to hide so much.

Two nights later we opened *The Crucible* and it was almost flawless. An eleventh grader missed a cue, but Liane improvised such a smooth save, the audience probably didn't even notice. Backstage after curtain call we fell into a tangle of limbs. Liane said, "You were perfect," and pressed her lips against my cheek.

Charlie had his arms around my waist. I leaned back against him so I could look into Liane's eyes. "So were you," I said, stunned that I was even friends with such a beautiful person.

Breaking from the mob, Tim lifted Tess off the ground and spun her in a circle. Liane kicked off her colonial boots and threw one at Charlie, who caught it against his chest.

"That was amazing," we kept saying.

"Can we go back out there?"

"Can we do it every night?"

"Does anything else feel this good?"

"Let's form our own company."

"We could tour America."

"We could tour Europe."

"Is makeup melting all over my face?"

"Do you think they could tell I was sweating through my costume?"

"Did you hear me hiccup? I actually hiccupped."

"Mr. McFadden was crying."

"I've always wanted to make that asshole cry."

"He's such a good director."

"The best."

"Can we go back out there?"

Killing the chaos, Charlie lifted a notebook above his head. "Let's make a pact," he said.

We looked up from our various embraces.

"A pact?" Tim tilted his head.

"A pact," said Charlie, "to never date each other."

Most likely my eyes went wide.

"Why?" asked Tess. She lifted a lock of hair from her lipsticky mouth.

Charlie looked at me. Everyone followed his gaze. They waited for me to explain Charlie's perfect, terrible idea.

"Isn't it obvious?" My words drifted toward the ceiling. "It would ruin everything."

After a second of silence, Tim agreed.

"It's not worth the risk," added Liane.

Tess shrugged. "I didn't want to bone any of you anyway."

Since Charlie wanted to be a lawyer, he basically wrote the pact himself.

> We, the five essential members of the Thespian Troupe of Bickford Park Alternative School of the city of Portland, solemnly swear to never kiss, grope, fondle, lick, caress, court, woo, seduce, or otherwise date each other. Should any actor develop unseemly feelings for one of his/her four costars, he/she will sacrifice his/her desires for his/her love of the stage and for the collective artistic potential of Rebecca Rivers, Charlie Lamb, Tim Li, Tess Dunham, and Liane Gallagher. The foregoing pact is hereby consented to by the five essential members of the Thespian Troupe as evidenced by their signatures hereto.

I had still been wearing my costume, plus a week's worth of makeup, which somehow made it easier to sign my name.

CHAPTER 5

DURING MY MOTHER'S BIRTHDAY DINNER I ACCUMULATED seven text messages, all from Charlie, all insisting I call him immediately. Alone in my bedroom I waited for him to pick up, my heart racing unreasonably fast. I had seen Charlie every day since September, but something still shifted whenever we were alone—on the phone or in person. Sometimes it seemed clear that he shared my lawless feelings. And then I had to remember that outlawing those feelings had been his idea in the first place.

When he answered, he was infuriatingly nonchalant. "What's up, Rivers?"

"You sent me seven text messages."

"Not seven," he argued.

"Seven."

"Well, you missed Slurpee day."

"Mr. McFadden gave me a ride home," I explained.

"Seriously?" Charlie's voice rose to an unlikely octave. "Did you listen to the sound track from *Sweeney Todd*? Did he tell you your movements were too stiff, your delivery inaudible?"

"He acted really normal. But his car was shitty." I described the garbage on the floor and having to lift my butt up. I went ahead and claimed that Barbra Streisand *had* blared briefly from the stereo. It was satisfying to share even these exaggerated details about our director.

After a while, Charlie redirected the conversation. "So how many swimsuits are you bringing to the Shining Stars Summer Camp for Performing Arts? I don't want to suffer from that problem wherein I'm ready for a swim, but my shorts are already wet."

"It's theater camp," I said. "I don't know how much time we'll have for swimming."

"Little kids have short attention spans," argued Charlie. "I strongly advise you to bring, at minimum, your least conservative swimsuit. It will dry fast."

Speechless, I pressed my forehead against the window.

An ice-cream truck was stopped on the shoulder of Elliott Avenue.

"Are you worried about the pact getting broken?" asked Charlie casually.

"Excuse me?" I was alone in my room, but I felt my cheeks flare.

"Do you trust the three of them unsupervised all summer? If Liane doesn't wear down Tim, you-know-who will."

In the street, kids were lined up for Mister Softee, waving their money in the air. "Right," I managed, hope deflated. The idea of Liane needing to *wear down* anyone was laughable.

"Did you think I was talking about you and me?" Charlie asked innocently.

My heart was still pounding. "Nuh-uh."

"I guess I'll see you on the bus," said Charlie.

After we hung up, I watched Mister Softee serve the last ice-cream cone and shift into gear. I lowered myself to the floor and let my imagination slip briefly into dangerous territory: a lake at night, Charlie shirtless, me in my least conservative swimsuit. It took that stupid song crackling through Mister Softee's speakers to bring me back to reality.

Admittedly, I adored Charlie. Touching his skin—even by accident—was the best thing that happened on a regular basis. But most likely he only flirted with me because he knew he would never have to follow through.

The pact might have been Charlie's idea, but the rest of us had signed our names for a reason.

CHAPTER 6

AFTER CLOSING *THE CRUCIBLE* IN DECEMBER, WE HAD suffered two months of tenth grade without theater. Mr. McFadden had told us that the break between the fall and spring plays was a chance for us to catch up on school-work, which was nonsense. We spent half our nights that winter at the hotcake house, longing for new scripts. Finally we got to audition for *The Seagull* and Charlie and I were cast as Nina and Trigorin: Russian lovers. By then I was so crazy about Charlie, I didn't know if I wanted to rejoice or vomit at the prospect of kissing him onstage.

For the record, the kiss didn't break the pact. We had realized a long time ago that we would sometimes have to act out certain intimacies. Preserving the integrity of our performance was what the pact was all about. Kissing Charlie couldn't be wrong when I was Nina Mikhailovna

Zarechnaya and he was Boris Alexeyevich Trigorin. Like how movie stars can be married but still have sex on camera—because the lights are so hot and there are so many people looming over you that it's more akin to being at the dentist.

Progressive as our school was, Mr. McFadden probably would have gotten in trouble for directing daily make-out scenes between students. Apparently there's a fine line between Chekov and pornography—at least when everyone involved is sixteen and fairly desperate. Which is why we didn't rehearse the kiss until a week before opening night.

Backstage, Liane was helping me with my English paper. I had begged Mr. Walker for an extension and he had complained about the thespian troupe thinking ourselves immune to academic standards. Ironic, given that Charlie was responsible for raising our school's standards so damn high in the first place.

And now the same Charlie was shuffling toward us, looking mildly nauseated and also very cute in his green corduroy pants. I wanted to bite his bottom lip.

"We have to kiss this time," he said.

My whole body went numb. I did not want to bite his bottom lip, after all.

Liane said, "You do?" right as I said, "We do?"

I hadn't been expecting our mouths to touch until opening night. I was relying on my performance high to make it possible. It wouldn't be me up there; it would be Nina parting her lips for a brooding Russian author, the silence of the audience like the whole world holding its breath.

But I couldn't kiss Charlie in front of Mr. McFadden and the rest of the Essential Five. Not with my presently greasy hair, which Tess had tried to remedy with baby powder, and which now appeared to be molding.

I started praying for a power outage, or an after-hours fire drill.

"Mr. McFadden wants us to practice one time." Horrified, Charlie splayed his fingers across his face and pulled at his skin until I could see the reds of his eyes. "He has to make sure our angles are right."

"Our *angles*?" I said.

Liane bit down a smile. Charlie just stared at his feet. His shoes were the kind your mom makes you wear to a funeral, only they were adorably scuffed at the toes.

"Okay!" I passed my notebook to Liane. "Whatever! We will kiss. I mean, this was always going to happen. If we had a problem with it, we should have said something a long time ago. Tonight, next week—what's the difference?" A note of laughter came out like a bark.

Somehow, this insane speech cured Charlie of his fear. He smiled with just one corner of his perfect lips. His spine straightened.

"Calm down, Rivers." His eyes darted from me to Liane and back. "It's just pretend."

Hearing his cue, he turned and sauntered stageward. I hated him.

"Are you okay?" Liane's eyes were wide. "Can you do this?"

Panic tightened in my chest.

"Remember, you're a professional." Liane gripped my shoulders. "Acting is what you want to do with your life, right?"

I nodded, barely.

"And you've kissed people before, right?"

Liane's assumption was understandable. Based on my reputation, any of my peers would have guessed I had a range of bodily fluid–based skills. This was hardly the time to correct her. I nodded again.

"Good, this will be easy. No feelings involved. You'll be fine." Liane gave my shoulders a confident shake, like she actually believed what she was saying. Maybe she did.

Onstage, Charlie shouted my cue.

We delivered the lines we had practiced a hundred times. I, as Nina, declared I was abandoning my father for the love of theater. Charlie, as Trigorin, told me I was beautiful. He called me his darling. We promised to meet again in Moscow.

Charlie as Charlie radiated nervous heat.

I was in love with him. It was only my second kiss ever. I couldn't tell which was the bigger problem.

The script had described the embrace as prolonged, and my god, was it prolonged. Allegedly Mr. McFadden had directed Charlie to hold the pose for three seconds, but I would have sworn Charlie counted to thirty before unplugging his face from mine.

The curtain would have fallen, but this was only rehearsal.

"Uniquely unerotic," observed Mr. McFadden.

I had been terrified he would make us do it again. But our director had waved his hand and dismissed us. We had scurried offstage—Charlie with his cheeks burning, and me, with all my burning secrets.

CHAPTER 7

AT FIVE IN THE MORNING, A WEEK AFTER THE LAST day of school, my parents dropped me off in a church parking lot to catch the bus to the Shining Stars Summer Camp for Performing Arts. They were only mildly emotional about the whole thing, which I thought was weird. I had never left home for any real amount of time. After they abandoned me with my bulky duffel bag, I located Charlie in the crowd of soon-to-be-exiled Portland high schoolers. He was all clean and tan and caffeinated.

"Good morning, Rivers!" Charlie bounded up to me.

"Charlie." I could never call him by his last name. It sounded too much like a term of endearment.

He passed me his travel coffee cup. "Are you ready to

nurture young souls? To expose yourself to all the diversity of the world?"

Taking a sip, I winced. Charlie apparently drank his coffee black. "Excuse me?"

"Didn't you read the pamphlet?" He looked genuinely concerned.

"There's no way the pamphlet says that."

Charlie seized my shoulders. "Did you, or did you not, read the pamphlet?"

"I did not."

He feigned exasperation. "I need you to remember one thing, Rebecca. At the Shining Stars Summer Camp for Performing Arts, we value community over competition. Ensembles over starlets!"

I nodded earnestly.

"Our mission is to show these children the value of their authentic selves," Charlie continued.

"I thought it was theater camp," I said.

"It is."

A raincoated woman began shouting orders through a megaphone. A kid nearby put a finger to his lips and shushed us, like we were going to miss vital information regarding how to board a bus.

"So nobody's going to learn the value of their authentic

selves," I said. "They're going to learn the value of pretending to be somebody else." I thought this was pretty deep, for five in the morning anyway. Charlie half bowed, ushering me onto the bus.

"Why are you in such a good mood?" I asked. We chose seats toward the back.

"It's summer. No honor societies. No speeches. No tests. No volunteer hours. No rehearsing every single night."

I was a little surprised. Charlie did not normally admit the awfulness of his overachiever's schedule. "You're about to spend the entire summer with eight-year-olds," I pointed out.

"But I'm about to spend the next three hours sitting next to you." His knee crashed into mine.

The bus pulled out of the parking lot just as the sun was rising. On the highway it didn't take long to get out of the city, but the scenery wouldn't be terribly exciting until we got to the gorge, and even the gorge—with all of its looming cliffs and red rocks—was only as exciting as anything you've seen a thousand times. Most kids plugged into iPods or tried to sleep. For a while, Charlie attempted the same, leaning against my shoulder and closing his eyes. When I glanced down I could see the very top of his head, where his hair grew in a perfect spiral. He smelled like laundry soap and cinnamon gum—smells that made me ache in unmentionable places.

But Charlie had consumed about a pint of coffee. After a few minutes he gave up on sleep and demanded we play a game.

I hesitated. I had never really liked games.

"We will take turns saying things about ourselves, and then the other person has to guess whether the thing is true or false."

"Are you serious?" I had a pretty good idea of where this was going.

He nodded. "You first."

"I've never ridden a horse." It was the most benign truth I could think of.

"Given that you have participated in exactly one extra-curricular in your entire life, I'm guessing that's the truth."

I nodded. "Your turn."

"I've been to Sally's Club."

"No you haven't." Sally's was the oldest, dingiest strip club downtown.

"I really have. With some of the guys from my German class."

I stared at him, incredulous. "What did you do there?"

Charlie blinked innocently. "Enjoyed the dance stylings of Chastity and Sage. Charming women. A little past their prime."

I shook my head. I didn't believe him for a second, but if Charlie thought he could shock me so easily, he was wrong. "Fine. When Mr. McFadden gave me a ride home on the last day of school, he put his hand on my thigh."

Charlie's eyes widened. "False. Completely false."

I squeezed Charlie's leg to demonstrate.

"Please tell me you're lying," he begged.

"Yeah," I admitted, withdrawing my hand. "Didn't happen."

"I lost my virginity at last year's regional debate championship," said Charlie.

"False." I had seen the girls on the debate team, and they weren't Charlie's type. After a beat too long, I said, "I have romantic history with another member of the Essential Five."

My goal was to trick Charlie into talking about Liane. The two of them rarely referred to their lifelong friendship, which was starting to make me suspicious.

"Romantic history?" He raised an eyebrow. "What does that even mean?"

I shrugged. "It's up for interpretation."

"You're lying," Charlie concluded. "Tim's a little out of your league, and you don't seem like the type to—"

"To hook up with Liane?" I suggested.

Charlie's upper lip curled. "I was going to say, to get sexually disoriented."

Sitting on that bus with Charlie made me all kinds of disoriented. "So have *you* ever hooked up with Liane?" I asked, breaking every unspoken rule of the game.

Charlie flopped back against the seat, like the question amused and exhausted him in equal measure. "Liane Gallagher?" he stalled. "The coldhearted giantess?"

I rolled my eyes. Liane was beautiful, and he knew it.

"No." Charlie drew out the word, making it sound like a gift. He pressed his knee firmly against mine. "Liane and I are just friends. Always have been."

I stared out the window, trying to weigh the likelihood of this claim. The Columbia River was peppered with windsurfers, their sails like neon sharks rising from the water. I wanted to believe him.

Charlie put his hand on my thigh. "But Tim and I have shared the occasional vulnerable moment."

I grinned, relieved to be back in the game. "Liar," I said.

"How can you be sure?"

"Tim wouldn't break the pact."

"The pact." Charlie smiled distantly, as if I had invoked a joke from years ago.

* * *

Eventually our game fizzled out and we listened to music, sharing a pair of earbuds, until the bus finally turned down a gravel road. We passed a wooden sign shouting SHINING STARS! in chipped paint. Somebody opened a window and the air smelled different—clean and bottomless. We had traveled a long way, I realized. Even if summer turned out to be terrible, at least it wouldn't be a rerun of last summer.

"I've got one." Charlie powered off his iPod and pressed his temple against the seat back. His eyelashes were long, his face freckled and so close. "I liked kissing you."

He was talking about *The Seagull*. Contrary to our excruciating rehearsal, the kiss had felt perfectly natural in front of a real audience. The only problem was that during every performance—for about a second of our three-second embrace—I forgot all about being Nina kissing Trigorin. Very briefly, I was Rebecca kissing Charlie, and completely thrilled. The feeling vanished when the lights went down—two years passed between acts three and four; we had to change costumes fast—but I thought Liane was probably aware of it, somehow.

"False." I rolled my eyes, like it wasn't even possible.

"Yeah." He yawned. "No offense, you're gorgeous and everything, but it was still weird."

Gorgeous and everything.

"I've got one." I took a deep breath. "When Mr. McFadden made us kiss at rehearsal? That was my first kiss."

"Onstage?"

"Ever."

Charlie's lips parted. He blinked rapidly.

"Oh my god!" I shoved him. "I'm lying."

"I know that." He laughed nervously. "I didn't believe you."

"You totally believed me."

"No." The bus lumbered to a stop in a dusty parking lot. "It's obvious you've had some, uh, experience."

I decided not to ask what he meant by that.

From this angle, camp consisted of a lake, an old barn labeled MESS HALL, a tented area labeled STAGE, and a number of sinewy paths disappearing into the woods. Charlie would never have to know that my last lie had come dangerously close to the truth. Somehow he still believed the rumors about me.

Charlie was staring out the window. "Look at that lake," he said. "And look at those boats!"

"Yeah?"

He turned to me, all wide-eyed and reverent. "I thought it was theater camp."

"I guess there's other stuff too. Didn't you read the pamphlet?"

"Boats weren't in the pamphlet!"

Confused by his sudden enthusiasm, I followed Charlie off the bus. Our schedule allowed for an hour of "mingling" with the other counselors before orientation. On the wooden porch of the mess hall, adults in cargo shorts passed out name tags. Coolers were propped open to display shimmering cans of Diet Coke, attracting the majority of female counselors the moment they arrived.

It was hot. Dust disrupted by the bus hung in the air and coated my skin and I already felt disgusting. I turned to ask Charlie what we should do for an hour.

But he had vanished. Shielding my eyes from the sun, I located him standing in a circle of boys wearing elaborate sneakers. They looked like they had dressed for the gym and reached theater camp by mistake.

Abruptly, the boys shed their duffel bags and bounded toward the lake. As they ran, they yanked shirts over their heads, shoes off their feet. Charlie was the first to embrace the water—arms stretched in an arrow, shoulders curling and disappearing. He emerged hollering like a lunatic.

All around me, counselors formed loose circles, clutching backpack straps and sharing cabin assignments. I could have shuffled toward any group of kids. Instead, I kept staring at Charlie, his shoulders bobbing above the surface of the lake as he conversed with a complete stranger.

"This is the life, man!" bellowed the stranger.

Charlie made his voice extra low and gravelly. "Hell yes," he said. "This is it."

CHAPTER 8

"I'M NOT DOING THAT," SAID ANNELISE. SHE WAS wearing a bikini top, jean cutoffs, and those bulbous shoes designed for skateboarding. We had been acquainted for approximately two hours but my fear of her was increasing rapidly. She was twelve years old.

"I think you have to," I apologized. "I mean, it's what we're doing."

"Are you doing it?" She pursed her lips and crossed her arms over her chest. As cabin mates, zip-lining was our first team event. The threat of imminent death was supposed to help my campers bond. I watched a burly staff member strap a pigtailed girl into a harness and push her off the cliff. She went zooming over the ravine, screaming bloody murder.

"No," I said. "But it looks really fun."

"I'm not doing it unless you do it," said Annelise.

Courtney, Margaret, and Peyton nodded their heads in agreement. They appeared to have already bonded successfully. On the other side of the ravine, somebody pushed Pigtails back to us. The muscly guy—presumably one of those weird lifetime summer campers—caught her by her skinny waist. She looked like she was going to puke.

"Who's next?" The zip-line master shook the empty harness. Annelise pressed her small hands against my shoulder blades.

Incidentally, it's very embarrassing to have a grown man guide your legs through a harness, which resembled one of those swings for infants. For a moment he held me, suspended at the edge. "Ready?" He blew hot breath into my ear.

I made a noise, somewhere between a laugh and a dying gasp. The girls snickered. He pushed.

The speed kept me from dwelling on the troubling distance between my butt and the ground. Everything was a blur of green and a blast of dry summer air. On the other side, strange hands pushed back before I could catch my breath. Despite the circumstances, I tried to relish my final seconds of soaring in solitude.

I would not be alone again for a very long time.

*** *** ***

My responsibilities began every morning at six: I had to drag the girls from their bunk beds and herd them into the showers. Each girl was allotted two minutes beneath a trickle of lake water. At orientation I had been instructed to preach the practicality of the "triangle wash," a method that ignored some fairly important body parts. The first time I tried to advise my campers on which regions to scrub, they looked at me with such intense disdain that I never, ever mentioned the triangle wash again.

Surprisingly, the Shining Stars Summer Camp for Performing Arts was not very heavy on the performing arts aspect. In the mornings we attended a rotation of random activities. Either hiking, swimming, the care and keeping of horses, nature identification, or zip-lining.

Once I had proved that zip-lining didn't necessarily lead to death, my campers never wanted to do anything else. When forced to spend the morning identifying poison oak or brushing the knots out of horses' tails, they spoke longingly of zip-lining. On a hike, Annelise declared, "Next summer, I'm not going to acting camp. I'm going to zip-lining camp."

Courtney, Margaret, and Peyton agreed.

Before dinner, everyone assembled beneath a large canvas tent and that's when we ostensibly rehearsed for our production of *Seussical the Musical*. Really it was absolute chaos: hundreds of kids crowded together, reading from their scripts, shouting to be heard over the din. Periodically I would spot Charlie across the tent, and I had a tendency to forget all about my campers and stand frozen, watching him.

His chorus of eight-year-olds couldn't memorize the songs. When the verse lagged, Charlie belted out the lyrics, looking partly like a little boy himself and partly like somebody's dad. It was endearing, but it also made me nervous. At home Charlie was all about volunteer hours and extra-credit assignments and controlled, ironic smiles. Here, he was inexhaustibly peppy. By the end of the first week he had been named official camp troubadour. He conducted a fireside sing-along, balancing atop a log to strum an acoustic guitar.

Charlie's performance of "This Land Is Your Land" for some reason involved singing the second verse in a drunken Irish accent. Halfway through the song he toppled theatrically from the log and continued to play from the dirt, pretending to be wounded. I felt kind of embarrassed on his behalf. Apparently Camp Charlie had no shame.

When the flames died down, senior staff members escorted the campers to bed. Since it was Friday, the counselors were allotted a few hours of freedom. I made the mistake of following Charlie down to the lake. I had this insane idea that he might miss me, like I missed him.

I found him with his gang of brawny boys, lowering a faded red canoe into the water.

"Hey." I stood in the sand with my thumbs in my pockets. "What are you doing?"

Charlie barely glanced at me. "Midnight canoe races," he explained, no time to waste. His friends looked annoyed, like I was interrupting a long-standing tradition.

When I didn't leave immediately, Charlie sighed. "Two men per boat paddle as fast as is humanly possible. Tip your vessel and you lose. Last dry men win the game."

Only he said this so fast I could barely follow.

And, I mean, we had only been off duty for a few minutes. How had they already invented a sport?

Charlie was climbing into the helm of the canoe. Somebody handed him an oar, which he laid gently across his lap. "You're welcome to stay and watch." He looked at me like I was a younger sibling, completely unwanted.

So I left, the truth hitting me hard. Charlie was officially ditching me for these new people, who believed he was the wildest of the wild-boy counselors: the most hilarious, high-speed, hell of a cool guy.

How did they think he learned to play those corny

songs by ear? How did they think he knew so many Shake-spearian insults?

Years of hard work and indoor activities, that was how.

Charlie had abandoned me. He was actually going to make me fend for myself at the Shining Stars Summer Camp for Performing Arts.

I should have known.

CHAPTER 9

THIS WAS A TYPICAL CONVERSATION BETWEEN MY twelve-year-old campers after dark:

Peyton: You're such a prude, Annelise.

Annelise: [*defensively*] Excuse me, I've kissed three different boys.

Courtney: With tongue or without?

Annelise: With one time, twice without.

Margaret: [*timidly*] What's better?

Annelise: If I say with, will you call me a slut?

Peyton: [*assertively*] I will.

Courtney: Three boys is nothing. I've kissed more.

Peyton: Rebecca, how many boys have you kissed?

Rebecca: [*silently wishes for swift death*]

Courtney: Have you done it?

Margaret: Does it hurt?

Courtney: Are you still a virgin if you just, um . . .

Peyton: Oh, like, oh! My sister says yes, you're still a virgin.

Courtney: But isn't that, I mean, how do you breathe?

Margaret: Yeah, Rebecca, how do you breathe?

Like I was some kind of expert.

This could go on for hours, individual voices flickering out until only Peyton and Annelise were still whispering and giggling, and generally being cruel to each other.

My status as a slut had been secured in the seventh grade.

The local news had just aired that stupid commercial, filmed over the summer, right before I gained twenty pounds in all the most suggestive places. Intrigued by my sudden fame, the most popular girls—Jenna Farley, Larissa Waxman, and Tina Vasquez—had invited me to the Pioneer Place Mall. I had been wary, understanding the invitation as a kind of tryout.

My mother, however, was beyond enthused; group shopping trips were the kind of thing she remembered from her well-spent youth. When Jenna and co pulled into our driveway, Mom peered approvingly at the Farleys' red convertible. "They must be from California!" she chirped.

This was back when my sister still lived in New York,

before my mother considered California the most sinister place on earth.

"How many bathrooms are in your house?" was the first thing Jenna's mother asked me, as I squeezed between Larissa and Tina in the backseat.

"Two," I said. And then, like an idiot, "Do you need to use the bathroom?"

"No," said Mrs. Farley firmly. "Just wondering how your family manages in such a small house, is all."

On the escalator, when we were free of adult supervision, Jenna announced the plan. "We're going to Victoria's Secret to buy thongs."

I felt Larissa's and Tina's eyes shift in my direction. Clearly they already knew about the plan.

"Why?" I asked. My underwear was usually cotton and full-sized.

"To know what they feel like," said Jenna. "So we're prepared for high school."

"The only thing is," Tina said cautiously, "I'm not sure I'm even allowed."

"Of course you're not *allowed*," said Jenna. "None of us are *allowed*. That's why we're not going to wear our thongs until the school sleepover."

The school sleepover was, for me, a massive source of anxiety. The teachers were billing it as a "mandatory girls-only evening of body positivity!" Meaning we had to wear our pajamas to school on a Saturday night, eat pizza off the gym floor, stop hating ourselves, and sleep on cots in the library. The sleeping part worried me the most. I didn't want anyone to draw on my face.

At Victoria's Secret, Jenna selected our thongs. For herself she picked plain and purple. She assigned polka dots to Larissa and nautical stripes to Tina. Of course, Jenna discovered my thong in the sales bin and, of course, it was leopard print.

As we left the store, pink bags hanging from our wrists, I attempted to make a joke. "So what *is* Victoria's secret?" I asked. "Like, do you think she killed a man?"

Jenna, Larissa, and Tina pretended not to hear me.

I stashed the leopard-print thong in the back of my drawer—behind old swimsuits and retired training bras—until the night of the school sleepover. On top of the thong I wore only a baggy pair of drawstring pajama pants.

At the sleepover, the guidance counselor explained to us that boys learn confidence through physical exertion and dominance—while girls are taught to hold still and take up as little space as possible, until we can hardly go down stairs without crumbling. Therefore, Mrs. Hoover somehow concluded, we needed to run a relay race.

The race required jumping rope and jumping jacks before climbing into a burlap sack and hopping to the finish line. I ended up racing against Jenna Farley. I almost won, but that's not the detail everyone remembered. Probably all of the hopping combined with the abrasion from the burlap sack loosened the drawstring of my pajama bottoms. When I pushed the sack to the floor, my pants fell down too.

Twelve-year-olds are not very creative, and could only interpret my leopard-print thong as evidence of my robust and indiscriminate sex life. Jenna Farley and co never spoke to me again.

The sleepover had been all girls, but ultimately it was the boys who took the slut rumor to heart—and who insisted it still applied, years after the incident. I wasn't sure how many people actually remembered the thong. Most likely, the anecdote had melted into a single hard fact. Like how we all knew that Charlie wanted to be a lawyer, or that Tim had a gluten allergy.

As a camp counselor, I realized quickly that modern-day twelve-year-olds were still obsessed with identifying the sluts and prudes among them. It was painful, listening to Peyton cast the other girls as she pleased. I wanted to tell her to knock it off, but I was supposed to be the adult—and from experience I knew adults usually let those things slide. Mostly I pulled my sleeping bag over my head and said nothing.

But after a few weeks of camp, my constant nearness passed for intimacy, and that's when my campers started dragging me into their dialogue.

"Which of the seventh-grade boys do you think is cutest?" asked Peyton from the bunk below mine.

"I don't think seventh-grade boys are cute," I said. "I'm sixteen."

"Yeah, but if you were our age, which one would you want to ask you out?" asked Courtney.

"I can't answer that."

Maybe I could have looked at the seventh-grade boys objectively and figured it out. But I preferred not to do that. They were always scratching at their mesh shorts and shouting the names of body parts.

"Okay," conceded Courtney. "Then which of the counselors do you think is cutest?"

In eerie unison, my campers chimed, "Char-lie!"

Camp had, unfortunately, only made Charlie more attractive. His skin had turned the color of milky coffee and his hair had grown into his eyes.

"He's one of my best friends," I said. "We do the school plays together."

"Have you ever kissed him?" asked Peyton.

"No."

Annelise, who was smarter than any twelve-year-old had the right to be, asked, "Have you ever kissed him *in a play*?"

An awkward silence ensued.

"That means yes," concluded Peyton.

While they lamented the lack of kissing in *Seussical the Musical*, I shoved my face into my stale pillow and mourned. Kissing Charlie was almost the last thing I wanted to remember. We hadn't spoken since the first Friday night of camp. Since then I had seen him periodically with a skinny, red-haired girl from Tacoma. At a campfire they sang a duet version of "Free Fallin'," awkwardly changing pronouns until the song didn't even make sense. Otherwise Charlie stuck to his loyal troupe of buzz-cut boys, messing around in canoes and calling everyone "bro."

"Rebecca!" shrieked Annelise. "Did you fall asleep or something?"

"No," I answered. Like it was even possible.

"Tell us how many boys you've kissed. Onstage or off. Doesn't matter."

"Shh. I'm sleeping."

The truth was that nobody had ever kissed me when it wasn't explicitly written into the script. Even last summer, the whole thing had been orchestrated not-so-masterfully by Tess. And it didn't even count, because after every kiss I had begged the boy to stop.

And that really was the last thing I wanted to remember.

CHAPTER 10

FOR REASONS NEVER MADE CLEAR, COUNSELORS WERE not permitted to make calls from anywhere but the public office phone, and we were not allowed to check our e-mail. At all. For eight weeks. Count this restriction among the things Mr. McFadden did not tell me about the Shining Stars Summer Camp for Performing Arts.

Toward the end of August, with less than two weeks to endure, the rumor of Dylan Larsen caught up to me. Dylan was employed by an online forum for some video game. His job was to comb the forum for fights and suspend gamers for violating the website's code of conduct. Somehow, Dylan convinced the office staff that his position was so essential to the well-being of the gaming community, he required an hour of Internet access each evening.

The point was that Dylan could allegedly be bribed into checking your e-mail and printing off anything important. Once the possibility entered my mind, I couldn't think about anything else.

At camp, I was something of a loner. Other counselors had managed to sort themselves into spontaneous, precious friendships, but I had been too busy fuming over Charlie to get with the program. I longed to hear from Liane, or Tim, or even Tess. I was desperate for confirmation that I had a real life untainted by the miseries of summer camp. Maybe, on some irrational level, I believed Charlie's regular self was still in Portland, studying for standardized tests that weren't even mandatory and writing me the occasional flirtatious e-mail.

So I approached Dylan Larsen in the mess hall, temporarily leaving my campers without supervision. Dylan sat hunched over a plate of oily scrambled eggs, displaying the easy calm of a man with Internet access. I tapped his shoulder. On a sticky note I had written:

rrivers@bickfordpark.edu
pw: diamondsforbreakfast

I figured I could change the password when I got home. Dylan Larsen glanced at the note before peering up at me through tiny John Lennon glasses. His gaze landed on my chest. I was wearing a black bra beneath a white tank top.

"No problem." Dylan took the note between two greasy fingers. His T-shirt bore the inexplicable phrase of 4CHAN.

Reportedly, kids had been offering Dylan everything from candy bars to blow jobs. I was stunned.

"I said it's no problem." He blinked at me.

"Seriously?"

"Yeah." His voice went syrupy cruel. "I'll read your personal e-mails for free."

Somehow, it hadn't occurred to me that I might not be the one benefiting from our arrangement. My mouth popped open and closed, but I thanked him anyway.

It was my night off, so after the sing-along I walked to the far side of the lake to swim. Swimming was one of the few things I did pretty well. I had learned from my sister a long time ago.

I swam aimless loops until I was out of breath, then hoisted myself onto a sagging, moss-covered dock. Lying flat on my back, with my toes dipped into the lake, I stared at the stars for a second. I guess I should have pondered their beauty and realized the rarity of a sky unsaturated by city lights, or something. But it occurred to me that you could probably see stars from the vast majority of the earth. It was the city lights that were actually rare.

I heard the boys laughing before I could make out their silhouettes, adrift in a canoe and coming closer. They must have wrapped up their idiotic games for the evening; I could hear beer cans hissing and see cigarette ends lighting up like fireflies. I had missed my chance to gather my clothes and slip away unnoticed. As quietly as possible, I lowered myself into the water and clung to the dock.

"That shit's not symmetrical."

It wasn't Charlie's voice. He never cared much about geometry.

"Which one was bigger?"

That was Charlie's voice. Apparently he cared a little.

After a long pause, the first kid said, "The left."

Almost everybody's left breast is bigger. We learned that in eighth grade, in the girls-only portion of health class. The news had been something of a relief.

"You know who I'd like to get with?" asked a third voice.

"Who?" The first.

"Rebecca Rivers."

I wasn't even surprised.

"Isn't she super-slutty?"

How had my reputation followed me to camp? Was it the white tank top, black bra thing? Was it something about my lower lip, roughly twice the size of the top one? Did I walk slutty? Talk slutty? Sneeze slutty? Sit in the mess hall eating my corn dogs and baked beans slutty? The label, which had been traumatizing when I was younger, was just getting annoying. Especially since I couldn't even seduce the boy I actually liked.

"Nah," said Charlie, spitting into the lake and sounding like a parody of boyness. "Rebecca goes to my school. That's just a rumor."

My heart skipped a beat.

"Really? Does she have a boyfriend?"

Like those were the options—rampant promiscuity or going steady. For a second, I missed Tess, who would have suggested we sneak through the water like torpedoes to dunk their boat, escaping into the woods as they mourned the loss of their smuggled Budweiser.

After a silence—during which I couldn't even guess Charlie's thoughts—he said, "Yeah, Rivers has a boyfriend."

"What's his name?" I could no longer distinguish between the other two voices. They sounded exactly the same.

"Stephen."

Which, incidentally, was Mr. McFadden's name. Was it just the first name that popped into Charlie's head?

"Well," said one of them. "Stephen's not exactly keeping his eye on her, is he?"

Definitely not.

The next night at dinner, Dylan Larsen silently dropped a handful of pages in my lap. Before I could thank him he had disappeared into the crowd—all the discretion of a drug dealer.

"What's that?" Peyton stretched out her skinny arm and I promptly sat on the pages. My middle school reflexes were still intact.

"Paperwork," I said.

My campers lost interest and turned to discussing the age of the guy who manned the zip-line. I figured it was safe to smooth the pages flat across my lap. The first few contained a thread between Tess, Tim, and Liane. They had actually copied me and Charlie on every message.

Dear Essentials—including Rebecca and Charlie,
who are technically useless until August but
who are always essential in our hearts, and

so shall receive every official piece of E5
correspondence—hotcake house? Tomorrow night?
Followed by *The Big Lebowski* at The Clinton
Street Theater?

Tim

I kept reading as my friends made plans and shared stories that hadn't included me, but now kind of did. In some of her e-mails, Liane begged me to confirm that I hadn't been eaten alive by mountain lions. She did not express the same concern over Charlie, which made me grin. My life would resume in a matter of days. All I had to do was survive a few performances of *Seussical the Musical* and learn to pretend that Charlie had, by no definition, broken my heart.

I did a double take when I got to the last message and realized it was from my sister. I didn't think Mary had my e-mail address, let alone anything to say to me.

Dear Rebecca,

I have abandoned a lot of people in my life.
(Just in case you thought you were special, rest
assured, you're not.) And for the most part, I
can't really go back and apologize. But you're

my sister, and we share approximately 99% of our DNA, which might mean that when I send you an e-mail, you at least have to read it? Maybe?

After I moved from New York to California I started going to therapy. Don't judge me. Just wait and see: You will be old, you will either be in New York or California, and you will spontaneously leave one for the other and start going to therapy. It's the hero's journey of the white, upper-middle-class, sexually confused, formerly rebellious child. Anyway, the therapist—who looked exactly like Maude from *Harold and Maude*—told me to write a letter to my teenage self, at the precise age I was when I first fell in love. But I couldn't write a letter to my teenage self, because it turns out you never really stop being your teenage self, so I wrote a letter to you instead.

Girls your age always think they will be rewarded for destroying themselves. And if that's what you believe, it's not your fault. But it also isn't true. And you probably have some calm friend you cling to—because she provides the peace that Mom can't, one of those "everything will be okay" faces—and you need her but you secretly think you're superior to her, because she is unromantic and never loses control. But seriously, Rebecca. Stop thinking your own wild heart gives you power over her. Consider the fact that she is stronger than you.

And if you have to destroy yourself—no matter what your aging sister says—if you have to give away what might otherwise be stolen, and abuse your body and your heart, please have an exit strategy. Your actions will never be reversible, but make sure they don't define your life, or prevent you from becoming who you're supposed to be.

Do you remember that night Nadine and I got home so late? (Do you even remember Nadine? It kills me to think you might not.) You were six, and I'm sure you didn't know what it meant to be messed up. But you knew that dilated pupils and weak knees did not equal your sister. Somehow, a ray of consciousness filtered through my private oblivion. I recognized you standing in the hall.

Nadine left me lying in a heap so she could tuck you into bed and convince you it had been a dream. Then of course she did the same for me. She was my anchor.

```
     Be kind to yours. That's all I wanted to say.

     And I swear to god, I barely know you but I
miss you so much. Do you think I'm crazy? I'm
99% sure you do.

                              Love,

                              Mary

                         (Your sister)
```

"I bet he has a girlfriend."

"I bet she's super-pretty. Prettier than Rebecca, even. He could have anyone he wanted."

"Rebecca, do I have to eat the carrots?"

The commotion of the mess hall swallowed my sister's voice.

"Three more bites," I said, because that's what somebody once said to me. I folded the pages and searched the cafeteria for the back of Dylan's head. It suddenly made sense that he had wanted to get away from me as fast as possible. My sister, who was a bona fide lunatic, had written to me like I was one too.

Somehow the e-mail managed to embarrass me, and fill me with guilt, and make me want to roll my eyes all at the same time. For one thing, I didn't need Mary's warnings. I might have been a certain kind of mess, but not like her. I wasn't on the verge of running away or cutting myself or snorting drugs, or whatever she was insinuating.

I forced myself to take a deep breath. Dylan Larsen was a stranger. In another week and a half, I would never have to see him again.

"Are you okay?" asked Peyton. On her plate, a single baby carrot had been nibbled three times.

"You're totally shaking," added Annelise.

"I'm fine."

"How old do you think the zip-line boy is?" asked Peyton.

She blew her bangs out of her eyes. She looked so hopeful, like a difference of one or two years might mean he was the perfect guy: A lifetime of harnesses and happiness awaited her. I felt an unlikely surge of affection.

"I would guess he's in his twenties." I reached across the table to steal one of her carrots.

She heaved a tragic sigh. "That figures."

After dinner we walked in a sloppy line toward the fire pit. The sing-alongs were so popular that they had become a nightly ritual. To me they felt designed to convince us of our inexhaustible love for camp. I guess it worked on most people—at least, my campers' cheeks turned pink and they sat with their arms laced, ankles crossed. Maybe it would have worked on me if things had been very different. For example, if Charlie had ever looked at me across the flames as he led the crowd in another round of "It Ain't Me Babe."

But he didn't.

I wanted to dismiss Mary's e-mail, exactly as you have to dismiss sappy birthday cards from your grandparents. And maybe I could have, if she hadn't mentioned Nadine. Because I did remember Nadine—but in these infuriatingly vague flashes, the way you remember a movie you haven't seen in years. Baggy jeans. A long braid against her spine. The two of them had their own scent when they were together—a sticky-sweet Christmas smell, which now I realized was definitely pot.

As far as I could remember, Nadine had always been nice to me, so I couldn't explain why her name triggered such a strong wave of anxiety.

I was sitting three feet from the fire—wedged between Peyton and Annelise—and my hands were turning cold.

On the final Friday night of camp, Charlie found me walking through the woods alone. I heard him before I saw him—a loud disruption of bushes and branches. Fearing some woodland animal, I upped my pace. I was wearing only a bikini top with my shorts because it was about a million degrees, so I felt fairly vulnerable to anything with claws.

When the source of the noise turned out to be Charlie, angry and panting and demanding, "So what'd you give him?" I wished for a mountain lion instead.

"What did I give *who*?" I asked, incredulous. Our camp troubadour wasn't so easygoing after all.

"Dylan Larsen."

"Nothing!" I shouted, relieved to be telling the truth.

"He says he printed your e-mails."

"He did!"

"Yeah, well, he didn't do it for free! That guy doesn't exactly do things out of the goodness of his heart. He's a troll."

I hesitated before succumbing to Charlie's insanity. "He's a what?"

Charlie embarked on the following rant:

"All that stuff about his moderating being essential to the well-being of the World of Warcraft community? Bullshit! He has two accounts: one as a moderator, and one as Doomclan94, which he uses to ask his enemies questions like, 'Why don't you idiot shamans ever battle rez?' Which everyone knows the shaman class isn't even capable of, so of course people get offended and start cursing, and then Dylan logs back in as moderator and suspends his opponents! Bam!"

I crossed my arms over my chest, wishing I had worn a shirt.

"He's a troll!" bellowed Charlie.

"What does this have to do with me?" I bellowed back.

"He won't tell any of us what you did! Every time somebody asks, the bastard gets all coy and acts like he's preserving your fucking honor!"

I looked up at the canopy of trees and swallowed my urge to laugh in his face. I had never seen him so upset. "Charles Lamb," I said, "you've been played."

Charlie inhaled deeply through his nose. "Pardon me?"

"I gave Dylan Larsen nothing. Absolutely nothing."

Charlie blinked. "So he—"

"Asked me for *nothing,* so that he could imply *everything.*" I was pretty proud of this analysis.

Charlie frowned at his sandals. "That's stupid," he said quietly.

I smiled and put my hands on my hips. "It worked on you."

"Troll," he whispered bitterly.

I turned and walked away. Beneath whatever amusement I felt at Charlie's expense simmered a summer's worth of rage. He didn't deserve my company. Not anymore.

"Rebecca." Charlie chased after me, planting a clammy hand on my arm. I threw him off as hard as I could.

"What business is it of yours whether I do Dylan Larsen, or anyone else, any favors? You've been pretending I don't even exist. You've been pretending *Charlie* doesn't even exist. It's like your body's been possessed by an imbecilic summer camp enthusiast who—"

Charlie was turning red from his cheeks to the tips of his ears, which were sticking out through his overgrown mop of hair.

"—doesn't even have a shred of interiority! Since when do you even play video games? The Charlie I know doesn't have time for video games! And, I mean, 'Free Fallin' by Tom Petty and the freaking Heartbreakers? I thought you loved Cat Power and Elliott Smith! Oh, and, *Tacoma*?"

I shouted that last part, like the city itself was a lewd act.

"Leave Madeline out of this," muttered Charlie.

"Like you left me out of your whole summer?" I was sweat-slicked, tear-slicked, kicking dirt at Charlie's perfect legs.

He averted his eyes, showing me the backslash of his cheekbone. "I'm sorry," he said, suddenly sounding sorrier than anyone had ever been. "I thought"—and his voice went deep and gravelly—"it would be fun or something to take a break—"

"From me?"

"From my whole life! From treating everything like it's my job! Hank told me I take myself way too seriously."

"Who the hell is Hank?" I asked.

"The guy in charge of the zip-line. He has an Xbox in his cabin. He's awesome."

I shook my head in disbelief. "I like you better when you're serious."

Charlie lowered his chin. "Serious like you?"

I had never thought of myself as serious. But serious sounded good, like it was Charlie and me against a non-serious world. "Yes," I whispered.

He stepped closer. Charlie put his hands on my waist, and I let him.

"You're not going to lick me, are you?"

He froze. His posture conveyed disgust. "Lick you?"

"The pact. Never to kiss, grope, lick . . ."

"Oh, that." He pressed against me. I felt his damp T-shirt on my skin. In that moment I could not remember if the pact was important or if it was more of a joke. I tried to weigh it against the urgency of his approaching lips.

"Did you ever think it was an elaborate scheme to get inside your pants?" His breath was hot.

"No," I answered honestly.

I thought of two things before I let Charlie Lamb kiss me.

I thought of my sister crawling into my bed when I was six years old. Her hair smelled sweet and smoky. She said, "Rebecca, I have discovered the reason for breathing."

And I thought of Mr. McFadden, shipping us both off to the most miserable excuse of a performing arts camp.

I would have to remember to thank him.

CHAPTER 11

CHARLIE AND I SAT TOGETHER ON THE BUS BACK TO Portland. None of his camp friends happened to be on our bus, but I think he would have sat with me anyway. He seemed somewhat relieved to have finally cut the act. Most counselors sobbed through their farewells, but Charlie doled out hugs with dry eyes. I guess it always feels good to go back to your real life—even if your real life requires playing classical guitar for the elderly, and sometimes retaking calculus exams because you got a ninety-eight percent.

I kept trying to find the words for the question I needed to ask him, which was something like, "What the hell are we going to tell our friends?" But I couldn't—partially because Charlie kept kissing me, and partially because I had no idea what I wanted. His lips were all loose and raw with something. Probably not love; it was too early for love. But with enthusiasm, and an obvious willingness.

As the bus lumbered down the highway, Charlie explored me with his hands. He rubbed circles on my back, and on my neck, and on the corner of my jaw. He dared to splay one hand across my stomach, so that his fingertips pushed against the underwire of my bra. Charlie's own skin was calloused from a summer-long affair with a canoe. If I closed my eyes, I could easily imagine he was somebody else, somebody older.

It was occurring to me that Charlie, as a person, wasn't exactly consistent. For our teachers at Bickford Park he was tirelessly studious; for the bros of summer he was all noise and sportsmanship; for his campers he played the clown. Still, our world onstage meant something to him. The Essential Five meant something to him. Maybe I didn't trust Charlie, entirely, but I trusted that part of him.

Now he was searching my back pocket. Paper crinkled. "What's this?" he whispered.

Damn. I had forgotten to throw out Mary's e-mail.

What really bothered me about it was the reference to my "wild heart." Like my sister knew me, just because I was sixteen and she had been sixteen once. Like because I was in high school it followed that I was deliberately cruel to everyone, and melodramatic, and prone to collapsing in hallways.

My sister was not a normal person. By the time she was fourteen she had thrown out all her clothes in favor of one oversized Joy Division T-shirt. By the time she was seventeen she had run away from home. As far as I could tell, she spent the in-between years sneaking out of windows and getting stoned and crying in the shower and screaming at our father.

When I closed my eyes I could still hear the pitch of her scream, the way you remember an ambulance's wail. Dad and Mary screamed at each other like howler monkeys, or like people on daytime television. I didn't know what they were fighting about. I guess it never occurred to me to ask. Even when they weren't making the windows rattle, the silence between them was loud. At the table in the mornings they braced themselves against their chairs, like they were just hoping to survive each other.

The night she left home, the screaming woke me up. I crept into the hall and watched them through the rungs of the banister. Mary was sobbing pathetically, like a child in the toy aisle of Target. Dad slapped her cheek and she cried harder. On his second attempt, Mom seized his wrist. "I will divorce you if you do that again," she said, so calm it was almost creepy.

I was seven.

Maybe my memory was not entirely accurate. For one thing, when I pictured the scene I saw hair cascading down Mary's back, but my sister never had long hair. It was always cut into a bob and parted down the middle, curls sticking up in odd directions. More importantly, our father wasn't the slapping kind. I had seen movies about abusive families. They had boats in their front yards, whereas our house bore a plaque from the National Register of Historic Places. We even hugged, sometimes.

I had overheard enough relatives describe Mary as a "troubled girl." But at seven years old, I couldn't have drawn the same conclusions I drew now—about substance and sex and downward spirals. As a kid, the most I could gather was that Mary was extra-charged. Something besides blood coursed through her veins and kept her heart beating fast.

After she ran away, she disappeared completely for a few years. I didn't know anything about it; the details were whispered far from my ears. But when I was ten she showed up unannounced, looking a little less grungy and—according to Dad—looking for money.

After that, Mary was around sometimes. Not often, and only about half the times she promised. But now we knew things about her life. At least enough so that when

Mom ran into people at the supermarket, she could pretend to be on speaking terms with her firstborn. Mary lived in Northern California. She worked as a waitress and was some kind of artist. Naturally.

As for her missing me, I didn't exactly grant her the right. My sister didn't know the first thing about me. We might have shared ninety-nine percent of our DNA, but who really cares, when that one percent clearly determines everything?

We had survived Mary and she had survived us.

"It's nothing," I told Charlie. I didn't want him to read Mary's e-mail. Either he would make fun of me for having a crazy sister or he would be attracted to her craziness. Either way, I didn't want him making the comparison.

Charlie might have heard things about me—people might talk in locker rooms—but from firsthand experience, he knew me strictly as a drama nerd, a director's pet.

Well, I guess now he knew me in one other way.

Lazily, as if by accident, his thumb slipped beneath the waistband of my shorts.

Charlie and I said sterile good-byes in the parking lot. We still hadn't discussed the issue of the broken pact.

"You'll call me later?" I asked, filthy duffel bag slung

over my shoulder. But Charlie was already jogging toward his parents' car, eager to resume his role as the perfect son, I imagined.

Sinking into my own father's arms, I was briefly, overwhelmingly happy to be home.

"Did they feed you?" Mom's brow furrowed as she reached for me. "You look awfully thin."

I was exactly the same size as always, but her concern was endearing.

Then I climbed into the backseat of the SUV, which still somehow smelled like a new car, even though it was approximately half my age. Dad started the engine, inched toward the road, remembered his turn signal, and batted my mother's hand away from the air conditioner controls. My eyes glazed over. I had been gone for practically the entire summer, but everything was the same.

We got stuck in traffic on Grand Street, right by the vacuum cleaner museum. I wasn't exactly well traveled—I had basically never left the West Coast—but I thought I might someday like to live in a city where there was no vacuum cleaner museum. It seemed like a reasonable goal.

My mother asked me a series of mundane questions about the girls in my cabin, and the types of food served in the mess hall, and our performance of *Seussical the Musical*. Abruptly, she turned in her seat with an "Oh!"

"What?" I asked, without lifting my head from the window.

"I ran into Hadley Clarke's mother at Whole Foods!" Like it was big news.

I barely knew Hadley Clarke, even though she had played small parts in both *The Crucible* and *The Seagull*. Outside of theater, Hadley belonged to a group of girls who wore vintage clothes and called each other *doll*. Unfortunately, our mothers had attended birthing classes together in the previous century and still maintained the belief that Hadley and I shared some kind of bond.

"Is Hadley the one with the inappropriate T-shirt?" asked my father.

"That's Tess," I said. For the record, the T-shirt said I ♥ MY VAGINA. Tess wore it constantly, on the grounds that it was a feminist thing.

My father went, "Hmmm."

Mom continued, "You know Tess. Her family took Rebecca to the beach last summer, before the girls had their little falling-out."

My father looked amused. "What did you fall out about?"

"Ask Mom," I said. "She seems to know everything."

"Oh, I don't know. Perhaps a boy?" Mom theorized.

I flopped back against my seat and groaned. It had been

over a year, but discussing the beach trip never appealed to me. "So what happened with Hadley Clarke's mother?" I asked, just to change the subject.

"Oh!" Mom switched back to her gossipy voice. "Well, according to Diane, Hadley thinks she has a shot at getting the lead this year."

"Why would she think that?" I asked.

"Well, why wouldn't she? She's got all that blond hair, and such pale skin. She's perfect for it."

"Perfect for what?" I practically spat.

"Blanche DuBois from *A Streetcar Named Desire*?" prodded my mother. "They announced the fall play in the school newsletter."

My mother had a habit of burying the lede. It provided her with some sick pleasure.

I commenced freaking out while she chuckled to herself. I didn't even know anything about *A Streetcar Named Desire*—except that it was another nonmusical, and something you might study in English class, just like all the plays Mr. McFadden chose.

"You don't think your director might want to give the part to a fresh face?" asked Mom.

"No," I said firmly. Although apparently the lead required blond hair. Maybe I could dye mine. Not playing Blanche was obviously not an option.

Sighing, Mom resumed fussing with the controls. Dad reached across the center console to lightly rest his hand on her thigh—and even though it was a completely perverse train of thought, I flashed back to the bus. For the last hour of the ride, Charlie had held me with his thumb pressed against the underside of my left breast.

For a second, I forgot all about the play and focused on the memory of that pressure.

Eventually I realized my father was staring at me in the mirror. "What?" I asked. I had been thinking about sex. Wondering if Charlie and I would be having it.

"We're happy you're home," he repeated. "The house felt too quiet without you."

CHAPTER 12

THE SUMMER BEFORE, WHEN TESS HAD FOUND OUT I was a virgin—despite our whole school's belief in my sexual prowess—she had at first been shocked and then determined to get rid of it. Like my virginity had been a rash, or a parking ticket—something simply cured or dismissed. I had only needed to appeal to the right person.

Her parents had invited me to spend a week at their house in Seaside, and Tess had sworn it was the perfect opportunity. I had made the mistake of questioning her logic: Why leave the city—which was theoretically swarming with beddable boys—for a town with a population of six thousand? My options would be reduced by one hundred times. Tess had rolled her eyes.

"The point is for the guy to be a stranger," she said. "You'll never have to see him again."

"And that's a good thing?" I asked.

Tess nodded sagely. "Trust me, you won't want to see him again."

"Why not?"

"Because it's going to be a disaster."

That made sense. When I thought realistically about having sex with a person, I couldn't imagine it being anything short of disastrous. Maybe if my first attempt was with a stranger, I would be better prepared to do it with a boy I actually liked. The first time would be like a dress rehearsal, only without any costumes.

But the coast was having a cold summer and Seaside was pretty dead. Toward the end of the week, when Tess had almost lost hope, we finally located some boys. Their names were Jason and Connor and they were loitering outside the sweet shop. They both had mouths full of saltwater taffy—Jason's with green apple, Connor's with tutti-frutti.

I thought you could probably tell a lot about a boy based on his preferred flavor of taffy. Tess stepped closer to Jason.

The four of us wandered down the main drag of Seaside, lined with dingy arcades and ice-cream parlors and stuff that was allegedly exciting to people a hundred years ago. Peering through the window of the Thingamajigs

Store was kind of like looking at old pictures of your parents—when your mom keeps insisting wooden clogs and red paisley dresses were the style, and you can't help but suspect she was kidding herself, even then.

The sun was high and the sky cloudless, but the wind kept biting at my neck. Outside of a clothing store, Connor felt up a mannequin. It was modeling a hoodie that said I'VE GOT SEASIDE SWAGGER. Jason hooted his approval so loudly the shopkeeper came outside to yell at us. The boys sprinted down the street, laughing like they had gotten away with something.

Riding the bumper cars was Tess's idea. She lifted her eyebrows as she made the suggestion, like bumper cars were common foreplay. We each gave four dollars to the boy at the gate. He was actually kind of cute, the gatekeeper. He had floppy hair and a mole like Marilyn Monroe's. I smiled at him as he helped me into a lime-green car.

We had the track to ourselves, because it was cold and hardly even fun. At first we just drifted around, Tess and I giggling self-consciously and the boys ramming into each other like goats. With a strange look on his face, Jason—who was supposed to like Tess best—crashed his car into mine as hard as he could. Then he looked at me expectantly, like how I reacted to the attack meant everything about what kind of girl I was. And I tried to be the right kind, by laughing and returning the crash with equal force.

"Ohhh," said Jason, in a this-means-war kind of way. His tone attracted Connor, and soon they were both slamming against me to a sound track of Tess's giggles. I attempted to maneuver my car away from theirs, inspiring them to back me into a corner. They took turns rear-ending me, shouting "We win!" and "Game over!" and other things boys take so seriously.

I could hear Tess getting annoyed. Nobody was paying any attention to her. "Come on, guys," she whined. "This is dumb."

It was in fact dumb, so I said, "Knock it off," and they did.

Bumper cars weren't so sexy after all.

On the sidewalk I reminded Tess we had to be back at the house for dinner. I was actually excited for dinner; we were having bouillabaisse.

Tess leaned close to Jason to whisper something in his ear, and whatever it was caused his eyebrows to leap and his lips to twist mischievously.

"What did you tell him?" I looked over my shoulder at the boys retreating, their heads ducked low.

"To meet us on the beach tonight," said Tess. "We're sneaking out."

The boys were likely already drunk when we arrived. They had built a campfire right on the sand and the flames were waist-high. The sky was black and the ocean, somehow, even darker.

Jason and Connor kept harping on a weird inside joke. It started when Jason touched Tess's hair and asked, "What kind of bird are you?"

"Huh?" Tess giggled. For someone who claimed to have once made out with David Bowie's nephew, she didn't seem that accustomed to having her hair touched.

"Probably a blue jay," said Connor.

Jason looked aghast and said, "Nuh-uh, pure robin."

Connor jerked his thumb in my direction. "This one's the robin."

"I can be a robin." Tess pouted. "They have pretty red chests."

Her cheeks burned; she had not meant to reference her own chest. Still, Jason couldn't hold out another second before attaching his lips to hers.

Perched on the end of a log, Connor was clutching a Heineken, staring at me like I was a poster on the wall of his science classroom, or his toothbrush. I sat down next to him—because what else was there to do, really? He slid his hand beneath my tank top, pressing against the small of my back. I had not realized that a stranger's hand against my skin could feel like such a good idea.

It was my first kiss ever and it was not good. Connor's mouth was all weak and wet and redundant. As we made out, my mind was occupied with the horrifying realization that kissing was terrible, it was humiliating.

It was mostly spit.

I wanted to revisit the simple pressure of his hand, which had felt so promising. But I couldn't think of a polite way to request he eject his tongue from my mouth, so I just kept going.

Jason unzipped his backpack to produce more Heineken. He held out a beer for me to take. I stared at the bottle glistening in the firelight, slick and green like kelp.

Abruptly, and without a word of explanation, I ran. I didn't slow down until I was over the grassy dunes and out of their sight. The road to Tess's house was gravel and, of course, I had left my shoes on the beach.

I managed to get inside and into bed without waking any of the Dunhams. About an hour later I heard Tess push through the window of the room next to mine.

Judging by the noise, she wasn't alone. It was fairly bold of her to bring Jason back to the house containing all of her sleeping relatives. But I was soon distracted by the door handle turning in my own room, the boy-shaped shadow appearing in the frame.

The door clicked into place behind him and he loomed wordlessly over my bed.

"Feeling better?" he asked, kneeling on the mattress. Connor wasn't wearing a shirt. It made no sense. The ocean was freezing. They couldn't have gone swimming.

"No." I raised my knees, defensive.

"I'll make you feel better," he said, simultaneously drunk and matter-of-fact.

"No." My fear was not the slow-creeping anxiety induced by horror movies. It was immediate and paralyzing. I was a rabbit, cornered. My heart beat in my throat.

I had this idea that I wouldn't be able to stop him. He had the advantage of size, and drunkenness. And probably Tess had promised him I wanted it.

His mouth tasted like metal and blood and something organic. I kept saying, "No," like even if it happened, at least it would happen to a sound track of no. I would never be able to convince myself I had said anything but no, the first time.

I said no to his hands on my thighs, and I said no when

he pulled my tank top straps down over my shoulders. I said it so many times that the word turned soft in the middle, like a tender piece of steak.

He grabbed the front of my pajama pants, and with a fistful of material he assessed the situation, which was nothing but cotton and elastic. I felt his smile grow against my neck, like the elastic meant yes. And I whispered my last no.

Thrusting my knee between his legs, I hissed, "If you don't get off me, I will scream so fucking loud."

There were a lot of people in that house: Tess's parents, her aunts and uncles and cousins and grown brothers. Connor respected the command, like a blade against his throat. He peeled his body from mine, never re-touching the places he vacated. He left through the window and I rose from the bed only to lock the door. It felt very important to lock that door.

Through the wall, I could hear Tess with Jason. I was still trying to determine if she was laughing or crying when I fell asleep. My brain shut down without warning, like the old computers in the school library. The next thing I knew—some number of minutes or hours later—the locked door was rattling. In my half consciousness, I saw Tess's face in the doorknob: two screws for her flooded eyes, a sad keyhole of a mouth.

Deep down, I knew it was wrong to feel so mad at her. I had never told Tess I didn't want to have sex. Before we met Jason and Connor, when sex was just an idea, it had seemed like a reasonable plan. Like a sure way of eliminating a painful moment in the future: me stuttering beneath a boy I liked, confessing, "My first time."

But I only liked Connor when he was an abstraction. Once I saw him with his flat-billed cap and those basketball shorts—which, from certain angles, revealed the contours of certain organs—I knew I couldn't sleep with him. The idea was kind of laughable, like doing it with a refrigerator.

Listening to Tess cry in the hallway, it had occurred to me that she was a virgin too. Or at least that she had been, moments earlier. And I should have felt sorry for her then, because I was okay and she wasn't—because I had changed my mind, and she couldn't. But instead I had fallen asleep, half believing her sobs belonged to my dreams. Later, after she had stopped speaking to me, I had wanted to blame my brain for malfunctioning.

Now I blamed my survival instincts.

CHAPTER 13

"ARE YOU AND CHARLIE STILL CLOSE FRIENDS?"

My mother attempted to ask this question very casually. I had been home from camp for approximately twenty-four hours. We were eating dinner on the patio.

I looked up from my plate. "Yup."

"Just good friends, or special friends?"

Charlie still hadn't called, but I had spent the last day thinking about his hand sliding down my shorts, so I guess he qualified as a special friend. I knew there was a chance Charlie would pretend we hadn't hooked up—and I knew that, in a way, it was our best option. I missed the Essential Five and did not particularly want to suffer the consequences of breaking the pact.

But my mother's professionally plucked eyebrows were

raised, all hopeful. It wasn't often that I had the opportunity to make her happy.

"Somewhat special," I answered, already cursing myself.

A grin stretched across her face. My mother looked thrilled, like until this moment she had fully expected me to die alone.

After dinner I walked toward Sixteenth Avenue, past sprinklers hissing and people drinking beers on porch steps. I lacked a clear plan. Guilt was threatening to displace the food in my stomach—but I didn't exactly intend to confess, and I didn't exactly intend to lie.

At Liane's house, a diminutive, sundress-clad version of Liane answered the door. The kid gave me a wide-eyed stare and said nothing.

"Uh." I peered into the house, hoping to be rescued. "I guess I'm looking for your sister."

Shrugging her bony shoulders, the kid said, "Liane's probably in her tree house."

"Yeah?"

"I was supposed to inherit the tree house." She sighed and kind of collapsed against the door frame. "But Liane's always in it."

"Where exactly is the tree house?" I asked.

Liane's sister gestured for me to follow her through the

living room, to a screen door off of the kitchen. An ancient tree took up most of the backyard, its roots warping the surrounding earth. Gracelessly I ascended the ladder and heaved myself into Liane's hideout.

She was hunched over, frantically trying to put out a cigarette. Jean shorts exposed her long legs and a new haircut emphasized the spherical tendency of her curls.

"Jesus!" she cried, relief washing over her face. "I thought you were Danielle."

'This is amazing," I said, looking around. "I've never been in a tree house." Beanbag chairs sat in each corner and two Coleman lanterns dangled from the ceiling. I stepped closer to a wall plastered with posters: Avril Lavigne, a shirtless man torn from the pages of *Cosmo*, a bear cub looking posed and pained.

"Middle school?" I summarized.

"Essentially," said Liane.

I sank beside her and issued a one-armed hug. "Hi."

"Hi." She squeezed me tight before producing a pack of cigarettes. "Want one?"

I accepted. Over the past year, my smoking skills had improved considerably. In the winter I had purchased a pack from the Lucky Stars Mart and practiced in the alley behind my house.

"So," said Liane, expertly harboring smoke in her lungs, "how was camp?" She emphasized each word, as if bracing herself.

"Awful," I said. "I'm going to have to shower for about a year straight to get the campfire smell out of my hair."

Liane lifted my braid and sniffed it. She wrinkled her nose.

"And whoever thought to make a musical out of the collected works of Dr. Seuss should maybe be arrested," I added.

Liane nodded knowingly. "Well, you didn't miss much here."

"Not true. I read your e-mails. I missed pancakes and movie nights."

"You missed pancakes and movie nights," Liane allowed. "But it wasn't really the same without you and Charlie."

Hearing his name kind of gutted me. Maybe I could tell Liane about us if I said it fast, like ripping off a Band-Aid. "Charlie and I—"

"He was weird, right?"

My heart pounded against my ribs. "What do you mean?"

"He's always weird around new people." Liane tapped

her cigarette. "It's like this tic he has. He becomes whatever they want him to be."

I remembered Charlie splashing into the lake, instant leader of the wild-boy counselors.

"When we were kids," she continued, "my parents let him come to our family reunion in Burns and Charlie spent the entire week sucking up to my cousins. He mastered *Magic: The Gathering* overnight, I swear. They still ask me about him."

I laughed a little and, taking a breath, told her all about Camp Charlie—how he had concealed the evidence of his overachieving, theater nerd self to become champion of the midnight canoe races.

"Yeah." Liane made her voice flat. "That's Charlie."

We sank into an awkward silence. I watched a buildup of ash fall from Liane's cigarette to the floorboards and I wondered if she suspected anything. Without even being here, Charlie had managed to dominate our conversation. I hated him for that.

"Of all my friends," said Liane evenly, "you are the only one who's been up here."

"Really?" I looked around, appreciative.

"Except for Charlie," she added.

"Charlie," I echoed.

"Not in years," she clarified.

"Oh." I tried to seem normal, like nothing about this conversation hurt me. "What was he like when he was younger?" I asked, hoping Liane would take the opportunity to assure me she had never, ever pined for him.

Liane shrugged. "Same as now. Exciting, exasperating. He was my first kiss."

Repressing a cough made my eyes leak.

"We were ten," she continued. "It was kind of a joke, or an experiment. We wanted to know what it felt like."

Wading deeper into the murkiest subject, I asked, "So, what did it feel like?"

"It was okay. It didn't feel like much. We were still little kids." Squinting at the ceiling, she spoke faster. "The weird thing is that I still get really jealous, like whenever he has a girlfriend, or tells me about hooking up with someone. I mean, I don't even want to be his girlfriend. I just don't want anybody else to be either."

I concentrated on smoking, taking increasingly deep breaths. There was a prickly sort of niceness to hearing someone else obsess over Charlie. Like it allowed me to take a break from the job.

"But we don't really *know* each other. Charlie might think he knows me, because there are pictures of us on the swing set together, and I once puked all over him at Oaks Park. But we've changed so much. He's been so intense about getting into Harvard. He used to be completely different."

"Different how?"

She didn't answer, but she shook out her shoulders and arms, as if to demonstrate a looser person.

"So what was it like for you?" she asked.

"What, my first kiss?"

"No." She smiled. "Kissing Charlie onstage."

Liquefying, I thought, combining that memory with more recent kisses: by the lake, and as we watched our campers take their bows, and for the last time on the bus. Out loud I said, "It was nothing. It was like kissing my hand."

"Huh." Liane ground her cigarette into a floorboard. Clearly she didn't believe me.

Tentatively, I asked, "Do you think you'll ever kiss Charlie again?"

She rolled her eyes. "He wouldn't kiss me again if his life depended on it."

"Why not?"

"Look at me." She fluttered her hand over her face, her body. "And look at him."

I had never been particularly versed in the language

of girls. I didn't really know if I was allowed to look her in the eye and say, "You're beautiful." Liane was a lot bigger than me. Meaning she had broad shoulders and wide hips. When she walked, she kept her spine perfectly straight.

"That's stupid," I said finally. "Charlie's not as hot as he thinks he is."

Of course, Charlie was precisely as hot as he suspected, but that wasn't the point. If my obsession with him was a disease, talking to Liane was the closest I'd found to a cure. Being with her put all former friendships into perspective—like they had been insurance plans against social destitution, nothing more. Liane was bold and careful and mysterious.

After a long silence, she said, "Hey, can I ask you something?"

"Sure." I steeled myself. If she asked me outright, *Did you hook up with Charlie?* I would tell the truth. Liane would have to determine the degree of my offense—whether I had broken the pact, or something more important.

"Do you have a problem with Tess?"

Not the question I had expected. For half a second, I hesitated. It might have felt good to admit that Tess and I had been friends before the Essential Five. At least one secret would be out in the open. Instead, I formed my most innocent face. "Of course not. Did she say I have a problem with her?"

"She might have said that you ignore her," admitted Liane.

"I like Tess," I said. "But sometimes she makes me uncomfortable. Like, I know that she enjoys being a seductress, or whatever—"

"She's *liberated*," said Liane.

"Well, when people call me *liberated*, I hate it."

"What's that about, anyway?" Liane and I had gone to different middle schools, and apparently nobody had told her about the incident.

"Oh, I wore a leopard-print thong to the seventh-grade sleepover."

Liane kind of choked. "Excuse me?"

"Jenna Farley thought I might be cool because I was on TV. She took me underwear shopping."

"And then . . ." Liane motioned for me to explain.

"My pants fell down."

She threw back her head and laughed. "Do you want to know a secret?" she asked.

"Yes," I said quickly. I would have paid money for her secrets.

"You're my favorite."

I felt a dumb smile stretch across my face and dimple my cheeks. "Blasphemy," I said.

Liane closed her lips around her cigarette. Her eyes drifted toward her middle school wall of shame. "Truth," she said.

CHAPTER 14

ON THE FIRST DAY OF SEPTEMBER I FOUND MY MOTHER in the dining room, hunched over a sheet of stationery. Sunlight seeped through the stained-glass window and fell in colored patches across the table. For a second I forgot that she routinely drove me crazy and I went to wrap my arms around her shoulders.

Mom stiffened before relaxing under my weight. I asked what she was doing.

"I'm looking over the guest list for the Labor Day barbecue."

I had forgotten about the Labor Day barbecue, which we hosted in our backyard every year, and which always turned my chronically sober parents into embarrassing, middle-aged party animals.

"Let me see." I moved to her side. She had invited all of the neighbors and all of her friends, plus Dad's old co-pilots from American Airlines. Toward the bottom of the list, Mom had written *Exclusive Five*.

I pointed. "What's this?"

"I thought you would want to invite your friends."

"We're the Essential Five, not the Exclusive Five."

"Oh." Mom frowned, like she wasn't sure if it was better to be exclusive or essential. "You want to invite them, don't you?"

Charlie still hadn't called, intent on pretending nothing had happened. My night with Liane had made it easier for me to play along, and for a second I considered inviting only her. The two of us could sneak shots of something into our Cokes and hide in my room.

Of course, that wasn't how the Essential Five operated. With theater starting up again, it seemed like I should follow the rules.

"Sure," I told my mother. "Invite my friends."

The night before the party, I left the house at dusk in pursuit of Rolos. Grocery shopping may have been my mother's favorite activity, but she always refused to buy chocolate lest she ruin her figure. For the record, Mom's was a totally normal fifty-six-year-old figure, perfectly capable of withstanding a few Rolos.

I smiled at the man behind the counter before squeezing into the narrow candy aisle. The door buzzed, but I didn't look up until I heard a familiar voice ask, "Could I get change for a five?"

His beard needed maintenance and he was wearing jean shorts, which surprised me for some reason. During the school year he stuck to slacks and blazers.

"Mr. McFadden!" I called, excited.

"Hello, Rebecca." He held out his palm to the cashier. "Good summer?"

"It was okay."

I was on the verge of asking him whether the role of Blanche DuBois truly required blond hair. I guess I was looking for some confirmation that he had me in mind for the lead. But Mr. McFadden was being weird, all fidgety, waiting for the cashier to make change.

"How was your summer?" I asked instead.

"Just fine, thanks." He was already backing up against the door. "See you next week, I assume?" He looked vacantly past my shoulder, like we barely knew each other.

"Uh-huh," I managed as he pushed through the doors. I watched him dart across Hawthorne Boulevard to catch an approaching bus. I wondered if his Toyota had finally bit the dust.

* * *

The next morning my mother burst into my room while I was still in bed. I had stayed up late watching TV and eating Rolos off my stomach.

"Rebecca!" she scolded, like there was something I should be doing with my life. "You've hardly gotten out of bed since you came home from that camp. Didn't you get any sleep there? It's almost noon. Why don't you call Charlie? There's plenty of time before the barbecue. I can give you some money to see a movie."

Harsh sunlight invaded the room. I squinted at the Forever 21 bag dangling from my mother's wrist. "What's that?"

"Oh!" She brightened, and from the bag she produced a lacey yellow dress. It had capped sleeves and a full skirt. "What do you think?" she asked.

"I don't know if it really screams *Linda Rivers*," I said.

"For you!" She ignored my sarcasm, hanging the dress on the back of the door. "For the party."

"Why would I dress up for the party?"

"Oh, Rebecca, it's really a casual dress. I just thought you might like something new to wear. I always like to buy myself something new when I'm about to see all my friends."

This was a common tactic of my mother's. She did not

seem to realize that my goal was not, in fact, to emulate all her habits.

"Okay," I said. "Thanks."

"So you will wear it?" She eyed me urgently.

"Probably not today. But sometime, sure."

"Rebecca!" she protested. "Don't you like it?"

"Yes, but all of my friends will be wearing jeans. Except for Tim, who will wear, like, boxers and a sweat-stained tank top."

My mother made a face like she had swallowed something rotten. "It's appropriate for the host to look a little dressier."

"I'm not the host. You are."

"Well, as the host, I request the pleasure of showing off my daughter at her best."

I didn't like where this was going. "Excuse me?"

Mom inhaled sharply and sat on the edge of my bed, much too close. "Honey, you've always been so serious. And you know we are very proud of you. You are a wonderful actress. But in the last year it's been such a pleasure to watch you blossom."

With that terrible and vaguely pubic word, I wanted to scream.

"Socially, I mean. Here you are with all your friends,

and your boyfriend, and you've turned into such a beautiful young woman. I just want everyone to see how far you've come."

She was blinking at me with this passive-aggressive smile. More than anything, I wanted her out of my room. "I'll wear the dress." I spoke through my clenched jaw, resigning myself to a night of ridicule.

Mom pressed her dry lips against my forehead. I could smell her sage-scented deodorant. She rose to leave, but paused with her hand on the door. "Tim won't really wear a tank top, will he?"

"I have no idea."

She faked a laugh. "Well, I suppose it doesn't matter, as long as Charlie looks respectable."

I let this sink in, before leaping out of bed and following her into the hall. "Mom, I have to tell you something."

She rummaged pointlessly through the linen closet, murmuring, "Hmmm," like she had suddenly lost all interest.

I took a deep breath. "Charlie and I are kind of a secret."

Slowly, she pivoted. "A secret?" She looked disgusted.

"It's possible we're nothing at all. But if we are something, it's definitely a secret."

"Why on earth would you keep your relationship with

that boy a secret?" She was disproportionately upset. "He's handsome, talented, his mother sounded sweet as could be on the telephone—"

"Despite the various charms of his mother," I interrupted, "it's complicated. We don't want our friends to think we're prioritizing our relationship over the thespian troupe."

"Rebecca, you're being ridiculous." Mom pushed at a stack of towels. Her efforts sent a basket of hoarded hotel toiletries falling to the floor. She glared at me. "You've been taking this acting business far too seriously for far too long," she continued. "Frankly, it's not normal for a girl to want to hide her boyfriend. You should be proud! This is a huge milestone!"

"Oh my god!" I erupted. "This is not your life!" I wanted to tell her to get her own. There had to be something she wanted to do, apart from obsess over my relationship status. Instead, I rattled, "Charlie is not officially or necessarily my boyfriend and you can't tell everyone he is."

Onstage, I loved the screaming and sobbing scenes. I had mastered a certain method of crying—my voice lifting attractively with each exclamation. But in real life, snot spilled from my nose and I struggled to breathe.

"Promise," I demanded.

"Promise what?" she sighed.

"That you won't say anything."

Behind her glasses, my mother rolled her eyes. "Okay, Rebecca, I promise."

I slammed the door of my bedroom. The message I texted to Charlie was straightforward, honest, and impossibly childish—basically everything he wasn't.

For the party I changed into the yellow dress and a pair of too-small heels. I wanted to prove that I, for one, could keep a promise.

Tess and Tim arrived together. Tim actually *was* wearing a tank top, but it was neither sweat-stained nor paired with boxers. The moment he saw me he bellowed my name—visibly startling the other guests—and squeezed me tight in his arms. Trapped against Tim's chest, I told Tess I liked her haircut. It was short and shaved above her ears.

"Nice dress," said Tim, pulling back.

"Very *Lolita*," agreed Tess.

"Excuse me?" I looked down at the yellow lace.

"It's the kind of dress you wear to seduce an old man," Tess clarified.

Across the patio, Charlie was presenting my father with a bottle of wine. Dad looked politely confused, unaccustomed to receiving alcohol-based gifts from children.

They shared a handshake before Charlie crossed the yard and joined our circle.

"Rebecca is in search of an old man to seduce," announced Tim.

Charlie didn't miss a beat. "How about over by the grill? It's like a mustache convention."

My father's friends were all retired air pilots. Their mustaches were permanent, the glue that held their faces together.

"Go ahead." Tess poked me. "Select your Humbert Humbert."

Charlie draped one arm over Tess, the other over Tim. He didn't exactly meet my eyes. "Where's Gallagher?" he asked.

The backyard was getting crowded. "I don't see her," I said.

"Who don't you see?" Liane came up behind me and slipped into our circle. She was stunning in a black-and-white-striped dress, her cheekbones glowing, hair untamable.

"Speak of the devil!" cried Tim.

"You're just in time to save Rebecca's innocence," said Charlie.

"That's funny." Liane turned to me, frowning slightly at my outfit. "I thought her innocence expired long ago."

"Same," said Tess.

"What is *Lolita* about, exactly?" asked Charlie.

I had missed this about the Essential Five—the way everything fell haphazardly into perfect order—but currently it was making me nervous.

"It's about pedophilia," Tess explained, "but also about desire and language and wanderlust and, like, America."

"Go America!" chanted my mother as awkwardly as possible. She was shuffling toward us, several friends in tow. The women clutched margaritas and peered at us with tight, lipsticked smiles.

"This is my daughter Rebecca!" Mom was using her tour guide voice, touching the top of my head like I was a prized rosebush. I could already tell she had been drinking. Not that I held it against her—probably my life would have been easier if Mom had been more of a drunk.

"And this is her boyfriend, Char-lie!"

Or maybe not.

Mom fondled Charlie's shoulder. Miraculously, he seemed unbothered. "Hello," said Charlie, shaking the hand of each completely indifferent woman. "It's nice to meet you all."

My mother flashed me a look that said "I told you so,"

and also "Aren't you a little drama queen?" and also "You can thank me later."

It was a lot of infuriating things for her to say at once. She attempted to drift away, but I stomped after her, my cheeks blazing.

"Are you kidding?" Panic cracked my voice.

"Oh, look at them! Nobody's even upset!" Mom whispered, before breaking from my grasp to assist Mrs. Almeida with the potato salad.

And, in fact, my friends did not look upset. Everyone except Liane was convulsing with laughter. Rolling her eyes, she beckoned me over.

"They already knew," Charlie explained, sliding his arm around my waist and pulling me close.

"What?" I backed away.

"He spent the last week of summer negotiating his way out of the pact," Tim said.

"He owes us," Liane said. "You both do."

I locked eyes with her, desperately trying to make sense of the timeline.

"But ultimately we couldn't really blame him," said Tess. "Camp sounded like torture and besides, you two are perfect for each other." She winked at me.

I looked at Charlie in disbelief. Camp was torture? On

the last night, he had won an award for being the Counselor Most Dedicated to Fun.

"You hate me?" he spoke into my ear.

"You wouldn't call me."

"I wanted to kiss you with a free conscience." He returned his arm to my waist, but he didn't kiss me.

"We have something for you." Liane directed this to Charlie. "Only we have to present it to you privately."

"Yes, privately," agreed Tess. "And we also need something to toast with."

She was swift, darting to the booze table and seizing a bottle of Jack Daniel's by the neck. "Nobody cares about the whiskey, do they?" Tess asked, climbing the steps to the back door. Stealing a glance at my parents, who were laughing uproariously beneath the plum trees, I led my friends upstairs to my bedroom.

They sank into a careful arrangement, as if we hung out in my room all the time. The girls sprawled across the bed, Charlie spun circles in my desk chair, and Tim perched on the wide windowsill. I hovered in the door frame, wondering what would happen next.

What happened was Tess uncorked the whiskey and took a swig straight from the bottle. Coughing and sneezing, she passed it to Liane, who was surprisingly more composed about the whole process. I wondered what would happen if my parents caught us. Presumably there was a rule against drinking hard liquor in my bedroom.

In the backyard, the party raged. An earnest U2 song replaced Carly Simon. If there was ever a night they wouldn't notice, this was it. When the bottle came my way I took a drink. Flames licked my chest, but it wasn't exactly a bad feeling.

Liane removed a folded sheet of paper from the pocket of her dress. She presented it to Charlie. "I haven't quite mastered the legalese," she said. "But I think I got the point across."

Charlie hummed to himself as he read over the note. Expressionless, he grabbed a pen off my desk and uncapped it with his teeth. "The deed to Rebecca?" he asked, scrawling something on the page.

"Every square inch of her," confirmed Tess.

"Use once and discard," said Tim.

I felt my eyes go wide with horror.

"The condom, that is."

I moved across the room to grab the note from Charlie, but he held it high above his head before passing it to Tess. Like the whiskey, the note made the rounds. I had to refrain from lunging like an idiot while everyone scribbled their names.

Finally, Liane dropped the page in my lap.

> Be it resolved that the five essential members
> of the Thespian Troupe of Bickford Park Alter-
> native School of the city of Portland shall amend
> their pact such that members "Rebecca Rivers" and
> "Charlie Lamb" are hereby authorized to perform
> the necessary acts associated with dating each
> other provided that these acts do not interfere
> with or compromise the collective artistic poten-
> tial of the Essential Five. The foregoing resolution
> is hereby consented to by the Essential Five as evi-
> denced by their signatures hereto.

I looked at Charlie, slumped in my desk chair. His lips
were twisted in amusement but his gaze rested somewhere on the carpet. Days ago, on the bus, I had wanted
to crawl inside his mind and see the scenery the way he
saw it. Now I wasn't sure I wanted anything to do with the
corners of Charlie Lamb's mind.

I tried to take a quick inventory of the ups and downs
of our friendship, or flirtation, or whatever it was.
The way he smiled at me outside of the hotcake house
last December: up. The way he ignored me all summer at camp: down. The way he kissed me on the ride

home: up, up, up. Followed by a long, confusing silence.

I kept trying to catch his eye, but he wouldn't actually look at me.

I signed my name. It was too late to do anything else. And besides, I told myself, maybe the pact had been the problem all along.

For a while our friends teased us. Tess wanted to know who had come on to whom. Tim asked, "Did you lock eyes across a crowded sing-along?" and Tess said, "No, I bet they were partners in a three-legged race."

"Hot," said Liane.

Tess asked if we used the top or bottom bunk.

Charlie, for his part, displayed the right amount of embarrassment and triumph on his perfectly proportioned face. But he also acted like I wasn't there, and I had to wonder why it felt so shitty to get exactly what I had always wanted. I guess I hadn't imagined it involving so much paperwork.

Liane kept reaching across the bed to reclaim the bottle. I watched her from the corner of my eye, looking for the moment she transformed from regular Liane to drunk Liane. But either I missed the moment, or there wasn't one.

Outside, the party was dying down. Somebody turned

Bruce Springsteen on full blast. Somebody turned the music off altogether.

When engines started rumbling in the street, my friends filed out of my bedroom and down the stairs. I lingered on the front porch while they went their separate ways. In the backyard, my parents slurred appreciation for their departing guests. My mother kept pushing left-over shrimp cocktail on people.

From behind, somebody draped her long arms around my neck. I smelled Liane's shampoo—the cheap, fruity stuff from Costco.

"Guesswha," she whispered in my ear.

"What?" I asked. I couldn't take my eyes off the street, where my boyfriend was saluting me good-bye.

"He told me first." She straightened her spine until she was a full head taller than me.

"Told you what?"

"That you kissed. That you . . ." She gestured with her hand, implying waves rolling, or some kind of sexual satisfaction I had never achieved.

"When?" I asked quietly.

"After," she confirmed. "He showed up at my tree house like twenty minutes after you left."

I looked at Liane in the porch light. Her jaw was tense,

her eyes glazed. There were a lot of things she could have said to me, and only one thing I owed her.

"I'm sorry," I said.

"It's fine." She shook her curls. "I mean, you tried to tell me."

"Not very hard."

"Not very hard," she allowed. "Good night."

"Can I walk you home?" was all I asked.

She dismissed my offer with a wave. "No thanks."

I watched her manage the porch steps one at a time. "We'll meet again in Moscow," she said, slurring a little so it sounded like "Moschow."

It was what my character said to Charlie's in *The Seagull*, right before our onstage kiss.

CHAPTER 15

SCHOOL STARTED AND MR. MCFADDEN ALLOWED THE FIVE of us to audition first, presumably so he could proceed to sleep through the sad attempts of the nonessentials. When it was Hadley Clarke's turn, she took the stage and clasped her hands behind her back, like somebody about to deliver her first book report. She wore vintage overalls and oversized glasses. The idea that Hadley and I had something in common just because our mothers had once coached each other through "deep, cleansing breaths" had never seemed more absurd.

"I would like to audition for the part of Blanche DuBois," said Hadley.

Total silence.

Mr. McFadden peered down the row of seats, where the five of us stared at Hadley in shock. "That's not how it works," he said, somewhat gently. "Everyone will get the role to which he or she is best suited."

"Right, I know the rules but I just wanted—" Hadley's voice wavered. "I just wanted to be clear about my intentions, and I—" She steadied herself and took a breath. "I intend to play Blanche DuBois."

Her eyes were focused on the back wall of the auditorium.

Mr. McFadden tapped his pen against his clipboard, clearly annoyed. "Please perform your selected material, Ms. Clarke."

I half expected Hadley to break the second cardinal rule of auditions: no material from the actual play. But she didn't. She performed the monologue from *Steel Magnolias* about how men are supposed to be made out of steel, but really it's women.

Afterward we filed out of the auditorium and stood in a circle on the steps. Liane was the first to comment on Hadley's transgression, saying, "That was so weird."

"Do you think she's trying to start an uprising?" Charlie asked.

"The revenge of the secondary characters," Tess warbled.

Tim nudged my shoe with his. "Do you and Hadley Clarke have some old score to settle?"

Everybody looked at me, I guess because Tim's idea would have made for an interesting story. But no; the bulk of my history with Hadley had occurred while we were both still in utero.

"Do you think she has a shot?" I asked, sounding more nervous than I really was. Physically, I was all wrong for the part. To blanch something means to drain it of color, and I was dark where Hadley was practically translucent. But I was also Mr. McFadden's favorite.

"No way," said Charlie.

Tess and Tim swept their heads back and forth. Even Liane put a comforting hand on my shoulder.

"Rest assured," she said. "The lead is yours."

On Saturday morning my mother burst into my room with a grave, "Rebecca, I have to tell you something."

I sat up and gave her my full attention. Because that's what you do when a person rouses you from the depths of sleep to inform you that your sister or somebody has died.

"Charlie is outside, and he brought yellow roses."

I gave my eyes a moment to focus on my mother's face, already caked with beige makeup at nine in the morning. Then I pulled the sheet over my head.

"It's okay," she said. "He probably doesn't know. Boys don't usually keep track of these things."

"Know *what*?" I groaned, unable to fathom why Charlie would think it appropriate to a) buy me flowers or b) deliver them at the crack of dawn.

"That yellow means friendship."

In my cocoon of sheets, everything was warm and cream-colored. I could pretend I had no unpredictable boyfriend and no melodramatic mother.

"He also brought doughnuts." She added an irritated sigh, like doughnuts were the nail in the coffin—the underline beneath *just friends*.

"Glazed or powdered?" I pulled the sheet away from my face. "Because glazed means *Marry me*, but powdered is more, *Join my cult*."

Handing me a hairbrush, my mother left the room.

Charlie was indeed on the front porch, smirking behind the bouquet. It was clear he meant the roses as some kind of joke, and not as an actual attempt to romance me. I went to put them in the kitchen and when I returned he handed me a doughnut—a maple bar garnished with bacon bits.

We sat on the steps, bare knees touching. Charlie didn't kiss me hello. We hadn't yet integrated kissing into our daily lives. If kissing wasn't the main event, it didn't happen at all.

"Why so early?" I asked between bites.

"I always wake up early." He sucked the sugar off his fingertips.

"Why?"

"Because otherwise there wouldn't be enough hours in the day."

Charlie and I didn't necessarily have a lot in common. Every time my head hit the pillow, I wondered why I had ever left my bed in the first place.

I could smell the soap on his skin. His T-shirt was perfectly white, perfectly unwrinkled, making me wish I had showered.

"Is that your bike?" I asked dumbly, referring to the one leaning against the porch.

"Yeah." He swallowed the last bite of his doughnut. "Go get yours. We'll ride to the waterfront."

"Don't have one," I said quickly.

Charlie stared.

"I mean, my sister's old one might still be in the garage, but I don't know how to ride it."

"How. Is. That. Possible?"

"One extracurricular, remember?"

"Riding a bike is not an extracurricular. It's like tying your shoes or brushing your teeth or putting bread into the toaster. A totally necessary survival skill."

I shrugged. Miraculously, I had survived sixteen years without mounting a bicycle. But Charlie was pulling me up from the porch. He righted his bike and patted the seat. "Get on."

"Nope." I had a strict policy against learning things in front of other people.

"Yup." Now he was tenderly stroking the seat.

I stood my ground.

"Afraid you can't do it?" he taunted. "Afraid of falling on your ass? Afraid that of the seven billion people on earth you are the one inherently incapable of riding a bicycle?"

"That won't work," I said, annoyed.

Charlie swung one leg over the bike. He stepped on a pedal and let the bike coast across the sidewalk, gently bumping over the curb. "Maybe you're wise to abstain," he said. "I mean, this takes talent." He pedaled in circles, barely yielding to a passing car. "Now that I look at you…" He crossed his arms over his chest, somehow managing to stay upright. "You've got the wrong build. Your body type just isn't conducive to cycling."

He zigzagged across the street, cocky and graceful.

"You're an asshole," I told him.

Charlie rested one foot on the ground so that he and his bike assumed the same quizzical posture. Matching his gaze, I went and seized the handlebars. Once he had relinquished the bike, I swung my leg over the frame and—like I had watched my sister do a million times—pushed off on the pedals.

Because the wheels were narrow and the street was wide—because I was dumb and the world was cruel—I promptly toppled over. I landed on my right side, still straddling the fallen contraption. Tiny pieces of asphalt were lodged in my flesh. Charlie folded in hysterical laughter, like my fall was the punch line he had planned.

I wanted to hurl the bike in his direction. I wanted to stomp inside the house and slam the door.

But I was sixteen years old. He was my first boyfriend. And I was still wondering, on a per-minute basis, what it would be like to sleep with him. So I walked back to the curb, wheeling the bike apologetically.

"Teach me," I said.

Charlie and I went into the alley where there wasn't any traffic, and for the next three hours we repeated the same exercise. I mounted the bicycle. He gripped the back of the seat and I pedaled forward, supported by the infallible physics of Charlie's feet on the ground. The problem was that he would eventually let go, and I would sail down the alley for approximately two seconds before gravity defeated me. The alley was littered with broken glass and bottle caps. By noon I was bleeding in three places.

"Every six-year-old can do this," Charlie said, losing patience.

"I know that!" I snapped. "Obviously you're a terrible teacher. If every six-year-old can do this *completely impossible* thing, then there is something you're not telling me!"

A flashback dropped me in our old Volkswagen, my teenage sister at the wheel. Dad was teaching her to drive stick. The car met almost twenty sputtering deaths before Mary erupted into sobs, screaming at Dad to tell her the secret.

"Just balance," said Charlie, pulling at his hair. "When you feel yourself falling, just don't fall."

I tried to keep a neutral face. I didn't want Charlie to see me realizing his total brilliance. He was correct; it had not occurred to me to balance—not really. To use my own weight against the force of gravity. That was the secret to riding a bike.

Wordlessly, I pushed off. When I felt myself falling, I balanced instead. It was like walking the elevated perimeter of the sandbox, or sliding down a railing. It was easy.

I wasn't so confident in my turning skills. At the end of the alley I dismounted and yanked the bike into position before pedaling back to Charlie.

"Thanks," I said coolly, returning the bike to his arms.

Grinning, he let the stupid thing fall to the pavement. It had taken so much abuse already. Charlie pulled me close and kissed me hard. I felt like I deserved that kiss more than I had ever deserved a kiss. All at once I forgave him for his coldness at school, the ironic flowers, and everything else.

"I have to go home and get some work done," he murmured.

I nodded. I wanted him to stay, but I also wanted to be a certain kind of girlfriend. Namely the kind who doesn't make demands—the kind you might describe as "low maintenance."

At home, a strange car was parked in the driveway, engine running. License plate with *California* written in that smug cursive.

A long, tanned leg emerged. She was wearing a pale pink sundress. She looked like a country club wife, which was approximately the last thing I had ever expected her to resemble.

"Rebecca." With one hand on her hip, my sister cocked her head. "Why are you bleeding?"

Charlie fled. His instant getaway put my new skills to shame. I guess that was the point of knowing how to ride a bike.

"Hi," I heard myself squeak.

"Why are you bleeding?" Mary repeated, like it was very disturbing to her. Like she had any way of knowing how unusual it was or wasn't for me to be bleeding on a Saturday morning. Her hair fell in loose, deliberate waves. A leather purse hung from one elbow and her eyeliner looked god-given.

"I fell off my boyfriend's bike."

We stared at each other. I cannot stress how much this woman did not look like my sister.

"About fifty times," I added.

"Were you riding down a staircase?" she asked.

"No." I gestured toward the door. Mary was really my parents' problem. "It was my first time."

She stood in place, frowning deeply. "You don't know how to ride a bike?"

"Can we go inside?" I asked.

She shrugged and obliged, clicking up the front steps and pushing through the front door like she did it every day of her life.

"Mooooom!" I bellowed in that helpless way.

My mother came running from the kitchen, wiping wet hands on her chinos, prepared for a yellow-rose-related crisis. When she saw Mary, her face went slack and froze that way.

Recovering, Mom pulled Mary into a hug. Mom's

shoulders relaxed and her eyes fluttered closed. She looked utterly content, like she had been doing nothing all morning except waiting for Mary. Like it was the most natural thing in the world for my sister—who had once gotten her tongue pierced on a school trip to Seattle—to show up dressed like a Kennedy.

My father wandered into the foyer holding the newspaper in front of his face.

"Mary is here," I announced.

He lowered the paper. "There she is," he confirmed.

After an unbearably awkward moment of silence, they hugged. Both of my parents turned to frown at me, lingering on the stairs. They wanted Mary and me to greet each other like sisters, but we had no idea how to do that.

"Well, would you like a drink?" asked Dad. "Or a snack? We have a fridge full of leftovers from the party."

"It's much too early for a drink, Glen," admonished my mother.

"Is it?" My father checked his watch. "So it is. Lunch then?"

"I'll whip us up some sandwiches." My mother clapped her hands together.

I followed Mom into the kitchen and watched her empty the fridge at an alarming pace. "Do we need anything from the store?" I whispered. "Maybe I should go out."

My mother looked up from the lettuce crisper, like strangling me was her deepest desire. "Or maybe," she hissed, "your sister is home for the first time in three years and you will get her some Perrier with lime and sit with her in the living room."

I got my sister some Perrier with lime and sat with her in the living room. I delivered the glass to her left hand, perfectly tanned save for a quarter-inch of pale flesh circling her ring finger.

Suddenly the whole thing made some amount of sense. She was married. Or engaged.

My father had taken a seat in his favorite chair, as far from Mary as possible. I had no choice but to sit beside her on the couch, leaving only a cushion of space between us.

"It's good to see you," said Dad belatedly, his gaze fixed on the ceiling fan. Mary smiled into her glass.

My father's watch was audibly counting each second. Outside, we could hear Mrs. Almeida watering her garden, even thought it was ninety percent cherubs.

"I learned how to ride a bike today," I announced.

My father flashed me a pained look, like I had burped without excusing myself. Abruptly he rose from his chair. "Linda probably needs my help," he declared. I watched him pad into the kitchen, one leg of his khakis tucked into his sock.

Alone with me, Mary breathed a sigh of relief, the opposite of how I felt. "Are they always this tense?" she asked.

"Uh." I inspected the hem of my shorts as if fascinated by the ripped material. "I think it has something to do with your unexpected presence."

When Mary giggled she sounded young. "Good point." She dipped her finger into her water and traced the lip of the glass. An old habit I remembered, one that used to get her into trouble at restaurants. "So that was your boyfriend?"

"Yes." I considered asking about her finger's tan line, but decided against it. I didn't necessarily share Mary's belief that we should have a heart-to-heart in however many minutes it took for our parents to return to the living room.

"How long have you been together?"

I paused. "Five days, technically."

"Technically?"

"There was a surprising amount of paperwork."

She giggled again. "Is he nice to you?"

It was a difficult question to answer. *Nice* wasn't a word people generally used to describe Charlie. More common would have been *brilliant* or *ambitious* or *improbably smooth*. But when he was nice to me, it meant more than if nice had been his default setting.

I nodded.

"Does he smoke cigarettes?"

Narrowing my eyes, I answered, "Sometimes."

"Good," she said. "Your first boyfriend should smoke some cigarettes."

On that note, Mom and Dad paraded into the room, each holding two plates of food. Lunch was distributed and then consumed in vast silence, punctuated only by Mom's squinty-eyed smiles in Mary's direction.

When Dad had swallowed his last bite, he wiped his fingers on his pants and cleared his throat, businesslike. "Well, Mary, what brings you to Portland this afternoon?"

Mary kicked off her shoes and pulled her legs onto the couch. "I'm visiting friends in Lake Oswego, so I thought I would drive down and say hello."

"Is anything wrong?" asked Dad. "Do you need help?"

"Oh Glen, does she look like she needs help?" snapped Mom.

Dad shrugged, like there was simply no way of knowing.

"I don't need help," Mary assured them.

"Something tells me you didn't drive all this way for leftover chicken salad," said Dad.

"You are welcome here anytime," added Mom. "And we hope you will stay the night."

Dad flashed Mom a look, like she was thwarting his game plan. I, for one, would prefer Mary not stay the night. This tension could not be sustained overnight. The air around us felt like glass, liable to shatter at any moment.

"I do have some news," Mary confessed. Finally.

My mother's eyes went outlandishly wide. I guess there are only a few pieces of news one's estranged child might have.

"I am getting married." My sister spoke with minimal emotion, but Mom's eyes filled instantly with tears. I expected her to smother Mary with affection, but for some reason she restrained herself, staying planted beside my father.

"To whom?" asked Dad. He had gone stiff.

"To Jeffrey," said Mary.

A look passed between my mother and father: some unspoken confirmation. Now Mom lunged at Mary, arms spread like wings.

"Who is Jeffrey?" asked Dad, once they had broken their embrace.

"My fiancé. We met at a party. I was working for the caterers."

"You're working for caterers?" Dad looked disturbed.

"I'm not anymore."

"Was this Jeffrey also serving food?" asked Dad.

"No, Dad," Mary sighed, sounding a lot like an annoyed daughter. "He was a guest at the party."

"What does Jeffrey do?"

"He's a very talented golfer."

"A professional golfer?"

"Yes, Jeffrey Cline."

My father made a face like he had just walked straight into a window. "You're getting married to Jeffrey Cline? Winner of three West Coast tours?"

For the record, my father was obsessed with golf. Jeffrey Cline was not a celebrity by any normal person's standards. Mary nodded, and then my father said something that made him sound extremely old:

"Well, I'll be damned."

A hush fell over the room. It was momentarily like being in church. From her purse, Mary produced a diamond ring the approximate size of a golf ball. My mother gasped theatrically.

"Whoa," I said, like a moron.

"I think it's time for champagne." My father stood and padded into the kitchen. To my surprise, he retrieved four glasses from the china cabinet and poured equal amounts of Dom Pérignon into each. I accepted mine without comment. Some screw had apparently come loose in my father's brain.

It was two in the afternoon when we toasted my sister and her golfer. My parents chanted, "To Mary and Jeff!"

I managed a "Yay."

"Jeffrey," corrected my sister. "He never goes by Jeff."

The tiny bubbles brushed against my lips and lingered on my tongue. I was developing something of a taste for alcohol. Admittedly this wasn't the best time to explore my new hobby, but when Dad offered, I accepted a second glass. The glasses were small anyway. Like the test tubes we used in science class.

Mom and Mary indulged in an airy conversation about dresses and flowers. Then Mom told the story of the Labor Day barbecue—how I had begged her not to expose my relationship with Charlie, how she had "accidentally" let it slip, how the joke was on me all along.

Amazingly, even a tiny amount of alcohol allowed me to laugh at this story. I wondered what a whole bunch could make me do.

Mom begged Mary to stay the night in her old room instead of driving the whole ten miles to Jeffrey's parents' house in Lake Oswego. With her cheeks flushed and her feet bare, Mary agreed. She stepped onto the porch to call her fiancé.

For a few minutes I was alone with my parents. It suddenly felt like I had never been alone with them in my life.

They turned to each other to acknowledge the events of the day and I felt like I was intruding on a private moment.

"She certainly seems happy," said my father.

My head was feeling strangely heavy. I let it fall back against the couch.

"Very happy," echoed my mother. "It's really much better this way."

Late that night, Mary knocked on my bedroom door. I let her inside. She was wearing a silk pajama set with a column of pearly buttons. She looked absurd, and my first idea was that she wanted to explain the weird e-mail she had sent me in August.

"Do you have a cigarette?" asked Mary, her eyes wide and urgent.

I started to shake my head, but then I remembered Charlie's jacket lying on the floor of my closet. I had borrowed it a few nights ago, when the temperature had dropped unexpectedly. I searched the pockets and found a pack of American Spirits, but no lighter. I left Mary alone in my room while I searched the hall closet for matches. It was strangely satisfying to supply my sister with her nicotine fix.

She leaned out the window to exhale. My muscles went taut with the possibility of getting in trouble. I had to remind myself that Mary was twenty-six: She was allowed to get engaged to middle-aged sportsmen and not come home for Christmas and smoke in my bedroom.

I sat cross-legged on the edge of the mattress. I was all ready for bed, wearing an old T-shirt and a pair of boxers. Mary stared moodily out at the street, her pajamas making her look like a vintage advertisement.

"So why did you . . ." I trailed off. What exactly did I want to know? Why did she assume my heart was wild? Why did it matter if I remembered Nadine? Why did she bother writing to me at all?

Mary was eyeing the taxidermied puffin perched atop my dresser. She pretended she hadn't heard me. "What's with the dead bird?" she asked.

I was on the verge of telling her the story, but then I changed my mind. I shook my head and the puffin became my secret.

She shrugged, the opposite of intrigued. Her eyes traveled around my room, making me very self-conscious. I remembered her own room in high school. The walls had been plastered with posters and pictures of her friends and her own paintings, the shelves crowded with ordinary things harboring mysterious value: empty bottles, dried leaves, rusted jewelry, cracked CD cases. Even as a little kid I had wanted to know what could be sacred about a receipt for two candy bars.

My room was plain, heaped with dirty clothes. The walls, once purple, had faded to a bruise color.

"I have to ask you something." She ground her cigarette against the windowsill. "Just answer honestly."

Finally, she was going to mention the e-mail.

"Do you smoke pot?" she asked.

A startled laugh escaped my throat.

"Just tell me." She spoke quickly. "Because if you don't smoke pot, there is something I need to do."

"I haven't tried it yet," I admitted, unwilling to commit to simply *not* smoking.

"One more question, then. Have you cleaned out your closet in the last ten years?"

My parents, for all of their tidiness, had always been secret hoarders. I had inherited their tendency to shove things into closets.

"Probably not." I sighed, irritated.

Mary crossed the room, tested the weight of the dresser, and climbed skillfully to the top. Her upper half disappeared inside the cavity of the closet; only her silk-clad legs remained in view. Stuff began falling from the shelves: mateless shoes, spiral notebooks. A stuffed dog landed on its stomach and began to sing, in a hauntingly mechanical voice, "Bingo was his name-o!"

Mary gave a cry of discovery. And then she tumbled to the carpet, clutching a small glass dragon to her chest. Mary sniffed the bowl-shaped end of the figurine—which now I realized was actually a pipe—and smiled.

"What. The. Hell?" I asked with Charlie-esque incredulity.

My sister shoved the pipe inside the breast pocket of her pajama top. "I was seventeen and they had developed this habit of obsessively searching my room every time I left the house. So I stashed my favorite pipe in here. Years later I woke up in the middle of the night and suddenly remembered I had left drug paraphernalia in your closet. I worried you would grow into the clean-cut kid you are, and Mom would decide to get rid of your baby clothes before the reality television producers came knocking, and in the process of cleaning your room would find it and assume you were a pothead and freak out accordingly."

I stared at her.

"I simply couldn't have that on my conscience," she added.

"What if I wasn't a clean-cut kid?" I challenged.

She shrugged. "I probably wouldn't have bothered. You would have to get caught for something, in that case."

I wanted to remind her that I had provided the cigarettes. I had consumed two glasses of champagne in the living room and suffered only a brief bout of hiccups in the process. Plus I had a boyfriend, and he wasn't even that nice.

"Can I have it?" I asked.

She looked surprised, but recovered quickly. "No way." She winked. "That's not what big sisters are for."

"What are they for?" I asked.

With one hand on the door, she considered this. "I guess you will have to wait and see." She leaned in to kiss my forehead, more like a mother than a sister.

She left me in her wake of perfume and cigarette smoke. She left me with the stuffed dog lying on the carpet, dismayed by its own resurrection.

Naturally I had observed that my sister was completely crazy.

But also, I noticed, Mary was completely in control.

CHAPTER 16

IN THE MORNING MY PARENTS TOOK MARY TO CAFÉ
Broder—which actually serves the most delicious breakfast the world has ever known—but I stayed in bed,
because I had started reading *A Streetcar Named Desire*
and I could not stop. It was completely different from the
plays we had done before. Meaning it was very intense.
Of course *The Crucible* was intense in a certain way; we
were always screaming, possessed by the devil. But it felt
like we were making fun of the way people used to be. *The
Seagull* was slightly more relevant to our lives, but nothing shocking ever happened onstage.

A Streetcar Named Desire is about a woman named
Blanche DuBois who shows up at her sister Stella's apartment in New Orleans and tries to convince Stella that her
husband, Stanley, is too poor and generally too violent
to be a good husband. Blanche herself is not particularly

sane—she's kind of a drunk, and prone to mental break-downs. But her excuse is that she was once married to a man who turned out to be gay, and who shot himself because of it. Afterward she became something of a slut, sleeping with everyone in her hometown, including a seventeen-year-old boy.

When Stanley finds out about Blanche's sordid past, he's upset that she was pretending to be so superior, calling him "brute" all the time. He's also tired of her hanging around their tiny apartment, hogging the bathroom and drinking all the booze. Things spiral out of control and toward the end Stanley attacks Blanche. The curtain falls.

I researched the play online and found out that he supposedly rapes her.

Afterward, Stella decides to believe her husband's word over her sister's, and they ship Blanche off to a mental hospital because she's completely insane by that point. Blanche's final line is delivered to the doctor who hauls her offstage: "I've always depended on the kindness of strangers."

Then the play ends.

Mary stuck her head into my bedroom to say good-bye before returning to Lake Oswego to be with her golfer.

"Aren't you going to get up?" she asked.

I was on the bed, holding my rolled-up script to my chest like a knife. "Eventually."

"Hey." She stepped into the room and shut the door behind her. She was wearing white pants and a yellow sweater, hair pulled into a smooth ponytail. She looked like a girl in a tampon commercial.

"Are you okay?" she asked.

I nodded. Having glimpsed the next few months of my life, I needed to be left the hell alone.

Mary dug around in her giant purse and produced the dragon-shaped pipe. She placed it on the mattress beside me, then backed away from her offering. "I changed my mind," she said. "You can have this."

"I'll probably never use it."

"Of course not."

I couldn't tell if she was making fun of me. Since my mother was prone to bursting in unannounced, I pushed the pipe beneath the covers. It was weird to think that it had been in my closet the whole time.

Retreating from the room, Mary pointed a finger at me. "I'll see you soon, okay?"

I grunted.

Downstairs, I heard Mom ask, "When do we get to meet this Jeffrey Cline?"

I didn't catch Mary's reply. Listening to my sister drive

away, I felt overwhelmed by the nauseating silence of Sunday afternoon, and also by fear. For the first time in my life I was terrified to play the lead.

On Monday morning, the Essential Five plus a small assembly of nonessentials waited outside the auditorium. None of us could really talk. It was like our real selves ceased to exist while we waited to be cast as new people. We couldn't interact before we knew our roles.

Minutes before the bell, Mr. McFadden appeared waving a sheet of paper above his head. He pressed the list into the cork and turned dramatically on his heel. He never stuck around to observe the damage.

I felt the usual kick of elation when I found our names at the top of the list.

- BLANCHE..................................... Rebecca Rivers
- STELLA..Liane Gallagher
- STANLEY.......................................Charlie Lamb
- MITCH..Tim Li
- EUNICE...Tess Dunham

Of the leftover roles, Hadley Clarke had been cast as the doctor, who only appears at the very end of the play. I could kind of feel her eyes boring into my back.

"You would have made a good Blanche," someone said to Hadley.

"I'll make a good doctor," Hadley asserted.

"Absofuckinglutely you will," said the same kid, clad in skinny jeans and a paisley button-down, who must have been Hadley's boyfriend. "This McFadden guy is totally blind to real talent. His decisions are all about nepotism."

"We're not his *children*," protested Tim.

"So then what are you?" challenged Hadley's boyfriend, draping a protective arm over her shoulder.

"The best," breathed Charlie. He was staring at the cast list, mouth stretched so wide I thought his face might crack. For days he had been talking about playing Stanley. The part involved a lot of cursing and swigging from bottles, which excited him.

"See?" said Liane to me. "I knew you were untouchable."

Tim and Tess were already drifting toward class. After patting me lamely on the shoulder, Liane jogged after them.

Charlie was grinning at me like a cartoon shark. "Well?" he said. "You think you can handle me playing another girl's husband?"

At first I was confused, and then horrified.

Because I had taken it for granted that Charlie would play Stanley, the male lead. But I had utterly failed to observe that if I starred as Blanche DuBois, somebody else had to play Stella, Stanley's devoted wife.

"Somebody else" happened to be Liane.

Before we could start rehearsing for *A Streetcar Named Desire*, we had to figure out what to do for the homecoming assembly. On Friday morning, each club would be required to demonstrate their special skills for the entire student body. Since the thespian troupe was technically a club, Mr. McFadden had put the five of us in charge.

We met backstage to discuss our options. Mr. McFadden was so upset about having to sacrifice rehearsal time for the "frivolous notion of school spirit" that he didn't really give us any guidance. He just sat at his desk, shuffling papers around.

Charlie insisted we perform a scene we already knew—like something from *The Seagull*—in order to save our energy for *Streetcar*. Tess, however, thought we should sing a song from *Hair*, the musical. Tim was enthusiastic about that idea because he was in one of those anti-haircut stages that boys go through. Every time one of us suggested something new, Mr. McFadden made a rude noise with his nasal passages. Eventually we agreed that this was hindering the whole process, so we seized our backpacks and left.

We wandered away from the school, halfheartedly throwing ideas around. Liane proposed that we refuse to participate altogether, but Charlie pointed out that the last thing we needed was to piss off the administration. Apparently they had been skeptical of Mr. McFadden's selection for the fall play, thinking *Streetcar* "too mature" for a teenage cast. Our director had written this whole letter in our defense, citing our reverence for the stage and his obligation to prepare us for our future careers, "not with the tap dances and painted-on smiles of a family friendly musical—but with Mr. Williams's prize-winning tale of deceit and delusion."

We were walking on Division Street, which was just south of our school and always made me feel like I didn't actually live in a big city. The apartment buildings were all worn out, interspersed with dive bars and auto shops. The problem with Portland was that, no matter how inner-city you got, you were still in Oregon.

"You know what would be funny?" said Tess. She was balancing on the curb, holding out her arms. "If we made, like, an advertisement for the fall play. We could take a camera on the streetcar during rush hour, and film all of the businesspeople looking bored. And then at the very back, Rebecca and Charlie could be, I don't know, making out. And a voice-over would be like: *A Streetcar Named*

Desire, coming soon to Bickford Park Alternative School."

It wasn't actually funny.

Eventually Liane said, "I don't know if we'll even have time for something like that." The rest of us mumbled agreement. I avoided looking Charlie in the eye.

We weren't exactly prone to making out on public transportation. Or really any place where people could see us. It was actually starting to bother me. I thought boys were supposed to want to touch their girlfriends, jealous costars be damned.

Of course, everything changed the moment we were alone—in the ink-blue darkness of his bedroom, or on my rusted porch swing that emitted bloodcurdling shrieks if we weren't careful. Then things got physical very quickly. His hands would be up my shirt and his heart would be beating fast against mine. It never seemed like a good time to complain.

At home I became invisible, which to be honest was kind of a nice change from the preceding sixteen years of my life. Mary and Jeffrey had decided to get married in December, at the Clines' country club. My mother was disappointed; she had apparently always pictured Mary getting married in the church downtown. Odd, given that we only went there on Christmas and Easter, and Dad always fell asleep halfway through the sermon.

Mary was officially staying in Lake Oswego until the wedding, but she had taken to coming over unannounced. Every time she burst through the door, Mom and Dad performed this whole ritual of exclaiming and hugging her. Like they were filming a scene entitled "Mary's Homecoming" and trying to get a take they were happy with. Mom was pretty desperate to meet the fiancé, whereas Dad was content to watch old recordings of Jeffrey's most crucial golf moments. Periodically he would whisper, "Jeffrey Cline. Well, I'll be damned." As a result, I had gotten a few good looks at the guy. The cameras tended to zoom in on his face, because a game of golf doesn't get more exciting than a twitching upper lip.

Jeffrey didn't look like much to me.

Finally Mary agreed to bring him to dinner on Thursday night. Mom made a leg of lamb braised in a red wine reduction. She said the phrase "red wine reduction" so many times that if quizzed on my deathbed, I will remember exactly what my mother cooked the night Jeffrey Cline didn't show up for dinner.

Mary arrived alone and said the lamb smelled wonderful but unfortunately Jeffrey had a work-related emergency. Dad huffed, untucked his shirt, and went into his office to spend time with the televised Jeffrey, who *never* let him down. But Mom, in her best chartreuse sweater set, promptly burst into tears. Mary launched into a defense, making Mom cry even harder, and I texted Charlie and asked him to meet me in the alley.

I realize it's not particularly classy to meet your boyfriend in the alley. But I needed to get out of there.

Smiling, Charlie pushed me against a garage door on which somebody had spray-painted *Call Your Mom*. We kissed. I had that feeling you get when you're exactly where you always want to be, and it's excellent, but also sad that things don't get any better. He slid his hands inside my jacket and then under my shirt. He unhooked my bra.

It scared me how much I liked kissing Charlie. There were so many moments when I felt sexy and powerful, like I could break his heart if I wanted. But then sometimes— like when his phone rang and he angled the screen away from me—I wondered if I was sorely mistaken.

I took a breath and looked up at him. He whispered my name, the sound somehow nicer than any compliment.

I decided to ruin everything by asking, "Why do you ignore me?"

With one hand beneath my bra, he squeezed, like that proved me wrong. "I don't ignore you."

"At school. Backstage. With everyone else."

He pulled back and kind of frowned at me, like he was trying to remember if I was telling the truth.

"There's so much going on," he said. "With the play, and junior year being the one that really counts. If I spent all day thinking about how you're my girlfriend, and how I'm allowed to touch you, I would just—"

He leaned in to kiss me again.

"You would just what?"

"Dissolve," he said into my mouth. "I would dissolve."

I wondered how it would make Blanche DuBois feel to kiss somebody in an alley full of broken glass and discarded furniture. I wondered how she should feel in the second-to-last scene of the play, when Stanley says something like, "We always knew it would come to this," and lunges for her. I was going to have to scream like I was actually scared of my own boyfriend.

Of course, by that point, part of me would be. What I loved most about acting was immersing myself in a character until it didn't even feel like acting anymore. Playing Blanche DuBois, I knew, would require me to go a tiny bit insane.

The assembly was held in the auditorium, *our* auditorium. First the debate team gathered onstage and sped through the pros and cons of the death penalty. It was clear they took themselves very seriously. Then the mathletes did something uncaptivating. A representative from Writers' Workshop whispered a poem about punching a mirror and gazing into the broken pieces. The so-called Heroes of the Hallway took the stage to outline their agenda for the year: LGBTQ support, aid to Africa, and flag football on Tuesdays.

Then it was our turn. The five of us, plus Hadley and another nonessential, stood seven abreast to sing the insufferable "So Long, Farewell" from *The Sound of Music* in which the Von Trapp children take forever to go to bed. It was Tim's idea, and it was somehow more rebellious than refusing to perform altogether. Certain members of our audience understood this, and laughed along. The rest stared slack-jawed, unable to comprehend why we would humiliate ourselves so thoroughly.

I was Liesl, and I caught Mr. McFadden's eye as I sang, "I'd like to stay and taste my first champagne!" He was sitting with the other teachers, arms folded, shaking his head as if in shame. But his movements were exaggerated, ironic. I could tell he was proud of us.

Tim, as Gretl, sang the final line with his lower lip protruding. "The sun has gone to bed and so must I!"

Charlie, as Friedrich, grabbed Liesl by the waist. I was surprised, couldn't help gasping into the microphone.

My boyfriend placed one hand on the back of my neck. He pressed his lips into mine.

First there was the silent shock of hundreds. Then one of the Von Trapp children—probably Gretl—applauded her siblings' incest. The rest joined and within seconds the whole school was cheering. My spine straightened, my heart beat fast with sudden elation. Charlie Lamb, Charlie Lamb, Charlie Lamb was kissing me.

And everybody knew he was mine.

CHAPTER 17

ON MONDAY MORNING, AN OFFICE AIDE INTERRUPTED first period to drop a note on my desk—*Please report to S. McFadden*—which normally would have meant he needed help unloading his car or moving scenery flats. But since Liane and Tim were both in my class and didn't get summoned, I was nervous. Kissing Charlie to the thunderous applause of the entire student body wasn't explicitly forbidden, but neither were a lot of things nobody ever tried.

Backstage, Mr. McFadden was sitting at his desk shuffling papers around. I always wondered if he did that for show. It wasn't like he had tests to grade.

"Good morning, Rebecca," he said evenly as I slid into the chair opposite his desk.

"Hi," I squeaked.

"How's school?" He sounded like an indifferent relative.

I surprised myself by saying, "It's torture."

This amused him for some reason. He flattened his lips and fiddled with a miniature stapler. "Do you know why I've called you in here today?" he asked casually.

"Not really," I admitted.

"It was a unique interpretation of *The Sound of Music,* to say the least."

Now we were essentially talking about kissing, and I didn't know how to talk to a teacher about kissing. "I, for one," he continued, "never sensed those kinds of tensions between Liesl and Friedrich."

My hair was hanging too far in my face. I pushed it back. "Look, Charlie kissed me, and I was caught completely off guard, and I'm sorry."

He held up his hand. "It's okay." He sounded suddenly sincere. "You're not in trouble. At least not with me. I just . . ." He paused, turning over the stapler like it was a fossil or a precious stone. "I wonder why Charlie did that."

I stared at him, incredulous.

"Can you think of a motivation?" he asked.

Was I that repulsive?

"He's my boyfriend now," I explained. "He probably just wanted to make that clear."

Mr. McFadden's eyebrows twitched. "To the entire school?"

I shrugged.

Casting aside the stapler, Mr. McFadden stared me in the eye. "Charlie is very smart, and very driven. He is the most ambitious teenager I have ever met and I'm sure he will go far in, uh . . ."

"Law," I supplied. "He wants to be a lawyer."

"Law!" Mr. McFadden brightened. "Charlie will make a ruthless lawyer one day, no doubt. But I've noticed he likes to win *every* game, to always get first place. Do you know what I mean?"

I nodded. "Charlie First-Place Lamb, we call him." Stupid and not true.

"Between you and me . . ." Mr. McFadden cleared his throat. "When you're onstage, Charlie gets second place."

My cheeks got hot and a kind of perverse joy seeped through my chest. "Charlie is a good actor," I said, like a loyal girlfriend.

"He is," agreed my director. "But you're better."

The funny thing was that, the moment he said this, I wanted to leave. Not because I was upset, but because I wanted to hold very still and let his words echo in my head indefinitely.

"Is that it?" I asked, flustered and flattered. "Can I go back to class now?"

He studied my face like he wanted to read my mind. I kept it blank, just in case.

"Yes you may," he said quickly. "Just remember to watch out for anybody who tries to convince you you're not talented. It's going to happen all the time, for the rest of your life. And come see me soon, so we can talk about college. You want to go for theater, yes?"

Slinging my bag over my shoulder, I nodded.

"Good." He resumed shuffling his stack of papers. "See you at rehearsal tonight. Be ready to block the first three scenes."

My chair screeched against the floor.

"And, Rebecca?" Mr. McFadden waited until my hand was on the door. I turned and a lock of hair attached itself to my glossed lips. "Don't kiss anyone on my stage."

I opened my mouth to point out the obvious. My director held up a hand to silence me.

"Unless I tell you to."

CHAPTER 18

"DO I LOOK TOO ECLECTIC?" ASKED MOM.

My parents and I were driving to Lake Oswego to meet Mary's fiancé and future in-laws. Mom was applying another layer of skin-colored makeup to her face, dressed in wool slacks and a beige sweater.

"Excuse me?" I asked.

"You know," she sighed. "Do I look like a hippie?"

I was so shocked as to be rendered temporarily speechless. "Mom," I said, after a second, "I can't imagine anybody looking less like a hippie than you do right now."

"Well, I'm worried the Clines will think differently. Mary told them we live in southeast." My mother said *southeast* like it was a dirty word.

"We do live in southeast," I said. "In a house that would sell for about a million dollars."

"Two hundred thousand in 1995," boasted my father. The appreciation of our house was a great source of pride for him.

"I just wish she hadn't called it that. Saying Ladd's Addition gives a better impression, I think."

"You'll have to find a way to mention our exact address," I said.

My mother heaved another gigantic sigh and squirmed in her seat. Her anxiety was bottomless sometimes. I worried about inheriting it.

"Mary has certainly grown up," remarked my father.

"Yes." Mom brightened. "She looks very respectable now. The Clines probably don't even associate her with . . ."

"With what?" I asked.

"Oh, she used to come across so—"

"Abrasive?" asked Dad.

"Alternative. She was very alternative."

I wanted to ask if either of them remembered the night before Mary's high school graduation ceremony, when she decided to experiment with homemade dreadlocks. But then I thought better of it.

The Cline residence turned out to be a suburban

mansion, the mailbox a diminutive replica of the house itself. We parked behind a pair of twin cars with personalized license plates that actually said HISBMW and HERBMW. My father blinked at these cars, as fathers do when they can't choose between disdain and envy.

As we climbed the steep driveway, I silently thanked my parents for raising me in the city. For one thing, there were no artsy alternative schools in the suburbs. And for another, being from one of those anonymous towns was like being from nowhere at all.

We rang the doorbell. My mother hung back, like she wanted the Clines to see my father and me before they saw her. Not a good plan, as my father's pants had a tendency to get stuck inside his socks, and I was not feeling charming.

A tiny woman threw open the door. "Good evening!" she cried theatrically. The woman introduced herself as Darlene Cline and kissed each of us on both cheeks, which seemed excessive. She was wearing high heels and pearls and a black dress. Her face had a kind of stretched look—not exactly like plastic surgery, but like she hadn't stopped smiling in years.

Suddenly I understood why my mother was worried about looking like a hippie.

Darlene whisked us through the foyer, past a fountain with spitting turtles. My mother looked at the fountain longingly—realizing, I guess, that our own foyer was sorely lacking in water features.

"Mary and Jeff are running a bit late, I'm afraid," said Mrs. Cline, urging us to sit on an antique couch. "Traffic on I5."

"Isn't there always," said my father. He coughed.

Mrs. Cline lingered at the bar cart, making sure each drink had the correct number of ice cubes. I accepted a Coke, prompting Dad to frown at me like I had demanded her finest cabernet.

"Bradley!" Mrs. Cline lifted her chin and shouted into oblivion. I expected a child to come running. But instead a tall, glassy-eyed man shuffled into the room.

"My husband," explained Mrs. Cline.

He was wearing a gray suit. He looked like the kind of man who always wore a suit—the kind everyone describes as stoic and hardworking until the Christmas morning he unexpectedly murders the entire family. He sank into an armchair and requested a whiskey sour.

I was kind of nervous about clutching the Coke while I sat on the couch. It was easy to imagine dumping it all over the floral upholstery. Even more troubling was the soft rug beneath my feet, which appeared to have once been a polar bear. I banished the glass to an end table and my father frowned again.

Now everyone focused on me, like I was a baby, or a dog with an impressive repertoire of tricks.

"What grade are you in?" Mrs. Cline leaned forward, like she had been longing to ask.

"Eleventh," I said.

"And what are your favorite subjects?"

"Well." I reached for my Coke and took a sip. "I'm a thespian."

Holding an ice cube in her cheek, Mrs. Cline looked at me like I was utterly insane. "You're a what?"

"She's an actress!" interjected my mother. "A very good actress! She stars in all the plays!"

"Well!" Mrs. Cline sucked her ice and looked smug. "That's an excellent skill for a young woman to have. You must be very confident."

"Um," I said confidently.

The front door banged open and I felt the cold draft on my legs. My sister and her mysterious fiancé took their time hanging up their coats, giggling about something. Probably about having forced their relations into so many minutes of painful small talk. As they entered the room, their laughter died.

My parents jumped to their feet. Jeffrey made an overly enthusiastic noise. I knew he was thirty-six: ten years older than Mary. His giant mustache made him look a lot older.

"So glad to finally meet you!" exclaimed Jeffrey, squeezing my mother's hands. She raised her chin and squint-smiled at him in a way that kind of made me hate her, just for a second.

After giving my father's hand a rough shake, Jeffrey turned to me. I stood up from the couch and pulled at my dress. It was a little short, I was just now realizing.

"My future sister," he said with exaggerated reverence. Like it was some great honor to meet a random sixteen-year-old girl. He hugged me, reeking of cologne. I wondered how Mary could stand riding in the car with him.

I also wondered how long this whole thing would last. I just wanted to go home and shed my itchy tights and too-short dress. I wanted to fall asleep with my ear pressed to the phone.

Mr. Cline cleared his throat to deliver his first line of the evening. "Dinner?" He twisted in his chair and looked hopefully toward the kitchen.

At dinner things took a dramatic turn for the worse. After serving Cornish game hens on beds of green stuff, Mrs.

Cline picked up her fork and said, "Well, it certainly is good to meet the three of you. Mary has always been so mysterious about her family! We were beginning to think she was raised by wolves."

She rewarded herself with a nasally chuckle. Mom and Dad looked embarrassed, and I wanted to come to their rescue, but I didn't know how to prove that Mary was, in fact, ours.

When nobody said anything, Mrs. Cline continued, "I don't know how you cope with seeing her so rarely! I would be beside myself if I didn't see Jeffrey at least four times a year. Luckily his career keeps him traveling back and forth."

"Oh, we've always kept in touch," said Mary lamely. She was running her finger along the lip of her wineglass.

"It's such a long drive to Santa Cruz," added my mother. "We never wanted to pressure her into coming home."

I had maybe never heard my mother tell such an outright lie.

"How did you end up in California, dear?" asked Mrs. Cline. "Of course I know all about how you met our Jeffrey, but it never occurred to me to wonder what drove you so far from home in the first place!"

Mary took a gulp of her wine. The question was so terrible and invasive, but that didn't stop me from leaning forward to learn the answer.

"Well, after high school I moved to New York. I wanted to try and get involved in the art scene there."

"You moved to New York all by yourself?" Mrs. Cline turned to my parents with a look of excessive shock.

The whole table fell silent. I wondered why Mary didn't just say yes. Was it really so shocking? Obviously Jeffrey's mother had firm ideas about what girls did versus what boys did, and that kind of thing bothered me.

"She went with a friend." My father spoke quietly.

I hadn't known that.

Mary dabbed at her lips with her napkin. "A close friend from high school. The two of us went out there together and shared an apartment. I got a waitressing job and tried to get my stuff into galleries. But it was such a battle."

My mom was watching Mary very closely.

"New York was changing me. Everything about it was so competitive—even just getting on the subway, or buying a coffee. It was turning me into someone I didn't want to be."

Mrs. Cline nodded knowingly.

Suddenly Mr. Cline squealed like he had been stung by a bee. Everyone looked to the head of the table, where we had almost forgotten he was sitting.

"What is this?" Speaking through a full mouth, he pointed his fork at his plate.

"It's kale," Mrs. Cline answered calmly.

Disgusted, her husband winced and swallowed. The silence that followed was excruciating.

"Anyway . . ." Mary heroically resumed her story. "My friend and I weren't really getting along anymore, and I had heard about the art community in the bay. So I moved home, and I've lived in Santa Cruz ever since."

My father couldn't help dipping his chin and muttering, "You didn't exactly move home."

Mary looked trapped, like a cat crouched beneath a car. "Well, after New York, it felt like home." Spearing her Cornish game hen, she avoided Dad's eyes.

My sister and I were seated diagonally, on opposite ends of the table. The distance forced me to raise my voice. "Who was your friend?"

Mom and Dad glared at me. I got the feeling that if I pulled at the right thread, Mary's entire history would unravel—a heap of sordid yarn on the dinner table. But I didn't particularly care what the Clines thought. I just wanted to know basic things about my sister, like the name of her first roommate.

"Nadine," said Mary.

I thought of her e-mail. *Do you remember Nadine? It kills me to think you might not.* In spite of myself, I had practically memorized that e-mail.

"I remember Nadine," I said out loud.

A smile flickered across Mary's face. The reference was not lost on her. She met my eyes, and for a second it felt like I knew her better than I had ever known anyone. Jeffrey, who had been chewing methodically between chugs of wine, looked from Mary to me with curiosity.

"Well!" said Mrs. Cline, sawing at her hen rather violently, causing sausage and fennel seeds to fly. "Mary's paintings are just gorgeous. I'm sure you know. She's only allowed us to keep one, and I had to beg her for it."

"Where is it?" asked my mother hopefully, like seeing a painting of Mary's would redeem the whole evening.

"In the guest bathroom upstairs. It's got so many warm, rosy colors. Matches the fixtures just perfectly."

Jeffrey at least looked embarrassed at all the right moments. He opened his mouth—most likely to say that my sister's painting deserved better exhibition than the guest bathroom. Mary had always been a good artist.

But before Jeffrey could defend his future wife, my father coughed out a golf reference. "I have to say, Jeffrey, I've been following your career long before"—he gestured haphazardly at his oldest daughter—"and, boy, my heart just stopped when you hit that eagle in Gold Beach three years ago."

Jeffrey's lips spread in delight. He had some kale in his teeth. "*Your* heart! Sir, mine nearly burst out of my chest. I don't think there has been a prouder moment in all my life."

Mrs. Cline looked at my mother expectantly. Like now that the men were engrossed in golf talk, my mother should compliment her curtains or something.

"Darlene." My mother took a sip of ice water. "Those curtains are just lovely."

CHAPTER 19

CHARLIE TOOK TO DELIVERING HIS LINES IN THIS really crazy voice. Sort of like he was drunk, or had a sock in his mouth. The first time he half slurred, half honked his words, the cast looked at each other in shock and waited for Mr. McFadden to protest. He didn't. We had to finish the scene wondering if Charlie had experienced some kind of stroke. At the end of rehearsal, our director said, "Nice job, Brando," and I couldn't tell if he was being sarcastic.

When I got home I did some research. Apparently the original stage production of *A Streetcar Named Desire*—and later, the movie—featured a ridiculously good-looking actor named Marlon Brando as Stanley.

I watched the movie and quickly deduced that Charlie's new voice was an eerily accurate imitation of Brando's. And by the end, I could understand why Charlie would steal another actor's interpretation. It was suddenly hard to picture Stanley any other way.

Every day Charlie grew more dedicated to his role. He started wearing plain undershirts beneath his signature sweaters and stripping down for rehearsal. The flimsy white sleeves revealed his increasingly muscular upper arms. He perfected a way of leaning against the set and staring at his female costars with animal hunger. It was kind of funny to watch from a distance, like when he was acting with Liane, and I was offstage. Charlie was a lot of things, but he had never been overwhelmingly masculine. His shoes were always very clean and teachers praised him for things like "shrewd insight" into Robert Frost poems. Even at camp, where he went barefoot and tan, he had been more boyish than manly.

But as Stanley he was rough and rude—shouting, stumbling, grabbing Liane by her wrist and yanking her across the stage. It was all very mesmerizing or embarrassing, depending on my mood.

As for my part, Mr. McFadden explained to me that Blanche was kind of a poser. She wanted everyone to believe certain things about her—like that she was innocent, so prim and proper that everything about Stanley's life scandalized her. But in reality she had slept with every man in her hometown, including one of her high school students, and always within the walls of a seedy motel. The first page of the script called Blanche a moth, which I knew was meant to describe her skin: all white and translucent. But when I played Blanche, I pictured the brown speckled moths infesting our front porch. Every time I slid my key into the lock, they rushed toward the light and beat their wings against hot glass.

Liane, for the record, made a perfect Stella. She was even better than the actress in the movie. Liane made it clear that Stella was not actually oblivious to the tension between her sister and her husband. Her silence was partly owing to the fact that she was pregnant and she wanted a good life for her baby. And the other thing you understood after watching Liane was that Stella's love for Stanley was not necessarily pure, or selfless. She used him just like he used her.

There was one scene we had together, a particularly iconic scene, in which Liane had an incredible line.

> **STELLA:** But there are things that happen between a man and a woman in the dark that sort of make everything else seem—unimportant.

I was so jealous of Liane for getting that line. She delivered it perfectly, like she knew all about it.

> **BLANCHE:** What you are talking about is brutal desire—just—Desire!—the name of that rattle-trap streetcar that bangs through the Quarter, up one old narrow street and down another . . .

Liane held an unlit cigarette at eye level and thrust her jaw slightly forward.

> **STELLA:** Haven't you ever ridden on that streetcar?

When she looked me in the eye, I would flash back to that night in her tree house. I would almost break character, wanting to ask if we could ever go up there again, or if my stealing Charlie from her had been one of those unforgivable things.

But I never actually broke character, not after we repeatedly nailed that scene. Because Mr. McFadden yelled at Charlie when his accent got sloppy, and at Tim for giving his character a limp, and at Tess for trying to make Eunice a bigger deal than she was. But he never uttered a word when we finished that scene.

Silence was the biggest compliment Mr. McFadden ever paid to anyone.

There was a day toward the end of October when Mr. McFadden kept interrupting Charlie midscene to say unhelpful things like, "You have to *be* Stanley, you can't just *parody* Stanley." And the problem was, Charlie didn't actually react that well to criticism. His skills dissolved right onstage, leaving him flustered and embarrassed. I guess I was the same way, and so rehearsed obsessively alone in my room. But Charlie had a hell of a lot of stuff to do when he got home—such as lift weights and learn German past participles—so I couldn't really blame him.

Rehearsal ran long that night. Afterward, Charlie walked me home, which was fairly out of character. It was unreasonably cold outside and Charlie didn't have a hat, so I took mine off and pulled it over his eyes. I just wanted to make him laugh.

With one angry gesture, he yanked it off and shoved it at me.

"S-sorry," I stuttered.

"Whatever." He pulled a cigarette out of his jacket and furrowed his eyebrows as he thumbed up a flame. He knew he looked good, mad and smoking. I could always tell when Charlie thought he looked good because he would avoid eye contact for a long time, staring moodily off into the distance. Mary did the same thing.

We walked down the boulevard in silence. Eventually the silence added up to forgiveness and Charlie snaked his arm around my waist, pulling me close. It was awkward in my new winter coat, but also nice.

My house was dark and obviously empty. This had been happening a lot lately, since my parents were always out with Mary, auditioning string quartets and wedding cakes. But tonight I wished they were home.

"Where's everybody?" asked Charlie. When I said I didn't know, he flashed me a wild grin.

"They might be home soon," I warned. "Let me check for a note."

Stepping to unlock the door, I tripped over a package left in the center of the welcome mat. Presents had been arriving for my sister on a daily basis. She and Jeffrey had sent out save-the-dates and all of my parents' friends, who hadn't actually seen Mary in years, were suddenly compelled to buy her expensive spatulas.

Inspecting this particular package, I realized it had been delivered by hand. There were no stamps and the label said only: TO MARY.

"What's that?" asked Charlie impatiently. "Did you order something?"

I shook my head and unlocked the door. I carried the package into the kitchen and set it on the counter, where I expected to find a note from my parents. There was no note, and no message on my phone. "Weird," I muttered.

Charlie was kissing the nape of my neck. "Let's go upstairs," he said. He slipped his hand beneath my sweater and flattened his cold palm against my rib cage. I could imagine how my bones felt to him, smooth and secret. Wordlessly, I led him upstairs.

He did not even pretend to scrutinize the photographs taped to my mirror, or the stacks of DVDs in my closet. He kicked off his shoes and dropped his bag to the carpet. Seizing my waist, Charlie pushed me to the bed. Before I could register any kind of emotion, he was attempting to pull my sweater off my shoulders. It was like he had never observed the physical properties of a sweater.

"Buttons," I struggled to explain through Charlie's frantic tongue.

Interpreting this as a command, he started to undo them.

I grabbed his wrists, somewhat forcefully. "I just meant that there *are* buttons."

He blinked at me. He slid his hand between my legs,

like I was a malfunctioning machine and he was searching for the switch.

"Stop!" My scream sounded pitiful, echoing through the empty house.

Annoyed, Charlie sat up on his haunches.

"What are you doing?" I reached for my bedside lamp. The sudden light caused Charlie to rub his eyes.

"It's pretty obvious what I'm doing."

I tried to determine which one of us was crazy. Obviously, we had come close to having sex before. I thought so, anyway; I wasn't totally clear on how many events came before sex. But there was always some reason to stop, such as being in a gross alley. Or being in Charlie's room, right off the kitchen and mere steps from where his mother always seemed to be washing silverware.

And now I thought there were still plenty of reasons. My parents and sister were likely to pull into the driveway at any moment. Charlie seemed mad at me, about the hat incident or because Mr. McFadden had criticized his performance and not mine. Plus, there was the simple fact that we had never *talked* about it. He didn't even know if I was on the pill or not. And I was scared. And he was scaring me.

"Are you a virgin?" was, for some reason, the question I asked. And I hated that word, *virgin*, which sounded all religious and fussy, like something you only said if you were one.

I could see Charlie trying to choose between the truth and a lie. "You are," he said. A statement, not a question.

I nodded.

He exhaled a ribbon of air. "Funny."

"Excuse me?" It wasn't funny.

"Everyone," he said, "and I mean *everyone,* thinks you sleep around."

I stuttered in disbelief. "That's just something people have said since middle school. I thought you knew that. You said you knew that!"

Charlie frowned. "When?"

But I couldn't answer, because he had been in a canoe with his friends, and I had been lurking secretly in the lake.

"Are you a virgin?" I asked again.

Slowly, Charlie shook his head. I knew he was telling the truth. He was the kind of boy who completed the correct milestones at the correct times.

"Only once," he said. "A long time ago."

And for a second, the truth seemed manageable. Even like something I could relate to. Because if I had slept with Connor at the beach last year, then the same thing would have been true for me: once, a long time ago.

Only now I realized Charlie had not gone to the beach to seek an anonymous stranger. No, Charlie had taken the opposite approach.

"Who?" I said flatly, already knowing.

"Liane."

Her name was like an open wound revealed beneath a person's Band-Aid. I wanted to groan and turn away and tell Charlie to cover it back up.

"Why?" I whimpered.

Charlie appeared exasperated. "We wanted to know what it was like. I don't know, it was like practice for—" He softened, clearly impressed by his own brilliance. "For when I really—"

I waited for *love*. The only word that might excuse him.

"—*liked* somebody. The way I like you."

He pressed his palm against my cheek. I backed away, leaving his hand in midair. "You have to go," I said.

For a minute, Charlie sat hunched over his lap, elbows digging into his knees. Then he left. I stayed cemented to the mattress while he clomped down the stairs and slammed the front door.

I moved to the window and watched him linger in the pool of light from the streetlamp. Slowly, deliberately, he pulled a pack of American Spirits from his coat pocket.

He cupped his hand so tenderly around the cigarette, like you would a newly hatched bird.

 Probably he knew I was watching.

Gnawing at me was the thought of the unlocked door. I turned from the window and flew down the stairs. The moment the lock clicked into place, I felt strangely calm.

My feet carried me into the kitchen, where my arms wrapped around the package addressed to my sister. I took it up to my room.

I don't know why, I just couldn't resist.

Dear Mary,

You might remember this tiny covered wagon from the day Mrs. Peterson's sixth-grade class took a field trip to the Pioneer Center. On the bus, you sat next to Kristina Hart. I sat behind you, next to Mrs. Peterson. How humiliating. The museum showed us a movie about hardship on the Oregon Trail. Then we watched a middle-aged woman in a bonnet churn butter. In the gift shop, eleven-year-old Mary Rivers slipped this diminutive souvenir into the pocket of her raincoat.

"Are you going to pay for that?" I asked, aghast.

"Are you kidding?" You rolled your eyes. "Who would pay for this?"

You robbed the Pioneer Center. Later, I robbed you.

In ninth grade, I lent you some books. What teenage girl doesn't force her favorite novels on her favorite friend? *Fried Green Tomatoes at the Whistle Stop Café* and *The Color Purple*. And then, just in case you were really dense, *Annie on My Mind*.

You did not read the books, too busy getting stoned with other girls' boyfriends. Too busy climbing over the counter at Everyday Music to kiss that cashier, who had gouged earlobes before everyone and their mothers had gouged earlobes. But you kept the books in a stack on your nightstand, like you might read them if you ever got the flu. You even brought them to New York, leaving them and everything else when you moved out of our apartment. Here you go. Maybe you'll read them this time.

What is *this* garbage? you might ask. It is a piece of a broken CD: P. J. Harvey's fifth studio album, to be exact. You wanted it so badly you would admit no other reason for agreeing to make out with

Heidi Cho when Derrick Woolf offered you each twenty-five dollars. I stood in the parking lot of the Meow Meow, rain making my coat smell like an old dog, and watched you cup Heidi's chin in your hands. You both feigned indifference as Derrick doled out the cash. He paid you in singles.

I wouldn't speak to you on the bus ride home, and I think you knew why.

"I needed the money," you said, pressing your forehead against the window.

Later, you burned me a copy of the album, entitled *Stories from the City, Stories from the Sea*.

I broke it.

This next CD is in one piece, but equally impaired from years of traveling in my Discman. The song "Cemetery Gates" has never sounded like anything less than lust since one night in eleventh grade. It was April, the rain was warm and tropical. You had just obtained your driver's license and were for some reason brimming with unchecked, desperate energy. Like an animal. We drove up Mount Scott to the National Cemetery. And finally you pressed me into the wet earth, on top of all those dead soldiers. Finally the force of Mary Rivers was in my favor.

A girl I dated when I was twenty-three told me that song is about plagiarism.

Whatever.

Remember how we ditched prom early and used our fake IDs at the Blue Moon? Here's a matchbook from the bar. We each drank four cranberry vodkas and tried to play pool. We were in it for the leaning, the squinting, the slender cues sliding between our fingers. Pure sex appeal.

But before we ditched prom, Kristina Hart observed us slow-dancing to Mazzy Star. Kristina told her mother, who told mine.

You may remember: About a month earlier Mom had been stopped at a red light on Burnside when she saw us emerge from the bookstore, hand in hand. At home she gave me a lecture: "I know how close girls your age can be . . . but you don't want people to get the wrong idea."

Well, if Eileen Hart had the wrong idea, Jesus himself probably had the wrong idea. Such good terms, those two were on.

Nobody had told my parents that they could attend Bible study, and vote for Bush, and buy all the right bumper stickers—and *still* their teenage daughter might turn out queer.

But prom night was fun, don't you think?

Oh yes. I kept the ticket stub. PDX -> JFK. 6:45 am. Gate D3. Everyone hated Grandma P for letting my trust fund kick in on my eighteenth birthday. Thanks, Grandma. For that and for everything else. (She died, if you were wondering. Took all my pride not to call you.)

And finally, the wooden ring I found in a flea market in Queens. Such a sentimental idiot, to think a ring would convince you to stay.

But you were smarter than me, Miss Rivers. You knew exactly what we had, and what we had already lost. I demanded the ring as you were leaving, like I might give it to someone else. (Never.) And you looked at me like I was so unreasonable. I wanted to strangle you then.

But later I understood: If I hadn't screamed at you to stay away from me, you might not have.

Congratulations, Mrs. Cline.

Love,

Nadine

When I heard my parents' car pull into the driveway, I repacked the box with all nine artifacts and the letter on top. I slid the package beneath my bed. Sobs—the ugly, shuddering kind—were rising up my throat. I swallowed hard and listened to my mother ascend the stairs. She pushed open my bedroom door.

"You're in here all alone?" She looked disappointed, like she had expected a celebrity guest.

I gestured to the empty room, heart still racing.

"Where's Charlie?" she asked.

My urge to cry mingled with an urge to scream. Why did everyone like that guy so much?

"Probably off legally changing his name to Brando," I said.

My mother looked equal parts confused and disturbed.

"Where's Mary?" I attempted to sound normal, and not like I had uncovered an alarming secret. Not like anything under my bed might sabotage my sister's wedding.

"She's with the Clines tonight." My mother rolled her eyes. "You should see the centerpieces that girl picked out. Completely obscene, if you ask me, which she didn't."

For a second, I was distracted, wondering what could make a centerpiece obscene. Mom shut the door. She was always doing that—entering unannounced, then exiting halfway through the conversation.

Curling into a ball, pathetic and fetal, I sobbed.

And I knew my feelings were all wrong. Because even

though Nadine's letter was extremely sad and fairly shock-ing, I wasn't crying about that. I wasn't even crying about Mary's impending marriage to an aging golfer, when she was maybe or probably or definitely gay.

I was still crying about my stupid boyfriend.

Charlie, who had slept with Liane.

Charlie, who had looked at me like I was a child unwill-ing to eat my dinner.

Charlie, who would never write me a letter like that—because he would never waste so many words on loving me or hating me or trying to win me back.

Charlie, who had believed the rumors after all.

CHAPTER 20

CHARLIE WAS SUPPOSED TO LOOK AT ME HUNGRILY. I WAS supposed to step tentatively toward him, then retreat. His line was: "Go ahead. I'm not going to interfere with you."

"Then again," he reconsidered. "You might be kind of fun to interfere with."

I was supposed to seize a lamp for self-defense. The script actually called for a broken bottle, but Mr. McFadden figured that might be dangerous. Charlie was supposed to lunge and pin my arms to my sides and say, "We've had this date from the beginning."

Only we couldn't do any of it. Charlie wore his wrinkled undershirt and his new Levi's, but there was nothing malicious in his eyes. He kept whispering his lines, like each sentence was an apology. I was dissolving in this terrible, naked embarrassment. I couldn't stop thinking about Liane listening backstage—Liane, who knew everything I didn't know about sex. And about Charlie. And about having sex with Charlie.

We fumbled through the scene, all the way to the end. Charlie held me in place, inflicting only the slightest pressure.

"From the top" was our director's verdict.

We tried again. Charlie forgot his line, and his face went blank like he had forgotten his own name. I was so miserable I wanted to howl.

Finally Mr. McFadden rose from his seat. "Okay," he said. "Let's quit. I'm going to look over the text tonight, see if I can find a way to water down this scene."

He sounded genuine. Still, Charlie and I held our breath and looked at each other. For once, I could actually read my boyfriend's mind. And he would never quit, not after the word had been said out loud.

"Wait," said Charlie.

With a cruel smile, Mr. McFadden sank back into the second row.

Charlie crossed his arms. He tilted his head to one side and then the other, closing his eyes against the strain of his neck muscles. Then he looked at me, his tongue lazily polishing his bottom lip. I could tell he had stopped seeing me and was now seeing only Blanche DuBois: frail, fluttering like a moth.

"I'm not going to interfere with you," he said. Without breaking eye contact, I reached for the lamp. "Then again." Charlie lunged at me without finishing his line. My gasp was real, but my fear was fake. Or it was the other way around; I couldn't tell anymore. I struggled against his arms, all tense and unyielding. In that moment I could have quit the stage forever.

Then Charlie's arms went slack. He cupped my chin in his hands, gently.

"We've had this date from the beginning."

His delivery was soft and sad—the exact opposite of Marlon Brando's. We held our pose until Mr. McFadden clapped his hands together three times. He actually clapped for us.

So far beneath his breath, only I could hear, Charlie said, "I'm sorry."

Backstage, Tess and Tim were playing a fast-paced card game that involved slapping cards against the floor and shrieking frequently. Neither of them had gotten to rehearse a single scene, and I realized that sitting needlessly backstage for three hours could drive anyone crazy. Still, their energy made my head hurt.

I turned to Liane, hoping to communicate my exhaustion and win her sympathy. Painful as it was to picture her with Charlie—and I had pictured it, a lot—the silver lining seemed obvious. I had concealed vital pieces of information that night in her tree house. But so had she.

Zipping her perfect, wine-colored leather jacket, Liane met my gaze. Did she know that I knew? With a half smile, she waved good-bye and left through the stage doors. I couldn't read her mind.

After disbursing cigarettes to Tess and Tim, Charlie offered me the open pack. "Ready?" he asked.

"Go ahead," I said, waving him off. "I actually have to get something from my locker."

I didn't, but I felt like walking home alone. The three of them exchanged semi-concerned looks before nodding and pushing through the curtains. They were presumably halfway across the auditorium, out of earshot, by the time Mr. McFadden said my name.

I jumped. He rarely followed us backstage after rehearsal. Casually, he leaned against the front of his desk, crossing his arms and then his legs. "Are you okay with all of this?" he asked.

I wanted to laugh, because there was an enormity contained in "all of this" and he didn't even know it. Instead,

I nodded. Maybe I wasn't okay, exactly, but I couldn't quit the play. I had formed an unreasonable attachment to Blanche DuBois.

"I realize I was manipulating you back there. I shouldn't have done that. I'm sorry."

Speechless, I shrugged my shoulders. Teachers were not supposed to apologize.

"I like what you did with that scene," he continued. "I think it's a valid interpretation."

"Charlie did it," I said.

"Charlie did part of it," he insisted. "You did the rest."

I couldn't remember doing much of anything, which worried me. Whatever Mr. McFadden had seen couldn't be repeated. Not without me breaking into sobs onstage, anyway.

He studied my expression. "Walk with me," he ordered.

Our footsteps echoed in the long hallway. Mr. McFadden walked fast, like he had somewhere to be. I half skipped to match his strides, which reminded me of following my father through the airport. But comparing Mr. McFadden to my father filled me with a slow-seeping kind of shame, so I stopped.

He shouldered through the main doors. The night was dark and damp, as cold as it could be while still raining. Farther down Hawthorne, a pack of chaperoned children blocked the sidewalk, their Halloween costumes obscured by ponchos. I had completely forgotten the date.

"Shitty night for trick-or-treating," I observed.

Mr. McFadden nodded distractedly.

I braced myself for the rain. I had brought the wrong coat. Nothing waterproof was warm enough. "Good night," I said.

"You can't walk in this." Mr. McFadden spoke more to the bloated sky than to me. "Let me drive you home."

I hesitated. My parents probably wouldn't mind if I used a credit card to pay for a taxi. Plus, Mr. McFadden looked kind of uncertain—like he wasn't sure if he wanted me to accept or refuse. But we had done this before. The same offer hadn't felt so bold in the spring.

So for the second time in my life, I followed Mr. McFadden to the staff parking lot.

When I remembered the small issue of his car only starting with no weight on the passenger seat, I regretted my decision. I wasn't in a butt-lifting mood.

I looked at him. He gave me a nod. I lifted my butt and he started the car and we merged onto the boulevard. It was all feeling very familiar.

"Why don't you get a new car?" I asked in a fit of candid irritation. "This is ridiculous. What if you have a date? Do you seriously ask her to lift her butt up?" I winced at my choice of pronoun. Mr. McFadden never spoke about his romantic life, so I didn't know for sure.

He didn't seem to notice. "No first dates in the Toyota," he admitted. "For a number of reasons." He gestured to the Starbucks cups littering the backseat, the gearshift held together with duct tape.

"It's weird that your car is so shitty," I said, apparently incapable of making appropriate conversation. "It doesn't even match."

"Doesn't match what?" His lips curled in amusement.

"You."

He was quiet for so long that I actually stopped waiting for a response.

At a red light, he took a breath. "I'm not sure my teaching style is entirely indicative of my personality."

I kind of snorted; it was the exact type of thing he said all the time.

"Seriously!" he insisted, sounding suddenly different, younger. "I'm not just a director. I play many other parts—captain of this fine automobile, for example. If my teaching style suggests a kind of . . ." He glanced at me.

"Hard-assery," I supplied.

He spoke through laughter, half pleased: "It's just because high school students respond well to criticism! The more I ask of you guys, the more you deliver. And in my experience, when young actors hit their stride, they offer something that adults just can't."

"Like what?" I asked.

"You're all so focused on trying to understand your characters. You always want to know how they feel. Adult actors are obsessed with understanding the author's message, or with the historical context of the play. They want to know exactly what they're preaching. High school students only care about getting mad, or falling in love."

I was conscious of the windshield wipers squeaking, and of Mr. McFadden's tongue clicking against the roof of his mouth, and of the stoplights reflected in the wet pavement. It was draining, in a way, noticing all of this at once.

"I don't think anybody in *A Streetcar Named Desire* falls in love," I said.

He chuckled. "You might be right about that."

I leaned over my knees and rummaged in my bag for my cell phone. The clock on the stereo was flashing the wrong time. I felt his eyes flicker to my arched spine and back to the road.

"What about you?" he asked. "What are you, besides an actress?"

"Huh?" I sat up abruptly, hair whipping against the seat.

"What do you like to do when you're not onstage?"

I liked making out with Charlie. And walking downtown with the Essential Five and eating candy off my stomach while watching Audrey Hepburn movies. I even liked running errands with my parents. Sometimes.

"Nothing," I said.

He raised an eyebrow. "That can't be true."

"There isn't time for anything else."

"That's my fault, I suppose." He cringed, maybe because the rain was picking up.

"I guess I don't mean time." I didn't want to offend him. "It's more like there's no space in my life for anything else. Theater could be like, just one thing. But instead I make it everything."

I looked over to gauge his reaction. His face was slightly pockmarked and I was strangely attracted to the imperfection of it. Staring at Charlie's face eventually got old, like looking at a lake on a windless day.

"Is it enough?" he asked.

"Sometimes," I said carefully. "Sometimes it's way too much."

Without warning, the rain became a downpour. The windshield wipers squeaked frantically from side to side, but water had flooded our view.

"Shit!" he yelped. "I can't drive in this."

"I told you, you need a new car."

Laughing somewhat hysterically, he manually rolled down his window. Rain rushed in, splashing against the dashboard. Mr. McFadden leaned into the storm and guided his fine automobile to a side road, where we wouldn't be blocking traffic. He parked illegally beside a fire hydrant and rolled up his window. He was half soaked.

"The rain will stop soon," he promised, unbuckling his seat belt and sliding down in his seat. He drummed his fingers nervously against the steering wheel. "I'm sorry. I should have just put you in a cab."

I shook my head, meaning it was fine. Or that he shouldn't have. It occurred to me to be scared. I could end up on the evening news: "Teenage Starlet Abducted Post-Rehearsal: Chopped to Bits in Station Wagon." But I wasn't actually scared of Mr. McFadden at all. And I didn't particularly care if the rain stopped soon.

I did wonder what my parents would think, if they could see me right at this moment. Given that I was almost always exactly where they thought, it was somewhat thrilling to be in the least likely place.

"Tell me something," he said suddenly.

I waited for the question.

"Just tell me anything," he clarified. "Anything you want."

I got the feeling that my choice would either impress or sorely disappoint him. Still, I said the first thing that came to mind. "My sister is about to marry Jeffrey Cline."

"Who is Jeffrey Cline?" he asked, emotionless.

"Winner of three West Coast tours."

Mr. McFadden shifted in his seat and blinked at me. Apparently not all men spoke all sports fluently.

"Golf," I explained.

"Interesting," he said, like it wasn't at all.

I tried again. "She ran away from home after high school and this is practically the first time she's been back."

"How old is she now?"

"Twenty-six."

"Huh." He gnawed at his thumbnail. His fingers were stained with ink. "What's her name?"

"Mary." I was driving our conversation into a wall, but I couldn't think of what to say. The rain persisted, pounding against the roof of the car.

"Mary Rivers," he echoed with faint interest. Then his eyebrows leaped toward his hairline. "Mary Rivers! I actually remember her!"

"What?" I kind of choked. "My sister was your—how *old* are you?" Panic tightened in my chest.

"No!" He looked equally horrified. "She wasn't my

student. I'm only twenty-seven! We went to high school together, at Cleveland."

Cleveland High was the public school in our district. My parents had decided against sending me there, probably on account of how Mary turned out.

"I thought you were from Spokane," was the first thing I thought to say. I could not, no matter how hard I tried, think of Mary and Mr. McFadden as peers. It wasn't that they seemed like wildly different ages or anything. More that I wasn't convinced they inhabited the same world.

"Why would you think that?" He turned up his hands, bewildered. I drew a blank. Why had I thought that?

"How do you know it's the same Mary Rivers?" I challenged.

Squinting, he leaned toward me. "You are, without a doubt, Mary Rivers's little sister."

I crossed my arms and looked straight ahead, at the water cascading down the windshield. It was like Mary had pushed me out of the car and stolen Mr. McFadden's attention.

"Were you friends with her?" In spite of my jealousy, if that's what it was, I was curious.

"Not really. But I remember, the one time she auditioned for a school play, she got the lead. She played Hermia in

A *Midsummer Night's Dream*. I was the duke of Athens."

"Oh my god." The realization was sudden and swift, made me feel both sick and elated. "Oh my god!" I started laughing. Tears threatened to slide down my cheeks. "Holy shit!"

"What?" he asked, offended. "What's wrong with the duke of Athens?"

I shook my head, gasping for breath.

"Tell me!" With tense hands, he strangled the air between us.

"I was in that play!" I managed to confess.

He frowned deeply before yielding to nervous laughter. "No you weren't. You would have been . . . five, six?"

"My parents volunteered me to be a fairy."

"Oh," he moaned, pressing himself against the window, looking nothing like my director. "Oh, that's so weird." He appeared physically pained.

I released a final, faded giggle. I tried to remember him as the duke of Athens, but I couldn't. My memories of *A Midsummer Night's Dream* included the warm, adoring presence of the crowd and my turquoise fairy costume. I had fallen in love, completely in love, with the stage that night.

I wanted to run out into the rain and tell somebody that I had once acted beside Mr. McFadden. It was the kind of revelation that wouldn't feel real until at least one other person acknowledged it. But as I considered this, I realized I couldn't tell my friends. Our director's attention had always threatened to drive a wedge between me and the four of them. I had never wanted him to like me best. But now, maybe I did.

The rain let up enough that we could see the car parked in front of us. Mr. McFadden reached for the ignition, but didn't turn the key right away. "Do you remember me at all?" he asked.

I shook my head and watched the tension leave his shoulders. "Good. I would hate for you to have a mental image of me at seventeen."

"Mary might have pictures," I teased.

He dismissed the possibility. "Not of me, she doesn't."

Once I had lifted my butt and, again, convinced the car I wasn't there, we drove back to Hawthorne. Instead of telling him my address, I waited to see if he remembered. The break in the rain felt temporary; wind still raged against the side of the car. We passed a lot of houses with Jack-o'-lanterns flickering hopefully in the front windows, but trick-or-treaters were few and far between, and they all looked devastated.

Mr. McFadden was calmer now. "I remember your sister was the kind of person who made you feel like it was okay to be exactly who you were." He swallowed, turned toward me. "Is she still like that?"

My sister, I thought, was the kind of person who would abandon her girlfriend in New York City and marry a man instead. My sister wasn't particularly honest about her own identity; the answer to Mr. McFadden's question had to be no.

But I had this strange urge to preserve his memory of her. I could imagine Mary and Nadine in our family's old Volkswagen, winding up Mount Scott Road, bravely choosing each other. Everything between them had been over for years, but I was still somehow rooting for them.

I said, "Yeah. Pretty much." Like by saying so, I could give them another chance.

And my director nodded, satisfied.

For once, the lights were on inside my house and I was glad. Staying home alone so often was starting to make me paranoid.

With the engine idling, Mr. McFadden turned to face me. "When you're a teacher," he said quickly, before he could change his mind, "everyone warns you that one day you will have a student whose future you can see so clearly. And that you will feel jealous, knowing they will accomplish what you didn't."

I stared at him. I had never expected anything like this to happen.

"I'm not jealous of you," he said bluntly, as if stating a fact. "But I am really looking forward to seeing your name in lights."

The car smelled of manufactured pine. His bottom lip was cracked in one corner and his hair, I suddenly realized, was unlike anyone else's hair. It grew in all directions and when he ran his fingers through it—which he did now—it changed shape, like beach grass rearranged by the wind.

I had thought that falling in love was a decision. Like first you noticed a boy was cute and smart and had good taste in movies. He kissed you and it occurred to you to love him. If a certain amount of time passed and nothing went wrong, then congratulations: love.

But apparently that was not how it worked at all. Apparently love happened accidentally, and without warning, and at the exact moment you were supposed to get out of the car.

CHAPTER 21

"WHY ARE YOU PUTTING A BOTTLE OF TEQUILA IN YOUR purse?"

Startled, I slammed the doors to the liquor cabinet. Mary was pointing at me with her car key, amused. My cheeks flushed with guilt. She still knew nothing about the box beneath my bed.

"School was canceled," I said, like that explained anything. Mary looked out the window and back at me. The storm was over and the streets were bone dry.

"Power outage. Nobody east of Thirty-second has electricity." I zipped the bottle into my bag. As long as Mary kept quiet, my parents would never notice. Tequila was not exactly their drink of choice.

She blocked the doorway, deliberating. Sisters were

overrated. Simple things, like robbing the liquor cabinet, became so complicated.

"Does Charlie live east of Thirty-second?" Her upper lip curled.

"Yes." I shouldered past her.

"Hey." Mary grabbed my purse strap. "Be smart, okay?"

I looked into her eyes, green with sparks of yellow. I wanted to say Nadine's name out loud, just to watch those sparks burst into flames. Mary was wearing leggings and pearl earrings, on her way downtown to find a wedding dress. Maybe, if she had retained a shred of her younger self, I could have explained my reasoning.

Which was that even though I wanted things I couldn't have, I had a couple of things worth saving. Such as the play and maybe the best-looking boyfriend in the state of Oregon. My plan was to surprise Charlie at ten in the morning with an apologetic bottle of tequila. I hoped it was the kind of thing Liane would never do.

"Smart?" I asked, like it was a foreign concept.

Our gaze broke against the sound of Mom stomping down the stairs, all perfume and anxiety. She was shouting, "Mary, honey, did I wear these slacks the last time we saw Darlene?"

Apparently, the hunt for Mary's wedding dress was a

group activity. Mary's index finger orbited her ear—our old sign of solidarity against our parents. Then she pointed at my bulging bag and whispered a flurry of instructions. "Pace yourself. Drink water. Stay with Charlie, don't end up alone with anyone you don't trust."

Our mother appeared, looking imploringly from her perfectly pressed pants to her firstborn daughter.

Mary assumed I trusted Charlie.

With a winter coat pulled over pink pajamas, Mrs. Almeida stood in her front yard, righting cherubs blown over in the storm. I lifted a hand in greeting and she frowned at my bag like she knew exactly what it held. All down the street pumpkins smiled toothlessly, or with their faces half collapsed and smeared across porch steps.

According to the local news, most of southeast had lost power around seven last night. Meaning Mr. McFadden and I had nearly been trapped backstage, alone together in total darkness. As I walked to Charlie's I imagined it happening that way: my director taking my hand and leading me to lighted safety. I gripped my own hand, pretending the pressure came from his. When that started to feel stupid I allowed my fantasy to slip back into darkness—to things that could happen only if I knew the lights would stay out forever. My heart pounded as I imagined his fingers crawling up my ribs. It was such an impossible scenario.

Charlie was home alone, thank god. He answered the door wearing jeans, wool socks, and a frayed cardigan. His house was shockingly cold.

At first he stared at me blankly, his mind still entrenched in the homework scattered across the kitchen table. I unzipped my bag and wordlessly produced the bottle of tequila. I watched the corners of his eyelids crinkle. He was beautiful, even if I was half in love with someone else.

"You never fail to amaze me, Rivers."

I melted.

He took the bottle from my hands. He worked on the cork until it slid out with a pop. Charlie led me to the living room and we sat on a sagging suede couch with space between us, passing the bottle back and forth. A vacuum cleaner lay overturned in the center of the room, like a murder victim. The coffee table was littered with warped magazines and remote controls and a wet sponge. I had been to Charlie's house a few times before. Normally his little brothers were noisy. Normally we would shut ourselves into his bedroom, but his mother would push on the door every time she passed through the hall.

At first, I just barely let the alcohol sting my lips. But when nothing bad happened, I swallowed more and more. Maybe the tequila didn't have to be an apology. Maybe the tequila could negotiate a deal between Charlie and me. Somehow I would end up naked, beneath him, and fine.

"Tell me something," I said.

"What?" He rubbed his socked foot against my leg.

"Just anything. Something I don't already know."

Charlie's forehead creased. "You have to ask me a question first."

"Just pretend I asked whatever question you would most like to answer."

I thought this was a pretty good offer, but Charlie looked annoyed. Throwing back his head, he took an impressive swig. "No," he refused. "I hate that kind of game."

Which was a complete lie. Or maybe the truth was that Charlie liked and hated everything equally. He reserved the right to change his personality at a moment's notice.

Across the room, a shelf held a row of photo albums, spines labeled by year. I rose from the couch abruptly— very aware of my skirt stretched across my hips, my sweater slipping from one shoulder: the things that would make him forgive me. I chose an album, as if at random. But sinking into the couch, closer to Charlie this time, I knew exactly what I was looking for. According to Liane, they'd been ten when they kissed for practice. I wanted to see what they had looked like.

After pages of baseball games, barbecues, and birthday parties, I finally found a picture. I recognized the setting as Liane's backyard. At ten she was taller than him, tight curls cropped close to her face. Charlie's lips were Popsicle red and bleeding into his chin. They had lazy summer smiles.

Obviously, they were just kids. I had no right to be jealous. But I would have given anything to erase those ties between them—for Liane to be my friend, and Charlie my boyfriend. Both of them mine and not each other's.

Looking up, I searched Charlie's face for some sign of nostalgia. But he wasn't even looking at the picture; he was staring at my neck, at the place where my sweater exposed my collarbone.

"I wish I was more like her." I covered Liane's face with my index finger.

"You're prettier than Liane." His words were slightly slurred.

He had seen her naked, I realized. He had never seen me naked. I wondered how he could know for sure.

"That's not what I meant."

Charlie tried again. "You're a better actress."

I shut the album and leaned back into the couch, which smelled like a dog, even though there was no dog. I searched for words to explain what Liane had that I didn't.

"She's so calm." I was instantly unsure if I had said this out loud.

"She's heartless."

"No," I giggled. "Just unflappable."

"That too."

Charlie leaned into me and our kisses were wet and loose. I tried things I hadn't before. I bit down on his lower lip. I moved my hands down his back, inside his jeans, to the front where things squirmed on their own. The more I did to him, the less he did to me. I hadn't noticed that pattern until now.

"Do you think she's mad at me?" Thoughts were rolling around my brain haphazardly.

"Why would she be mad at you?" Charlie spoke into my open mouth.

"I stole you."

"I ain't nobody's property," he joked, Marlon Brando style.

For a while, we lingered in an unlikely state of excellence: the right amount of alcohol, the right amount of kissing, the right amount of sinking between couch cushions. Daylight barely bled through the window, and it was like our hands belonged to people who knew what they were doing.

In the kitchen, a cat was shaking a bird to death. "What the?" I sat up, shocked and panting.

"We have a cuckoo clock," explained Charlie.

The clock proceeded to screech twelve times for noon, which was excessive and also hilarious. All of the excellence dissolved in my laughter. I struggled to catch my breath.

"Do you want some water?" asked Charlie, mildly annoyed.

I nodded. He disappeared and I listened to the water rushing through the pipes. When Charlie came back, the weather on his face had changed completely. I wondered if he could reverse my drunkenness too.

He thrust the glass into my hand. "I meant to ask you something."

I looked up at him.

"We waited for you after rehearsal last night. Why did you stay so long?"

I drained the glass, and then I had to speak. "I was talking to Mr. McFadden. He liked our scene."

Charlie sat with his elbows digging into his knees. "Then how come he only talked to you?"

My brain was cluttered with cobwebs, and I wanted to say "pass," like in school. I shrugged instead.

"Director's pet," Charlie sneered. And officially he was joking, but really he wasn't. I could tell by the way he angled his knees away from mine. "He goes so far out of his way to be nice to the girls, it's ridiculous."

"What?" My pulse raced.

"Well, it would look bad if he favored the guys." Charlie was pulling at a thread on his sweater, like his words mattered less that way.

I thought I understood him, but I hoped I was wrong. "Why would it look bad?"

His head fell back against the couch. He spoke to the ceiling. "Because he's a faggot."

I wanted to leap for the light switch, like you do at the end of a scary movie. But the power was out. "What the hell," I mumbled. It was awful, the way everything ached behind my eyes.

"Don't be naïve, Rebecca."

"I just don't think you should call me that."

Charlie blinked.

"I mean, call *him* that. Or call anybody that!"

Charlie shrugged. "It's just a word."

"To you." I stood up. The room tilted like a carnival ride. I was so much drunker than I wanted to be. "He yells at Tess and Liane just as much."

"Because they're not such great actors."

"And you are?"

"I'm as good as you." He sucked in so much air, I waited for his next line. "Maybe better." Charlie sat with his arms crossed, legs splayed: untouchable as always.

"You actually think"—I was crying, unfortunately—"that Mr. McFadden criticizes you because he's *attracted* to you?"

Charlie shrugged. "Some people are, you know."

"Oh my god!" I could hear myself screaming. It sounded somehow louder than all of the lines I had ever screamed onstage. I could feel our argument, hazy from the beginning, morphing into something else: something about sex, something about the fact that Charlie always had to win. He would never forgive me for being the better actor, but I was. Mr. McFadden had told me so.

"He's not even gay!" I shouted.

My cheeks flushed with immediate regret. I watched the truth occur to Charlie. His eyes narrowed before they went wide. He pointed at me. "You have a thing for him."

"Fuck you." I had left my boots by the front door. The house had a no-shoes rule, even though it was such a mess. Charlie's family was poor. Or mine was rich and his was normal. Whatever it meant that my mother paid someone to vacuum our floors and Charlie's mother didn't even have time to do it herself.

Charlie followed and silently watched me tie my laces. I was ditching him with the tequila. A bottle half depleted was more conspicuous than a bottle missing. Everyone knew that.

I pulled on my coat and patted the pockets, counting my belongings. I had shoes, and a coat, and a cell phone, and a wallet, and a problem. Such a massive problem.

"I don't have a thing for Mr. McFadden."

I made this statement for the record. We couldn't break up, that was the problem. We practically hated each other, but we couldn't break up.

"I know." He cooperated. "I'm sorry."

We had to keep pretending. Losing each other was one thing, but we could not lose the play. I had put so much of myself into Blanche DuBois. I was closer to her now than ever: drunk at noon, clinging desperately to what I still had, flapping my paper-thin wings against hot glass.

And theater was the passion Charlie couldn't hide. He needed the applause as much as I did. Maybe more.

"Can we act like this never happened?" he asked.

I leaned forward and, without touching him anywhere else, brushed my lips against his.

"Sure." I pushed open the door and a blast of cold air slapped our faces. "I'm good at acting."

CHAPTER 22

CHARLIE'S HOUSE HAD NEVER FELT SO FAR AWAY. I could have taken the bus, but I thought maybe I should walk off the drunkenness. Fortunately my feet knew the way home. My mouth was dry and if there had been anything to laugh at, I would have laughed hard. There happened not to be.

I tried to stop thinking about Charlie. On paper he was still my boyfriend, which was all he had ever really been: a signature on a dotted line. I understood our contract now. He had offered himself in exchange for the stage. As Charlie's devoted girlfriend, I was supposed to step aside, to ensure his status as Bickford Park's most talented thespian. It was *almost* the only thing he had ever wanted from me.

Waiting to cross Division Street, I shut my eyes against the morning. I tried to focus on getting home, on the box beneath my bed growing more consequential by the second.

I wanted to read Nadine's letter one more time. And then I had to show it to my sister.

By the time I made it home, I was more cold than drunk. Mary and my mother were still out, but my father's parka hung by the door. I shouted a greeting and he answered from his office. I didn't want him to see my face, which I was sure contained a history of the last few hours.

Safe inside my room, I sank to the carpet and pulled the box into my lap. Carefully, I set aside the tiny covered wagon, the books, the CDs, the matches, the ticket stub, and the ring. I unfolded the letter and examined every word, blood surging in my ears.

When I finished, I lay back against the floor, feeling the throbs of my very first hangover. I could still hear Charlie spitting out the word *faggot* with such dense, angry pride.

I closed my eyes and tried to remember the details of the night Mary left home. Still, all I could see was my sister and father screaming in the living room—my father lifting his hand and my mother seizing his wrist. I couldn't remember anyone naming Nadine as the reason, but it was so obvious now. My sister had left home because she loved a girl.

My parents had allowed me to grow up without a sister. And when she finally did come home to announce her engagement, my parents looked at each other so warily, unwilling to pour a drop of champagne until she clarified: he, him, his. Jeffrey Cline.

I listened to my father climb the stairs and shut himself inside the bathroom. He blew his nose in the most elephantine way possible. Suddenly, I hated him for things that had never particularly bothered me. I hated him for the hours he spent in front of the evening news, and for the giant khaki pants he always wore. I hated him for wrinkling his nose at Tess's I ♥ MY VAGINA T-shirt, even though I also hated that shirt, which forced me to remember certain things about Tess every time she wore it.

Maybe everything my father had ever done was in support of his palm against Mary's cheekbone. Maybe he was no better than Charlie.

The tequila had a strange way of clarifying things I normally ignored.

I heard the car in the driveway, doors slamming, my sister barreling through the house hollering my name. I practically broke a sweat trying to re-pack the box and shove it under the bed.

Mary burst into the room, all giddy and breathless. She seemed to have forgotten that I was supposed to be at Charlie's, draining a bottle of stolen tequila.

"Oh my lord, Rebecca, if you ever get married, do not go wedding dress shopping with our mother and your future mother-in-law! Too many matriarchs! Go with your fiancé. Go alone. Go with me! I have excellent taste."

Mary had two garment bags draped over her arm.

"Seriously, once I'd made up my mind, Darlene asked me 'Are you sure?' so gravely I could tell she was already revising her last will and testament, prepared to leave everything to the gardener. Or maybe the cook. She hates the gardener."

"You have two," I said.

She blinked.

"Two dresses."

"Aha!" Mary's eyes lit up. She unloaded one dress onto the bed and dramatically presented the other. "This one"—she lowered the zipper on the bag—"is for you."

Mary—formerly of the homemade dreadlocks and unwashed Joy Division shirt—did have good taste, after all. She had picked a simple black dress with a boat neckline, worthy of Audrey Hepburn in her prime. And because I was the most perverted girl alive, my first thought was that I wanted Mr. McFadden to see me in it. Badly.

"Do you like it?" Mary asked, even though I clearly did. "It's a little too big but that's on purpose. We'll go back to the shop to have it fitted."

"Yes," I said, fingering the fabric. "It's perfect."

"Are you ready to see mine?" Mary's eyes were bug-wide, like a little kid after too many Skittles.

She surprised me by stripping down to her underwear, then turning away to step into her dress. It's not that I was such a prude I couldn't handle watching her change. The problem was that Mary, naked, looked a lot like me naked—down to her slightly heavy calves and freckled shoulders. Did she know?

And if she knew what I looked like naked, what else did she know?

Mary's gown was sleeveless with a V-neckline that met in the center of her chest. The dress narrowed at her waist, barely grazed her hips, and fell straight to the floor. She could have gotten married like that—with her top-knot falling apart, her makeup several hours old, and her feet bare. There was no way Darlene Cline would give the family fortune to the gardener. Mary was beautiful.

"It's perfect," I said again.

Mary grinned. She grabbed my hands. "It feels real now," she whispered. "I'm getting married."

My head ached. I opened my mouth. I meant to produce Nadine's package. I meant to claim I had opened it by mistake—that I hadn't read a word but had shoved it beneath my bed in a moment of guilt-stricken panic, just seconds ago.

Mary was blinking back tears. She grabbed my arms and forced me to do a celebratory dance. I moved jerkily, like a hungover puppet.

And then I laughed, because insanity is contagious. Or maybe hereditary.

"You're getting married," I echoed.

CHAPTER 23

BEFORE REHEARSAL ON MONDAY, I ENTERED THE BATH-room to find Liane and Tess sitting on the counter with their feet in the sinks. I had never caught them alone together and my stomach twisted, I guess at the idea of them forming some kind of alliance.

Trying to appear unfazed, I waved hello and locked myself inside a stall. Tess resumed telling a story.

"So as you know, my grade in history is less than perfect—"

"You can't be in the play if you're put on academic probation," interrupted Liane.

"Exactly. So Mr. McFadden somehow heard, and called me in to discuss. He said I'm invaluable to the *Streetcar* effort, and that he wants to help me however he can. He kept being like, 'I want to help you! Tell me how to help you!'"

"What are you talking about?" I asked, emerging from the stall.

Liane pulled her feet out of the sink so I could wash my hands. "Mr. McFadden might have hit on Tess," she said.

"Oh he definitely did," said Tess.

I looked at Liane. On the wall above her head, somebody had written *Cross my heart and hope to diet*. She reeked of cigarettes and cinnamon gum.

"That's ridiculous," I said.

"Why is that so ridiculous?" Liane crossed her arms. She and Tess blinked their freshly outlined eyes, actually expecting an answer.

"Because he's probably gay?" I suggested.

Tess shrugged. "Well, maybe he's bi. I'm pretty sure he was hitting on me."

"He would never do that!" I could feel my cheeks getting hot.

Liane cleared her throat. "He would never hit on a student?" She was playing with the metal hoop in her nostril. "Or he would never hit on Tess?"

I stared at her in disbelief, but her gaze was

impenetrable. At that moment, I did not feel remotely bad about stealing the boy she liked. I would have stolen him a hundred times.

"Mr. McFadden would never hit on any of us," I asserted slowly.

Liane kind of snorted and smirked at her shoes. Something had broken our silent truce and now, instead of ignoring me, she was just being mean. Liane was too good at being mean. Shaking my hands dry, I rushed out of the bathroom. In addition to being absurd and offensive, my friends had made me late for rehearsal.

Tess followed, calling my name. We were alone in a deserted hallway between the main corridor and the auditorium. Her voice sounded amplified.

"Are you okay?" Tess looked very earnest, cupping a hand over my shoulder. I wondered if we had been alone together since the beach trip. I tried to remember what I had liked about her when we were fifteen. I could only think of her *Grey Gardens* impression. She did a perfect Big Edie.

"I'm fine," I said.

"You know I don't *actually* think Mr. McFadden was hitting on me."

"Obviously."

"You'll always be his leading lady," she teased.

I didn't respond.

Tess half closed one eye, like she was looking at me under a microscope. Now that Tess identified as a fourth-wave feminist, she presumably had new theories about virginity and how to dispose of it. I wondered if she still cried about the way she had lost hers. I felt kind of ruthless toward her, right then.

"Is everything okay with you?" She used her best guidance counselor voice. "Because if there's anything you want to talk about, I'm always here."

My instinct was to flip her two middle fingers, but I refrained. I could already imagine the wounded face she would pull. Like it wasn't her, but some other girl who had advised a drunk, shirtless boy to enter my bedroom and have sex with me.

Just once, a long time ago.

As the week dragged on, an idea got stuck in my head and wouldn't leave. It started with a dream that I kissed him.

The situation was all weird, not really romantic at all. I was at a school assembly in honor of a kid who had died. Our principal, Mr. Gladstone, was relaying the tragedy into a microphone—something about pills and Internet bullies. For some reason I was sitting next to Mr.

McFadden—which would obviously never happen in real life—and I was crying. Maybe the dead kid was a friend of mine. Maybe it was Tim. I fell across my director's lap and cried into his knee, the same way I used to cry into my mother's knee. He was wearing his favorite pair of pin-striped slacks.

I rolled over and looked up at his chin, faintly stubbled. He looked down at me. My eyelashes were attractively matted—you can see this kind of thing in dreams—and suddenly we were kissing.

Forget about the kid who died. Forget that the entire school could see. The kiss was actually stupefying. I woke up feeling kind of desperate and raw, like it was a great tragedy to be alone in my bed. And also like if I moved my leg in any direction, something inside of me would erupt.

It was a Tuesday morning. I got dressed and ate the toast my mother made me, feeling fairly criminal. As I walked to school, everything looked dry and blanched: the pavement, the tree trunks, the blank billboard looming over Hawthorne Boulevard.

What I wanted to know was, why couldn't I kiss him? Of course there were a lot of things that couldn't happen—at least not until I graduated. And probably he didn't think about me the way I thought about him. But men usually wanted to kiss girls, didn't they? And if we kissed once with no audience and never breathed another word about it, nobody would have any proof.

So what started as a strangely colored dream turned into a full-blown obsession. All through math and science and history I sat with two fingers pressed against my lips. At lunch I let Charlie drape his arm around me, because that was what our boyfriend-girlfriend act required. But I wasn't really part of the scene in the cafeteria. I ignored the smell of boiled hot dogs, and Tim's performance of a rap he had written about the quadratic formula, and the way Tess angled her wallet so we could all see the condom she kept tucked behind her money. None of it really mattered anymore.

We could kiss once in his car.

We could kiss once backstage after everybody had left.

We could kiss once in that convenience store where we had met by chance at the end of the summer. Just once, and then I would give up. I would go back to being his favorite student, his leading lady, sustained by a single memory.

There was one night that week when I couldn't sleep. Probably because my obsession with Mr. McFadden's lips had seeped into my bloodstream like too much caffeine. So I crept downstairs and slid out the back door, thinking I might get to witness the year's first snowfall.

I smelled the smoke before I registered Mary leaning against the plum tree, wrapped in an old winter coat of our mother's. She smiled when she saw me.

"I thought you were in Lake Oswego." I joined her beneath the bare branches.

"I was, but for some reason I really wanted to be here instead. Now I can't remember why. I'm so restless. I can't wait to go home."

"Home?"

"California."

"Oh." I had kind of forgotten that Mary and Jeffrey had a house in Santa Cruz. She never talked about her life there.

"Do you want a cigarette?" She held out the pack, looking amused with herself, like someone offering salad to a dog. I accepted anyway. Props were always helpful.

"Man," said Mary, thrusting out her jaw and exhaling skyward. "I used to hate this house when I was a kid. I fantasized about trampling Mom's tulips and breaking the stained-glass window and throwing the crystal champagne flutes against the Spanish tile. Do you ever do that?"

"Do I ever throw the champagne flutes?"

"Or fantasize about it?"

"No." Lately I only fantasized about one thing, ever. "I think I'm going to kiss my director, though." I presented this as a natural train of thought.

Mary's jaw dropped. "Excuse me?"

"Just once." I shrugged. "On the lips." I wanted her to think it was a cool idea, like something she would have done in high school.

"You can't," she insisted.

"One time," I said.

"Nope. Rebecca, listen to me. Your director is an adult."

"He's your age."

"I'm an adult."

I shrugged. I knew that she was, but it was easier to believe some days than others. Looking into her eyes for as long as I could stand, I felt like I was begging her to shed her adulthood like a snakeskin.

"You can't kiss your director," she said slowly.

"One time?" Like the terms were negotiable.

"Rebecca," Mary admonished me. "It's not funny. He might have kids, or a wife—he at least has a job. Those are the things at stake when you're an adult. Don't you get that?"

He didn't have kids or a wife, did he? The question didn't seem to matter. I had absolutely no desire to sabotage Mr. McFadden's life; I just wanted to feel his lips on mine.

"Do you think I could get him to kiss me if I tried? Hypothetically?"

"*Hypothetically,* I think you could get a lot of people to kiss you. I don't know who your director is. I would advise you to stick with people who can kiss you legally."

"You do know him, actually."

Mary took a shallow puff on her cigarette. She frowned, like it was bad news already.

"He went to high school with you," I added.

She frowned even deeper. "*Who?*"

"Stephen McFadden."

"Oh."

I studied her face. For some reason, I badly wanted to know what she had thought of him back then. "Were you friends?"

"We were aware of each other," she said carefully. "I think we once went to a concert with a bunch of other kids."

"At the Meow Meow?"

Mary looked startled. "How do you know about the Meow Meow? I thought they shut that place down."

I ignored the question. "So you knew him."

Shaking her head, Mary claimed, "I hardly knew anybody, even when I thought I did. I was self-absorbed. But I guess that's normal." She looked at me pointedly. I wondered when my sister had changed so much.

"Don't kiss your teacher," said Mary, as if in summation. "Go to bed. Study hard." And then, like the lecture exhausted her, she flashed me a wan smile. "And don't smoke cigarettes with anyone but me."

I stomped into the house, not caring if she followed. But I didn't go to bed.

I stayed up for another hour, staring at Nadine's letter and flipping through the torn paperbacks. Each of the novels was about a secret relationship between two girls. I tried playing The Smiths CD on my computer, but after a lot of angry noises it spit out the disc, which was too badly scratched.

I knew it was complicated, loving a girl. Loving anyone was probably complicated. Mary had most likely broken up with Nadine for a lot of different reasons.

But nothing could explain her transformation—from the wild kind of person who would kiss her best friend in a cemetery, to the handbag-toting fiancée of the world's most boring man. My parents might have welcomed this new, country club version of their daughter, but I preferred Mary as remembered by Nadine.

That girl, I was pretty sure, did what she wanted.

CHAPTER 24

REHEARSALS HAD BEEN GOING SURPRISINGLY WELL. Charlie and I might not have been born to play our parts, but we were perfect for them now. Onstage he looked at me like I was a bug he could smash beneath the heel of his palm. Enduring that look made me practically hysterical, exactly as Blanche was supposed to be.

It's not that I was scared of Charlie, the way my character was scared of his, or the way I had been scared of that boy two summers ago. Charlie was human. I knew he wouldn't hurt me. Sometimes still he gave me that melted-candle feeling, by touching my arm when the script didn't call for it, or moistening his lips as I delivered my lines. But when things between us crept toward normal, he would remind me that he knew too much. With a look from Mr. McFadden to me and a disgusted roll of his eyes, he would assure me.

He knew.

On Friday, rehearsal was awful. First Mr. McFadden got mad at Liane for touching her hair too much. Then, halfway through the poker scene, Mr. McFadden cleared his throat.

"Charlie, it's true that Stanley might be prone to vain flexes of the biceps, but you are approaching *Popeye* levels of gratuity."

Charlie looked equal parts embarrassed and enraged. For a second I thought he was going to erupt, and backstage, my heart leaped into my throat. But after taking a deep breath and tensing his arms for good measure, Charlie continued with the scene.

Tim soon got in trouble for looking "as bewildered as a suburbanite on the subway." For Tess, Mr. McFadden recycled a favorite criticism: "You're supposed to be acting as Eunice, not acting as an actor acting as Eunice."

It was typical for us to have a bad rehearsal in the weeks leading up to opening night. But that didn't make it any less agonizing. I could feel everyone resenting me for escaping Mr. McFadden's wrath, as usual, but I guess my loyalty had shifted. At least, his approval meant more to me than the Essential Five's. Maybe it always had.

Charlie and I were rehearsing the first scene, in which Stanley interviews Blanche about her mysterious past, when Mr. McFadden cleared his throat. He said my name.

He was reclining in the second row, making a big deal of massaging his temples. "Miss Rivers," he groaned, "please stop acting like you know how the whole play ends! It's only scene one. Blanche DuBois still has her dignity—tell me, what happened to yours?"

My jaw dropped. From backstage came a collective gasp. Did he actually expect me to answer that?

Mr. McFadden was all exasperation, pulling at his hair and fidgeting in his seat. Charlie looked frantically from him to me, performing some kind of calculation in his head. Before I could endeavor to read Charlie's mind, our director gestured for us to get on with the scene.

My costar's eyes burned, furious. "Have a shot?" He delivered his line, offering me a bottle half full of apple juice.

I couldn't figure out why Charlie was so upset. Wasn't this what he had always wanted? For Mr. McFadden to embarrass the hell out of me?

"N-no," I stammered as Blanche. "I rarely touch it." I steadied myself and tried to look at Charlie like I was seeing him for the first time. Like I had just walked into my sister's messy, un-air-conditioned apartment in New Orleans and there he was—this narrow-eyed, snarling man she had married.

Like he could turn out to be anyone.

After rehearsal everyone wanted to go to the 24-Hour Hotcake and Steak House. Saying no was most likely a bad idea. I could feel the loss of the Essential Five's respect, draining as I claimed my parents were forcing me to come home. I couldn't tell if my costars believed me or not. Charlie stepped forward to give me a perfunctory peck on the lips—him being my boyfriend and all.

I remembered to grip his biceps, like I wanted him closer. When we pulled apart, Tim clapped his hands. "Very convincing."

Tess yawned. "Your love is an inspiration to us all."

Liane didn't look like she gave a shit, whether Charlie and I were acting or not. She looked simply and intensely bored.

"I have to go to my locker," I lied. "I left something in it."

I turned, feeling their eyes on my back and also determination warming my blood. I was actually going to do it.

After rehearsal Mr. McFadden always dashed to the teachers' lounge for a final cup of coffee before the janitor emptied the pots. I knew I could catch him if I waited in the staff parking lot.

A mixture of snow and rain had fallen throughout the day. Now a thin layer of ice covered the asphalt. I lifted my knees high and stepped hard, cracking the ice and kicking it aside. I leaned against Mr. McFadden's car, but stopped when I realized how that probably looked. With my arms spread wide, I walked along the concrete barrier, trying not to slip.

Mr. McFadden's laughter echoed across the empty lot. "You look like you're about seven years old."

Startled, I shoved my hands into my coat pockets. I hoped he wasn't going to ask about my dignity again, because I really had no idea.

"What's up?" he asked.

I shrugged.

"Are you worried about rehearsal? It's normal to have a bad one right before opening night."

"Can you—" My pulse raced. I felt my sweat turn cold. Nothing made me more nervous than being alone with him, and I hated myself for that. "Can you explain why that happens?" I asked, like a puzzled student.

"I think because we start to realize that what we have made is very different from what we set out to make. It's part of the creative process. Now we just have to accept that what we made might be even better than our original vision."

"Do you think that it is?" I barely knew what I was saying.

"I hope so." His breath looked like smoke. He seemed torn between saying something teacherly and something deeper, which was always the problem. None of the adults in my life could decide if they were actually adults.

My resolve surged. I placed a hand on my director's coat sleeve and leaned in close.

He tried to back away but slipped on the ice. We fell against his car, gripping each other. He regained balance and firmly, gently, distanced me. It all happened very fast.

"Slippery," concluded Mr. McFadden, generously blaming the whole thing on the ice. Embarrassment flooded my cheeks. I couldn't kiss him. I would never kiss him. He was old. He was my teacher. He was looking at his watch and still not offering me a ride home.

But I couldn't help wanting something from him. It still seemed to me like he was the one person who could turn a bad day into a good day.

"Is everything okay?" he asked, like I hadn't just tried to kiss him. "You seem distracted."

"Right now or all the time?"

Amused, he said, "I guess I meant today."

"Do you remember a girl named Nadine?" I asked.

He looked confused. "No? Was she a student?"

"She went to your high school."

He twisted his neck until it made a popping sound. "Oh, that Nadine. Sure. She and your sister were joined at the hip."

"They were?"

"They were best friends, I mean."

"Were they a couple, though?"

A startled noise escaped his throat. "I don't think so? But I was a year older than your sister. I graduated first, so I wouldn't necessarily know. Aren't girls your age often inseparable from their best friends?"

"I don't have a best friend," I said.

He squinted at me. "You must be fiercely independent." For a moment, he balanced my entire world on the tip of his tongue. "Most artists are."

I stared down at my shoes. "So you don't remember if they were dating?" I asked.

"I have no idea," he claimed. "Isn't your sister getting married to a tennis star?"

"Golf."

"So why the sudden interest in her past?"

Now I stared at him. He seemed to have missed the part where I suspected my sister of being gay. But I didn't know how to be any clearer, so I just said, "The golfer is pretty boring." Like boredom was the problem.

"True love often is." Mr. McFadden sighed and unlocked the door to his car. He looked tired. I felt utterly incapable of walking away.

"Look," he said. "I recently learned that I'm not allowed to drive students home without notifying the office and obtaining permission from the student's parents. They implemented the rule just this year, so I'm a one-time offender. But I'm probably not supposed to leave students in dark, icy parking lots after hours either. So do you want to break the rules for now and confess in the morning?"

He looked at me, his eyes glazed with indifference. My head moved slowly from side to side.

"Okay." He shrugged. "But don't walk home alone. Promise me you'll call somebody?"

He gave me a half smile as he climbed into his car, like I was something small and lamentable—a missing pet, or a dead bird on the sidewalk.

Just because I was completely in love with Mr. McFadden didn't mean he could tell me what to do. Not in real life, anyway. I walked home alone, even though it was dark and the streets were frozen.

My parents weren't expecting me, but fortunately

there was enough chicken and salad and Moroccan couscous to go around. Apparently they ate all the food groups whether I came home or not. Probably they had retired too early.

My mother was so thrilled by my homecoming that she set the table with cloth napkins and crystal water glasses, like it was someone's birthday. Dad tucked his napkin into his shirt and sawed into his chicken breast while Mom asked me routine questions about the play and school. My answers weren't very satisfying and soon we were all just listening to each other chew.

"Tell me about Charlie!" chirped Mom in desperation. "What's he up to?"

I blinked. "I have no idea." I spoke through a mouthful of couscous.

Setting down her fork, Mom glared at me. There was no surer way to offend her than by insinuating that Charlie and I were not the greatest love story ever told. Before she could put words to her disbelief, the front door banged open and closed. Dad looked frantically from Mom to me before his eyes focused on Mary, now looming above the table. She wore a Burberry trench coat tied at the waist. She smelled like outside.

Mom pushed back her chair. "I thought you were staying with the Clines all weekend! Let me get you a plate."

Mary's refusal was sharp as ice.

Dad squinted at his oldest daughter. "She looks upset," he observed.

"Did you and Jeffrey have a fight? Sit down, honey." Mom wore her "compassionate-receptive" face, which she had actually learned from a book on raising teenagers. I once found the book on her nightstand, the diagram on a dog-eared page: lift the eyebrows, flare the nostrils. Don't forget to smile.

"No." Mary's features were tense with restraint. She got directly to the point. "Did you maybe forget to give me a package about three weeks ago?"

I bit down on my tongue so hard I tasted blood.

Mom frowned. "When gifts arrive for you, I leave them in your room. You know that."

Mary focused on the ceiling. "Let me rephrase. Did you maybe *decline* to give me a *certain* package, about three weeks ago?"

Seeing Mom's confusion, Dad interjected. "What's this about, Mary? I'm not sure I like the tone in your voice."

"Nadine!" Mary erupted, fists balled at her sides. "Nadine Pemberley! She sent me a package and out of the hundreds of packages I've received, you expect me to believe that *hers* got lost in the mail? Are you serious?"

Now my father looked at my mother quizzically.

Mom took a long drink of water and wiped her lips on the back of her hand. "No package arrived from Nadine," she said calmly.

"What makes you think Nadine would send you something?" Dad crossed his arms authoritatively.

"Well, first of all, I invited her to the wedding."

Dad looked pained.

"And second of all, she called to ask if I got the package!"

A phantom alarm wailed in my head. I had no idea how to fix this.

"I'm not sure it's appropriate to invite that gir—that woman—to your wedding," Dad lectured.

My sister throttled an imaginary throat. I hid my face in my hands, pinkie fingers pressed against my eyelids.

"What your father means to point out," said Mom, "is that Nadine is associated with some of your toughest times, and weddings are meant to celebrate the best of times! Why invite anyone who doesn't know you and Jeffrey as a couple?"

Mary shrieked, "The Steudle-Trapps! The Feldmans! The Popinos!" She was listing the names of our parents' friends, all of whom were apparently invited to the wedding.

"You may have forgotten," interrupted Dad, "but the

Steudle-Trapps played a large role in raising you. Don't you remember first Thursdays?"

Mary turned to me, looking for an ally. I stared very hard at a ceramic bowl in the center of the table. It was the successor to an expensive piece of pottery I had broken as a child. Mom had sobbed like the bowl was her firstborn.

"On the first Thursday of every month we had dinner with the Steudle-Trapps and during dessert you and Juliana liked to stand up on the hearth and perform popular songs for our amusement. What was the one where they held out their hands like traffic guards?"

"Amy Grant," answered my mother.

"Nadine!" bellowed Mary. "Nadine Pemberley! We don't ever have to talk about it for as long as you live. Frankly, if she were an old boyfriend you hadn't liked, we all would have moved on a long time ago. So that's what we're doing. I don't care how you see it. I really don't. I just want my motherfucking mail."

My father squeezed his eyes shut, like the pairing of those two words had ruptured something inside his head.

"I have it." The confession escaped my lips.

Mary looked like she had been slapped. "Excuse me?"

"It's in my room. The letter and everything."

Dad frowned. "Letter? I thought we were talking about a wedding gift."

Mom's eyes were wide with absolute panic. Mary stepped closer to me. "Did you read it?" She seemed more shocked than mad.

I nodded.

"And what did it say?" demanded Mom.

Mary's anger swelled. "And you *kept* it from me?"

My eyes were leaking against my will. I could not locate the words to explain what had felt logical at the time. Nadine's letter had the power to ruin everything. No more gorgeous wedding dress, no more Jeffrey's mustache, no more Mary bursting into our house unannounced. I had kept the letter so I could keep my sister. Hadn't I?

"She was trying to hurt you!" I claimed.

Mary stared at me.

"I mean she wants—" I glanced at my trembling parents, and then I let the words spill anyway. "She wants you back!"

Mary lifted her eyebrows, intrigued in spite of herself. "That's impossible," she said, before racing out of the room and up the stairs, crashing like a thunderstorm.

I followed Mary and was, of course, trailed by our mother. In my room I sank to my knees and unearthed the box from beneath my bed. By now it was half crushed.

"Thank you," said Mary.

"What's in there?" demanded Mom.

Mary lifted the cardboard flaps and pawed through the contents. "Just stuff," she said.

"What stuff?"

Pressing her lips into a coy expression, Mary clutched the box to her chest and sashayed out of the room. We followed.

"Rebecca, honey." In Mary's doorway, Mom put a hand on my shoulder. "Did you share that letter with anybody?"

Sinking upon her old bed, Mary rolled her eyes. "Yeah, Mom, she typed it up and sent a copy to the Steudle-Trapps."

Mom looked horror-stricken. Temporarily, Mary and I were on the same team, just willing our mother to leave. No matter how much she wanted to play a part in the drama, it was, for the first time ever, between sisters. Finally Mom got the point. Turning on her heel, she stomped back downstairs.

Feeling light-headed and desperate, I watched Mary shrug off her trench coat and pull the box into her lap. I lingered in the doorway while she read the letter straight through. A smile tugged at her lips, gradually becoming a grin.

"I'm sorry," I said, the moment she finished. I repeated myself like a cuckoo clock. "I'm sorry, I'm sorry, I'm sorry."

"Look." Mary let her head fall back against the wall,

laughing feebly. "I'm not ashamed of this, if that's what you were thinking."

"I wasn't—"

Mary cut me off. "You should never have read it. No matter how you justified hiding it, the package was for me. Not for you. For me."

Indignant and ashamed, I started to scowl.

"I assume you're not stupid," continued Mary. "You have a slightly more contemporary understanding of the world than our archaic parents? You and your—" She gestured haphazardly. "Your theater minions. Your thirst for tequila. You drew conclusions about Nadine and me years ago, correct?"

The truth was that my parents had withheld the necessary information. I had never known Nadine had anything to do with Mary running away. But how could I tell my sister that our parents had stopped saying her name? That I had stopped caring?

Simply ashamed, I lied and said yes.

"Good. But just so you know, this letter isn't the whole story. It probably seems that way to you, but trust me. You don't know what happened."

I didn't necessarily believe her, but I wasn't about to argue.

"I'm sorry," I said again. With my hand curled into a

fist, I rapped my knuckles against the door frame. I didn't want to leave. I wanted her to invite me into her room and tell me everything.

"She's not trying to hurt me." Mary closed her eyes. "And she definitely doesn't want me back."

"Then what does she want?" I asked.

Mary looked at the box, like it was a beloved, sleeping pet. "She wants to forgive me."

CHAPTER 25

THE ESSENTIAL FIVE SPENT A FEW PERFECT MINUTES together before everything went to hell.

Mr. McFadden was late for rehearsal on Monday. In all the months he had been our director, he had never once been late. "Where do you think he is?" asked Liane, her face scrunched with concern.

Charlie yawned. "Maybe his seventh cup of coffee propelled him into cardiac arrest."

"Maybe," proposed Tess, "he and Mr. Walker admitted their true, flamboyantly gay feelings for each other and are necking in the supply closet."

"Necking?" Liane looked skeptical.

"Necking can be nice sometimes." Tess sighed, like necking was a lost art we didn't appreciate.

Charlie startled us by collapsing across the stage. Prostrate, he announced, "I haven't slept in a week. Wake me if the bastard ever shows."

Tim lay down beside him. "O true apothecary!" He quoted Romeo's last words. "Thy drugs are quick!"

"Don't kiss me," preempted Charlie.

"You can kiss me." Tess settled with her head against Tim's chest. He kissed his own fingers and pressed them to her cheek. It occurred to me that nobody had mentioned the pact in a long time.

Nonessential cast members were slumped in auditorium chairs, unsure if they should climb the stage while the five of us lay there in a territorial arc. We must have looked like kids in the grass, staring at clouds.

With his apparent ability to read my mind, Charlie cried, "I see a donkey!"

Tim didn't miss a beat. "I see an ice-cream cone!"

In unison, the four of them delivered my infamous line: "And I see overcast skies with a forty percent chance of precipitation!" Their laughter sounded like something that could cure me, even if it came at my expense.

"I haven't seen that commercial in months," said Charlie.

"Me neither," realized Liane.

"Good," I said bitterly. "I hope it's gone forever." But I knew that, on the off chance I ever wanted to see it again, my mother had a copy stashed somewhere.

"Where is he?" Charlie actually sounded worried. "He's twenty minutes late."

I took a deep breath. "Maybe," I theorized, "he's not our real director. He's just a man acting as an actor acting as our director."

Everyone laughed again. I didn't dwell on the fact that something had to be seriously wrong for Mr. McFadden to miss rehearsal. Because before I had ever wanted his lips on mine, we had been the Essential Five. Before I had even wanted Charlie's lips on mine, we had been the Essential Five. And for the first time in forever, I thought that might be enough.

I felt Charlie's knuckles bump lightly against my hip. I lifted my chin to smile at him.

We were practically blinded by a flash of light. The auditorium doors flew open and clanged shut. Rising on my elbows, dazed, I watched the school secretary make her frantic way down the aisle.

Her announcement was shrill. "Boys and girls, rehearsals are officially canceled until further notice!"

A flat chorus of disbelief echoed across the auditorium. I wasn't sure if I was responsible for any part of the sound.

My heart clenched like a fist. I was rising to my feet, like it was my job to find him.

"Rebecca Rivers." The secretary's eyes met mine, briefly. But in that second I felt the ice-cold sting of her judgment. Like she knew every messed-up fantasy I had ever entertained. "Please report to the principal's office."

A cop was stationed beside Principal Gladstone—her arms crossed, her head hanging slightly to one side—but it was the sight of my parents on twin metal folding chairs that prompted fresh panic to balloon in my chest. My mother was sobbing and my father was staring at his feet.

"Where's Mary?" I asked. I couldn't make sense of my parents' presence, unless something had happened to Mary.

Principal Gladstone cleared his throat. "Who is Mary?" He looked past me to my parents.

"Our older daughter," Dad answered softly.

"Rebecca, please sit down. This has nothing to do with your sister."

The balloon lost a tiny bit of air. I perched on the edge of the only empty seat.

"I would like you to meet Detective Bunt." Gladstone nodded to the cop at his side. "She's going to ask you a few questions. It is very important that you answer one hundred percent honestly."

"Tell me what's happening." My voice came out forceful, like it does when I really, really need it to.

"You're not in trouble," lied Gladstone. "Detective Bunt, you may proceed."

The cop removed a pad of paper from her breast pocket. I wondered if she had a gun. I wondered if she had ever used it. Pen poised, she appraised me with narrow eyes. "I understand you're the star of the school play?"

I had expected her to speak soothingly, like a therapist. She spoke like a man.

"Yes," I whispered.

"And you, along with a number of other students, have been rehearsing under the direction of Stephen McFadden every day after school from three to six p.m.?"

I nodded.

"And how long have you known Stephen McFadden?"

"I don't know. I mean, he's the drama teacher, so." I looked to Principal Gladstone. He was concentrating on making a straight wire out of a paper clip.

The cop repeated herself. "How long have you—"

"I just mean, I've been going to this school since ninth grade, but you can't audition for the plays until—"

"Miss Rivers." The cop made no attempt to hide her

irritation. "Please answer the question. When did you first speak to Stephen McFadden?"

"Last September."

"So you have known him fourteen months?"

"Yes."

"And how many times has he driven you in his personal vehicle?"

I glanced at my parents. "Twice." My mother released a fresh sob.

"When?" The cop was scribbling into her notepad. She had to be scribbling so many more words than I was saying.

"The last day of school, last year. And on Halloween this year."

Her pen moved in the shape of a checkmark. "Why did your director drive you home?"

"Which time?" I stalled.

"Both."

"In June I stayed late to help him pack up old props. He was giving a lot of stuff to Goodwill. I carried a box to his car and then he drove me straight home."

Without lifting her pen, Bunt looked up at me. "Were you aware of the school rule prohibiting a teacher from driving students without pre-obtained permission?"

I shook my head.

"Why did he drive you home on October thirty-first?"

"There was a bad storm."

"Did he offer rides to the entire cast?"

It was a stupid question; there were too many of us. "No." I was trying hard not to cry. "Everyone else had left."

The cop raised one eyebrow—a muscular capability that, as an actress, I envied.

"I stayed late to talk about the play," I explained.

Principal Gladstone pinched the bridge of his nose. I listened to the scratching of Bunt's pen and my mother's rattled breaths. Finally, Bunt fired her next shot. "Where did Mr. McFadden take you after rehearsal on the thirty-first?"

"Home," I insisted.

"Did he take you to the 24-Hour Hotcake and Steak House?"

Laughter escaped my throat. "Of course not. He would never take me there."

After a long pause, Bunt asked her next question slowly, like English wasn't my strong suit. "So you're saying he drove you straight home?"

"Yes."

Detective Bunt's stare did not waver. People always

think kids will tell the truth if you stare at them hard enough. I matched her gaze, even as my hands shook.

"How many times have you made arrangements to see Mr. McFadden outside of school?"

"Never." Because even though I had seen him outside of school, it had never happened on purpose.

"Has he ever spoken to you or interacted with you in any way that made you uncomfortable?"

I shook my head.

"Has he ever touched you?"

Now my father threw his hands in the air. "This is ridiculous!" he cried. "How could he touch her without making her uncomfortable?"

The cop stared at my father like he was the biggest idiot. "Mr. Rivers, a student claims to have seen your daughter riding in Mr. McFadden's personal vehicle, dining with him at a popular restaurant on Powell Boulevard, and embracing him in the staff parking lot. Our source is a responsible student who does not appear to be motivated by anything other than concern for a peer."

Feeling faintly dizzy, I gripped the edge of the principal's desk.

"Who was it?" I demanded. Minutes ago, Charlie had

been lying beside me on the stage floor, looking almost like he didn't completely hate me. No part of me wanted to believe he could do something like this. "Because whoever said that stuff is lying. He drove me home, straight home, twice like I said. We never went out to eat. He would never suggest that in a million years, I swear to god."

The cop stared vacantly at the opposite wall, like she was playing back my words inside her head. "Well?" she asked. "What about the third claim? The student witnessed you with Mr. McFadden in the staff parking lot, last Friday."

"We had just finished a really bad rehearsal." I kept my eyes shut against the crowded office. It took all of my concentration to select the right words. "I—I hadn't done a very good job. I messed up my lines. I mean, I remembered them but I delivered them wrong. I just wanted to talk to him afterward."

"Why didn't you see him at his desk?"

"He wasn't at his desk." Could I reveal my knowledge of Mr. McFadden's routine? After rehearsal he went to the staff lounge for coffee, and then to his car. Would I keep track of these things if I wasn't in love with him? "I didn't know where he was," I lied, "but I knew I had a chance of meeting him in the parking lot."

"So you waited by his car?"

Nodding, I opened my eyes. Bunt dropped her chin and wrote frantically. "What did he say to you?"

"He said it was normal to have a bad rehearsal before opening night and that everything would be fine."

"What did you say to him?"

"I don't remember."

Of course I remembered asking Mr. McFadden about Nadine, but I knew I could not under any circumstances mention our unlikely history. That he had known my sister, that the three of us had once performed onstage together, was a total coincidence. But maybe it was also the thread that could unravel everything.

"Did he kiss you?"

"Of course not." I faked confidence. I did not explain how I had slipped on the ice, because it didn't make sense. You don't slip if you stand still.

"He didn't kiss you, or hug you?"

My father raised his voice for the second time. "Why would my daughter lie about this? The theater program at this school means everything to her."

And for the second time, the cop oozed condescension. "Mr. Rivers, in situations like these, students will often lie to protect their teachers. Especially when . . ." She nodded at me, like my love for my director was written all over my face.

Beads of sweat had formed on Principal Gladstone's temples. He cleared his throat. "You don't need to protect your teacher, Rebecca." Had he even known my name before this meeting? "Our priority is to protect you and your fellow students. This is a safe space."

Dad leaned forward to squeeze my shoulder and then quickly withdrew his hand. The cop was chewing her bottom lip, squinting at me like I was a television show on the verge of resolution. Mom whimpered.

"Nothing happened," I said.

The cop sighed, tucking her notepad back into her pocket, her pen behind her ear. "Do we have your permission to search Rebecca's cell phone?" She directed this question at my father.

I could feel Dad's eyes on my back. I could tell that, despite his display of loyalty, he wasn't sure what to believe. Wrangling my phone out of my hip pocket, I sent it skidding across the desk.

Bunt seized the phone with her left hand. She wore a gold wedding ring. For a second I was distracted, wondering what it was like to be married to her. If her husband forgot to bring home the milk, did she interrogate him at the dinner table?

"We will be searching the school e-mail accounts of

both parties," she said briskly. "If your daughter has a personal laptop, we would appreciate the chance to search that machine as well. The sooner we get to the bottom of this, the better for everyone involved."

The school had always encouraged us to use those e-mail accounts, insisting they were private.

Begrudgingly, my father promised to drop off my laptop in the morning. I didn't protest. Nothing on the hard drive revealed the fantasies in my head. My e-mail account would show the handful of e-mails Mr. McFadden had addressed to all the actors, plus a bunch of relatively pointless stuff from my friends.

Maybe the lack of messages would be enough to clear my name. How could we have had an affair without making plans?

Of course, we could have. I had imagined it a hundred times.

I was surprised to find stale tears clinging to my cheekbones. Wiping my face on my sleeve, I asked, "What about the play?"

I knew it was stupid, but I couldn't help myself.

Bunt looked at Principal Gladstone, who grimaced. "It's not happening," he admitted. "I'm sorry."

A Streetcar Named Desire starring Rebecca Rivers. I

had never worked harder on anything in my entire life.

"Why?" I asked. My eyes produced fresh tears, which should have been impossible.

"Even if we find zero evidence to back this student's claims," said Bunt, "it will take us at least a couple of weeks to be sure."

My father asked what would happen to Mr. McFadden in the meantime.

"Forced leave," said Bunt.

"Unpaid, of course," added Principal Gladstone, giving my father a good-guy nod.

Dad looked offended. "I'm on my daughter's side here," he asserted. Mom didn't say anything about being on my side. She had gone completely mute.

"Sir, with all due respect"—the cop stood and refastened a rubber band around her hair—"we're all on your daughter's side."

The house was freezing because my mother kept turning off the heat to combat her hot flashes. My father marched into the kitchen and lifted the dial on the thermostat. Wordlessly, Mom filled the electric teakettle with water. Neither of them acknowledged my sister, who was leaning against the counter, hunched over the seating chart for the wedding. My parents operated on autopilot, even when their teenage daughter was accused of sleeping with a teacher.

Because that's what they thought, right? If we had done it, he was a criminal. They would lock him up. I had to remind myself that I had only ever attacked his clothes in dreams. Still, I had been dreaming hard enough and often enough that somebody had noticed.

Oblivious, Mary piped up. "Do you think I can sit Aunt Karen with the Steudle-Trapps? There's no room for her to sit with the rest of the family."

Nobody answered.

"I didn't do it." My voice cracked. "Nothing happened, I swear. He's, like, a good guy."

Mary's spine straightened and her eyes went wide.

My mother mumbled something under her breath. She kept her shoulders squared, her hips pressed against the oven, away from me.

"What?" I asked.

She didn't answer.

"Mom. What did you say?"

"Rebecca." My father stopped me from moving past the butcher's block, from grabbing my mother and shaking her hard. Dad looked very old and tired and like he had not signed up for this. "Go to your room."

I guess it was shock that made me obey. I felt my

sister's eyes on my back as I left the kitchen. For once, it was my life to which she played the silent witness. Between the two of us, it had always been the other way around.

After a few minutes, Dad burst into my room and seized my laptop. I opened my mouth to protest—he couldn't give it to Detective Bunt until morning—but he stopped me with a look. Any reluctance to follow the rules would count as evidence against me. A point on the side of sleeps-with-her-teacher. Dad, I realized, still wasn't sure what to believe.

I lay flat across my bed and stared at the cracks in the ceiling. I had forgotten a lot of Detective Bunt's lines, but what I remembered I replayed in my head. I wanted some evidence that everything would be okay. All my life, the bad things had ultimately been okay.

The play being called off was a certain kind of okay. And I could learn to live with my mother refusing to speak to me. But Mr. McFadden might lose his job. He might be charged with a crime. He might go to prison.

Not okay.

My friends had watched the school secretary drag me offstage. Rehearsal was canceled, leaving an unplanned window in all their lives. Presumably they had stuck by each other. Presumably they were still together right now.

Maybe smoking cigarettes in Liane's tree house, wondering. Maybe dialing my number, over and over.

Maybe not.

I started falling asleep. Panic denied every comforting thought, except for one.

If the four of them stuck by me, I would be okay.

CHAPTER 26

PUSHING THROUGH THE HALLS AT SCHOOL THE NEXT morning, I hardly cared about the looks people were giving me. I knew I wasn't an attractive crier. The whole process always turned the whites of my eyes a really infectious-looking pink. But apart from finding my friends, nothing really mattered right then.

The four of them were huddled around Charlie's locker, which wasn't completely unusual. But their huddle seemed tighter than normal, all bodies gravitating toward Charlie, who was convincingly and despairingly slumped.

I froze. I knew, with nauseating clarity, that they had heard the story. They were not waiting for my defense.

I had wanted to trace the accusation to a jilted senior, never cast. Or to Hadley Clarke's boyfriend, who was always talking about nepotism. But those were weak theories. Who would tell such a lethal lie, just for having been denied participation in a high school play?

Standing still in the shifting crowd, I caught Tim's attention. His shoulders tensed; he looked anxiously from Charlie to me. The rest of them followed Tim's gaze to my face, most likely bloodless and horrified. Liane threw a protective arm across Charlie's back; her eyes bore into me and actually crumbled the strongest parts of me. It was the way you look at someone who has hurt the person you love most.

I stood still, waiting for Charlie to acknowledge me. Finally he lifted his chin and met my eyes. With obvious disgust, he just barely shook his head.

"You're a liar!" I screamed at him, like it was the worst possible thing he could be. "You made it up!" I lunged at him, slamming my fist into his shoulder in that helpless way.

So many surrounding conversations died as everyone turned to watch the scene. Maybe the rumor had spread fast enough that they already knew our roles: the girl who slept with her teacher, the wounded boyfriend. Or maybe they just saw the offstage drama, our two worlds finally bleeding together.

Charlie angled his head like he had been slapped,

showing me the ridge of his jaw and the pink apples of his cheeks. My costars tightened their circle. They actually believed him. He had presented the evidence to our friends as convincingly as he had to the school administration.

Farther down the hall, a teacher squinted in our direction. My outburst had disrupted the benign hum of the morning. The teacher's posture threatened detention, or the principal's office.

I knew I couldn't get into trouble, not now. Not until they proved Mr. McFadden innocent.

At first I retreated slowly, unwilling to turn my back on Charlie. Then I ran.

As it turned out, there was only one essential thespian at Bickford Park Alternative School—and it was Charlie Lamb, all along.

The whole school had always more or less agreed that Mr. McFadden was gay. Girls didn't talk about it that much, but I knew Charlie and Tim had endured a certain amount of locker room abuse over the issue. As if Mr. McFadden wasn't just teaching thespians to enunciate *through* their emotions and to "move across the stage without the stiffness of adolescent shame" but also to have sex with men.

Now, somehow, everyone forgot Mr. McFadden's status as the resident homosexual. Suddenly every girl in school had a story about Mr. McFadden hitting on her. In the hallway after first period I heard Zoe Waters say, "I mean, I could have been a victim!"

She hid her face in her hands. Melody Etherege patted Zoe on the back. "You're not alone, sweetie. Remember when my sister was in *Antigone* three years ago?"

Zoe nodded and blinked at the ceiling, like only gravity could stop her tears.

"Well, he once gave her a massage after rehearsal."

Zoe shook her head in speechless disbelief.

Others claimed to have seen us together—at an Italian restaurant on Twelfth Avenue, or riding the MAX train toward Clackamas—only they hadn't been sure at the time, because we had been kind of far away, but now they were definitely sure.

It would have been fascinating, the way everyone threw their own lies into the mix, if it hadn't made me sick.

An aid interrupted second period to summon Tim and Liane to Principal Gladstone's office. My costars refused to meet my gaze as they lifted their bags and marched dutifully past my desk. Liane was shaking, but with the determination of someone heading off to war.

Clearly they weren't planning to stick up for me. They

were going to overflow with evidence—how he had set me apart, and hardly ever criticized me, and given me the lead in every play. "We can't say anything for sure," Tim would add. "But it kind of makes sense."

Maybe, when it was her turn, Tess would tell Detective Bunt about the time Mr. McFadden called her backstage to talk about her grades—how he had repeated her name in lecherous desperation. "We need you, Tess. Tell me how to help you, Tess." And later in the bathroom, I had defended him. Of course I had.

For the duration of my morning classes, I hid backstage, curled into the corner where we normally piled our coats and backpacks. A long time ago, an adaptation of *The Great Gatsby* had involved dumping large amounts of sand everywhere. Grains of it still sparkled between cracks in the floor. I wondered what would happen to my Blanche DuBois costume.

The five of us always pretended like the costumes weren't a big deal. Like as long as they were true to our characters, we didn't care about looking awful. But of course, whatever Mr. McFadden picked, we had to wear in front of the entire school and all of our families, multiple times. Not to mention the yearbook always included a two-page photo spread of each production. Basically, when we said we didn't care about costumes, we were lying through our teeth.

Mr. McFadden had revealed my Blanche DuBois costume last week. It was hauntingly beautiful: a long white dress with an empire waist and tiny lace sleeves. A little too big in the chest, but Tess had promised her mom could take it in.

Now I knew it was a bad choice. He should have chosen something ugly.

In fifth period I was called back to the office. Principal Gladstone and Bunt sat in the exact same places—like they hadn't moved all night or day. I sank into the interrogation chair, where I imagined each of my friends had betrayed me already. In a voice that was half embarrassment, half apology, Gladstone explained that Bunt had a few more questions for me.

I didn't nod or do anything to show comprehension. Bunt was unfazed. "Would you describe yourself as Stephen McFadden's favorite student?"

I shook my head, willing my eyes to stay dry.

"You never felt like he singled you out in any way?"

"He's a tough director," I said. "He has really high expectations for us. Some kids think he should be, like—" I couldn't handle the way she was looking at me, like every

277

word I said proved either guilt or innocence. "—Nicer."

"But you always thought he was nice enough?"

I turned up my palms, blinking back tears. "Yes?"

"Can you think of a time he criticized you in front of the other students?"

"Yes." She waited. I closed my eyes, embarrassed. "The other day he told me that the way I was acting, it was like my character already knew how the play was going to end."

I opened my eyes. I could tell Bunt didn't know what to do with this information. Without any context, it didn't necessarily seem like criticism. The detective wouldn't know that my character's delusions defined her. Blanche couldn't appear to know the ending; she had to believe with all her heart that she had everything under control.

Bunt tapped her pen against her chin. "Where does Mr. McFadden live?" she asked casually.

"I don't know." I glared.

"Does Mr. McFadden have a long-term partner?"

I repeated myself.

She tested me, to see if I knew his exact age, or where he grew up. And then without warning, she switched strategies altogether. "Did he touch you the first time he drove you home?"

"No."

"Did he kiss you good-bye?"

I let my head shake back and forth and tried to block out the sound of her voice. The rapid-fire questions were meant to break me. She knew nothing, but the sharp edge of her voice implied the most personal interrogation. Each question mark cut into me, and all I heard was: *Did you do it on the backseat of his Toyota Corolla?*

And: *Have you done it with men before? With your boyfriend, Charlie Lamb? With those boys in the canoe at camp? How about the boy at Tess's beach house?*

This type of thing maybe didn't happen to other girls. Bunt was taking a deep breath, preparing for another round of questions.

"Who told you?" I demanded for the second time. "It was Charlie Lamb, right? Because Charlie's my boyfriend. At least, he *was* my boyfriend and he's extremely mad at me now. He made it up. If it seems like he's telling the truth, it's just because—"

The weather changed on Bunt's face. Her lips curled into something like a smile. It was a terrible sight.

"—he's a really good actor," I finished.

Principal Gladstone, who had been feigning invisibility, looked up with dazed surprise. Bunt's lips stretched triumphantly across her face. They were both staring at me like I had just confessed to the whole thing.

Bunt tucked her notepad inside the breast pocket of

her uniform, right behind her badge. "Thank you for your cooperation, Rebecca. That will be all."

"So what happens now?" I asked.

Nobody answered. Principal Gladstone inspected the pink stub of a pencil eraser.

"I mean, how long is it going to take?" I asked. "When can he come back to school?"

Pretending not to hear me, Bunt shook Principal Gladstone's hand and made her exit.

"Am I supposed to leave, or . . . ?" I looked at Gladstone desperately. I wanted the date on which this would all be over. I was starting to wonder if a person could die from panic.

"Not yet," he apologized. "I have someone else who wants to speak with you." He stood and slipped past the door frame, leaving me alone in his office. Feeling destructive, I briefly considered pulling open his desk drawers, or waking up his computer screen. Instead I just sat on my hands, obedient.

When Gladstone returned, he was trailed by a woman in a cable-knit sweater and plaid pants. She had a boring face and short gray hair parted down the middle. Her eyes were so blue they looked almost unfocused. Gladstone introduced her as Mrs. Meredith, a social worker from the City of Portland's youth services. Gladstone smiled and winked, like we were going to get along fabulously, and then he abandoned me altogether.

Calmly, the social worker perched on the edge of the desk. She splayed her fingers across her thighs. I stared at the leather band of her watch.

"Hello, Rebecca." She spoke like a recording. "How are you doing today?"

I hugged my knees tighter to my chest, shielding myself. I didn't want to be alone with this person.

"Do you feel like talking?" she asked. Her raised eyebrows were meant to look inviting but were actually condescending as hell.

"No."

"Okay," she said, like it made no difference to her. Like her job *wasn't* to reduce me to a mess of tears and confessions. "We don't have to talk this time. But I want you to look these over, and call me immediately if you feel like talking."

From her purse she produced a handful of pamphlets. She held them between us, and I forced her to keep her arm outstretched. When she started to tremble, I grabbed the pamphlets.

The one on top was entitled *Speaking out About Sexual Abuse*. It featured a girl sitting under a tree, staring intensely at an orange leaf. She looked kind of stoned.

The caption began, "Amy's stepfather was coming into her room every night . . ."

I read far enough to know that Amy and I had nothing in common. Mr. McFadden had never come close to hurting me. One night, weeks ago, he had given me a compliment I would remember forever. That was the worst of his damage.

"Shit," I whispered, thrusting the pamphlets back toward the social worker. When she refused to move, I let them fall to the floor between us.

"Rebecca," she protested evenly, "there is some very useful information in there."

"No." I slung my bag over my shoulder and looked into her weirdly blue eyes. I tried to appear much bigger and more consequential than I apparently was. "None of this is useful to me."

On the front steps, I bummed a cigarette from a kid known for his endless supply of Marlboro Reds. We had ridden the same bus in eighth grade. A seat near the back had borne the phrase REBECCA RIVERS GIVES GOOD HEAD for the entirety of the school year.

The kid stood with his friends and it was obvious, what they knew about me. His hand shook as he held out the pack. He tried to conceal his nervousness behind a crude tongue-popping noise.

"Here you go," he said.

I thanked him.

"Oh, it's my *pleasure*."

His minions erupted with hyena laughter.

My status as school slut had officially been renewed. I moved farther down the steps to smoke my cigarette. At the first inhale, my stomach wrung itself out, dishrag tight. There was nothing that could make this day a good one.

The Essential Four emerged from the building, Tim on Charlie's left and the girls on his right. Frankly, my ex-boyfriend didn't look brokenhearted. He didn't even look like he was having a particularly bad day.

They turned west on Hawthorne, pretending not to see me. An afternoon without rehearsal was uncharted territory for all of us. I wondered where they would go and what they would say about me once they got there.

Tears stung in my eyes as I remembered that morning at Charlie's house—the tequila in our blood, the power out. Charlie's hatred had emerged then, burning through all his usual charm. So had my loyalty to Mr. McFadden.

I had heard people say that if there's onstage chemistry

between two actors, nothing's happening offstage. It's when they're suddenly lacking sexual tension that you know actors have started sleeping together in real life.

Mr. McFadden and I were not costars. But something had definitely shifted during our last rehearsal. For the first time, he had found fault with my acting. Charlie must have caught on to something new between us— something suspiciously intimate when Mr. McFadden lamented my lost dignity.

When rehearsal had ended, Charlie had followed me to the staff parking lot. He had watched me aim for Mr. McFadden's lips, and rushed to the office to tell them everything he knew.

Everything he knew, and then some.

CHAPTER 27

TWO DAYS AFTER THE ACCUSATION, I WOKE TO FIND my father perched on the edge of my bed. I sat up and pulled the blankets to my chin. I could not remember ever waking up with Dad in my room.

He took a deep breath. "I need you to tell me whether there is any truth, any truth at all, to the claims this student made against your teacher."

From the street, I could hear Mrs. Almeida's sprinklers whirring. She watered her lawn every day that it didn't rain, like otherwise her stone cherubs would be parched.

I wondered if my mother had appointed my father to wrangle the truth from me. In two days she had said as many things to me: my name in exasperation when I left a wet towel on the floor, and later: "Have you heard from your sister?"

For the record, the answer was no. Mary had disappeared at the first sign of trouble, which wasn't exactly unusual.

"Did he ever take an inappropriate interest in you? Ever?" My father wasn't looking at me but at our reflections in the mirror.

I met his eyes in the glass. "No," I said so sternly, there was no way he could doubt me.

Dad's shoulders relaxed. Through the blankets he rested a hand on my shin. He told me the truth was all that mattered. The truth would make this whole thing go away.

The part of me that was young and terrified wanted to throw her arms around her dad. But the rest of me was just waiting for him to leave. I needed to be dressed in order to hug my father. I needed to have brushed my teeth, to be wearing a bra and eyeliner—basically to have put myself together, so he didn't mistake me for the little kid I used to be.

Patting my leg for good measure, he left the room. I wondered what would happen if I confirmed his worst fears. My parents had never talked to me about sex, not once. I knew that when Tess was twelve, her parents had sat her down for a lengthy lecture on condoms and consent and disease, concluding with awkward hugs and big bowls of ice cream. Like, *You did it, champ! You listened to your mother say "vagina," so enjoy some Rocky Road.*

Mom preferred "private parts." But even if she had bothered to tell me about sex back then, it would hardly make a difference now.

This was something of an unforeseeable situation.

When I got home from school—where rumors had swelled so far past the bounds of plausibility, we were apparently planning to elope in Canada—I found a neon sheet of paper on the kitchen counter. Beside it lay an envelope ripped straight down the middle. It wasn't like my mother to tear into the mail so recklessly.

The memo, from the office of Bickford Park Alternative School, was regarding the "disturbing allegations brought forth on Monday afternoon." It was supposed to assure everyone's parents that student safety was Bickford Park's top priority. "At this point in time, we have a very limited amount of evidence in support of the claims. But if a staff member is found guilty of breaching student-teacher boundaries, he will be swiftly terminated and our hiring policies reevaluated."

There were about six hundred students at Bickford Park, meaning that six hundred copies of this memo had been printed on fluorescent green paper—which seemed sloppy; didn't the occasion call for something more neutral?—and dropped in the mail. Six hundred sets of parents had read it and asked their kids for more information. And the kids, of course, would combine the only rumors they had ever heard about me and say it was probably true.

My mother, presumably, was upstairs dying of humiliation.

The memo also included a list of boundaries Bickford Park teachers were advised to maintain.

- Never compliment a student on his or her physical appearance.
- Never touch a student.
- Never meet with a student behind closed doors.
- Never be alone with a student.
- Never appear to have a favorite, or a "teacher's pet."
- Never give a student a ride home, except in emergency conditions.
- Never encourage a student to reveal personal information.
- Never appear interested in social relations between students.
- Never react to a student's emotion with equal emotion.

I thought probably Mr. McFadden had done all of those things. And I thought probably no teacher had ever avoided all of those things. Still clutching the memo, I wandered through the house until I came to the closed door of my father's office. I lifted my fist to knock, but stopped when I heard his voice.

"There's no evidence, Linda. The principal just admitted that the kid can't get the story straight. First it was that they had hotcakes together on Halloween. Now it's supposed to be last Friday. Rebecca came home for dinner last Friday! You cooked the Moroccan couscous from the box."

It seemed unlike Charlie to get his stories mixed up.

"This is such a mess," moaned my mother. Then, softly, "You could tell it came from the box?"

Dad ignored this last part. "If you ask me, Linda, this whole ordeal is nothing more than dramatics between teenagers. Somebody wants to teach our daughter a lesson, so they've gone and fabricated this whole implausible story, with no concern for the consequences! What we should be asking Rebecca is why somebody would want to punish her like this!"

As much as I did not want to answer that question, Dad's words filled me with hope. I had never heard him so passionate about anything—aside from a few pivotal golf moments. No evidence, drama between teenagers. Yes, please.

My mother's voice dropped an octave. "This is unreal," she said, like she hadn't even heard him. Dad was silent. I imagined him massaging her shoulders, his fingers smoothing the wrinkles from her lavender cardigan.

"Everyone is always going to remember this," Mom added.

The only safe way to contact Charlie was to take the land-line into my room. I figured there had to be something he wanted, something I could offer him in exchange for his confession. At this point, there wasn't much I wouldn't do.

I imagined Charlie's cell phone vibrating against his thigh. I knew he wouldn't recognize my home phone number on the screen.

A woman answered. She was all out of breath. Surprised, I hesitated before asking, "Is Charlie there?" I tried to sound like Liane.

The woman paused. "Who is this?" From her voice I could tell she was young for a mom. At least ten, maybe more like twenty years younger than mine.

"It's Rebecca," I whispered. I was developing this terrible habit of telling the truth.

Another pause. "No, honey." In the background, a microwave was beeping. "You can't speak to my son."

Beneath the hardness in her voice was something like sympathy, which made it even worse when she hung up.

CHAPTER 28

SCHOOL ON FRIDAY WAS MOSTLY A BLUR. EVERY TIME the bell rang and the halls filled with the usual frantic energy, it seemed impossible to me that everyone was just carrying on with their lives. It was like being in bed with the flu and watching TV characters run around and fall in love, when you can't even remember what it feels like to be healthy.

The day ended and I still had no information, no idea of what was going to happen to Mr. McFadden. My feet carried me to the office. The secretary's face hardened when she saw me, but I figured if they could ask me so many questions, I could ask some of my own.

"I need to see Principal Gladstone." I stood up straight, trying to appear indifferent to the secretary's irritation.

"He's very busy."

"Please."

"You need a referral. First make an appointment with your guidance counselor. When and if he decides it's necessary, you can see Principal Gladstone. He has an opening next week."

The resolve of a much braver person seeped into my voice. "You know why I need to see him!"

She squinted at me, clearly annoyed that I had shattered her shield of formality. "Do you have new information?"

"There is no *new* information because there is no *old* information!" I shouted. "This whole thing is a joke and I need—" The blood was rushing to my heart, and I paused to catch my breath. "I need to know when it's going to end."

Every muscle in her face went taut. It was really pathetic, I thought, that she would voluntarily work in a high school. She should get a life. When I was her age I wasn't coming anywhere near this place.

"Here's some advice," she hissed. Behind her, the copy machine released a groan. She swiveled in her chair to confirm our privacy. "Don't appear so concerned about your teacher. It looks really bad. If nothing happened between you two, you've only got yourself to worry about."

I brought my hands to my face. Anger rattled my skull.

Through the tips of my fingers I could feel my pulse, racing.

"Just go home," she said, taking a stab at kindness. "This will be over soon."

I could see how, from her perspective, if I had done nothing wrong I had nothing to fear. But she didn't know about the things I'd done that were maybe wrong, or a little wrong, or at least not prudent. She couldn't trace my lawless feelings back to the moment I first loved him—or to the moment I became the kind of girl who would fall in love with her teacher. This situation was a mess, but it wasn't complete chaos.

The secretary rolled her chair toward the copier, done with me. I tried not to scream. I tried to ground myself in a world where everything was ultimately okay and I was always safe.

But this was not that world.

I meant to go home, I swear. But when I left the office and stepped into the mostly empty hallway, I saw Charlie at his locker, clutching a basketball. Because of course, now that the play was canceled, might as well shoot some hoops.

With my spine straight and my shoulders squared, I went to him. Shielded by his locker door, he didn't see me until I was inches away. His eyes went wide and he half jumped, like he was actually scared of me. But Charlie Lamb gained composure quickly, running his fingers through his hair and twisting his mouth into a smirk.

"Rebecca Rivers. To what do I owe the pleasure?" He sneered at me, like I was Blanche DuBois, exposed as the whore of the Hotel Flamingo.

"Tell them you made it up." I stuck out my jaw. "Go to the office right now and admit it. This could ruin Mr. McFadden's life. What did he ever even do to you?"

Charlie sighed, like he was sick of this game. "I didn't tell them anything," he said. "It wasn't me."

"Yeah?" I challenged. "Then who was it?"

For a second he looked thoughtful, then shrugged. "Honestly, I have no idea. But if you want to tell everyone I'm the rat, go ahead. Works for me."

I shook my head frantically. "Nobody else could have made this up," I asserted. "You're the only person who knows how I—"

Charlie slammed his locker shut, grinning. The clang echoed in the empty hall. "Maybe nobody could have made it up," he said slowly. "But anybody could have seen you."

"There was nothing to see." My voice wavered.

He released a fake, adult-sounding chuckle. "Please."

He shook his head. "You think I can't tell when you're lying?"

My lips parted. A thousand comebacks dissolved on the tip of my tongue.

"Besides," he said, bouncing the ball hard against the floor, "we all saw the way he looked at you."

CHAPTER 29

ON SATURDAY MORNING MY MOTHER BROKE HER VOW OF silence to inform me that Mary was on her way over. She was taking me to get my dress fitted. My feelings regarding my sister were mixed at the moment, but at least I could hope for a distraction from drowning in panic. Mary was good for nothing if not talking about herself.

Before I went outside to wait, my mother forced a dumb hat over my head. The hat had a pompom, but it was freezing outside, so I didn't protest. It wasn't like I had anyone to attract. It would be better, I reasoned, to never attract anyone ever again.

Mary pulled into the driveway blasting The Smiths. She didn't really look over as I sank into the front seat. I knew she had her own reasons to hate me. Obviously, I should never have read Nadine's letter or hidden the package, but lately, I had kind of forgotten to feel guilty about it. The crime I had committed did not exactly measure up to the one I hadn't.

Mary lowered the volume on the song about the double-decker bus crash. "Hey." She sounded all too casual.

"Hey," I said warily.

"Nice hat."

I yanked it off. "Are you still mad at me?"

Mary turned onto Grand Street, where we immediately got stuck in traffic. "For what?" she asked.

I rolled my eyes. "For reading a letter from your ex-girlfriend."

"And then hiding it under your bed," Mary added.

"Yes."

Mary changed lanes abruptly, cutting off a cabdriver. "I'm not mad at you."

I stared hard at her profile. Mary was pretending to have no peripheral vision.

"You're not?"

"It was a terrible thing, what you did." A smile played at her lips. "But given that a number of authority figures think you slept with your teacher, I am going to give you a break. You have my permission to stop feeling shitty about it."

"Wow, thanks," I deadpanned.

"To be honest, it amuses me that you took her letter so seriously. When I was your age I took those kinds of things very seriously too."

"What kinds of things?"

"Love things."

"Love isn't serious?"

Mary put on an excessively coy expression. "Sometimes love is dead serious," she said. "But mostly it's a joke."

"That makes no sense," I said.

The bride-to-be slammed on her horn; a Range Rover was taking half a second too long to react to a green light. Then Mary's voice sank an octave. "I'm sorry I disappeared the other night," she said. "After you got home from your meeting with the cops, I could sense that Mom and Dad were going to lose it, and I didn't trust myself to react appropriately. But I should have stayed. I should have made sure you were okay."

I waited for the question. She was the only person who knew I had considered kissing Mr. McFadden to be an actual possibility. But Mary didn't ask me any questions.

Drops of rain died against the windshield. Mary uncapped a tube of lip gloss and stretched her neck toward the mirror. Weekend traffic was at a standstill.

"Aren't you going to ask me if I did it?" I wasn't as

nervous around my sister as I used to be. With my own scandal on record, I felt more like her equal.

"Nope," she said.

"Why not?" I was practically pouting.

Spotting a parking space on the next block, Mary veered in front of a competing car. "Because I know you didn't do it."

Expertly, she backed into the space.

In the dress shop, the seamstress referred to my sister as "the future Mrs. Cline," which made me feel kind of sad. It hadn't occurred to me that my sister and I wouldn't share a last name anymore. The mirror in the fitting room was edged with lightbulbs, just like the mirrors backstage. I let my ugly winter clothes fall into a damp heap on the carpet and I slipped the bridesmaid dress over my head. For the first time in forever, I liked the way I looked. I didn't know if the dress was more beautiful than my Blanche DuBois costume, but it felt somehow like it had been made for me.

When I emerged from the fitting room, the seamstress made me stand on a pedestal while she examined the dress from every angle, pinching and poking at the fabric. Mary stood with her arms crossed, nodding along with the seamstress's plans.

I allowed myself one good look into the three-way mirror. For a second, pleasure kept my stomach from gnawing at itself. Even my headache threatened to fade.

"She looks very beautiful," concluded the seamstress.

Back in my stale clothes, I stood beside my sister while she made the final payments on our dresses. The seamstress whispered the price and Mary slid our mother's MasterCard across the counter.

"Don't worry about it," said Mary, noticing my surprise. "Mom spent more updating the guest bedroom last year."

"How do you even know that?" Mary had not exactly been a frequent visitor last year.

"Because when I asked if the dresses were too expensive, Mom said, 'Don't worry about it, I spent more updating the guest bedroom last year.'"

Behind the counter, the seamstress pursed her lips in disapproval. She told Mary the dress would be ready in a week.

On the sidewalk, I remembered Bunt saying it would take two weeks to determine if there was any evidence against Mr. McFadden. One week had already passed. So far, I hadn't really believed in the possibility of evidence. Mr. McFadden had never sent me a suspicious e-mail; he had never called or texted me personally. But suddenly, it occurred to me to wonder: What if he had wanted me like I had wanted him? And what if there was evidence of that?

A collection of unsent letters.

Pictures of me from last year's shows.

His own dreams, transcribed in some kind of dream journal.

Mary was walking toward the car, saying, "So at my last fitting that woman tries to tell me I can't take the dress home, because Jeffrey will see it, which apparently is bad luck. And I wanted to laugh in her face. It's not the 1950s, and not only has Jeffrey *seen* it, but he's already torn it off of me multip—"

She realized I was not moving. "What's wrong?" she asked, backtracking. "Have I scandalized you? Did you think I was saving myself for my wedding night?"

I just stared at her, paralyzed by the possibility that he actually loved me back.

"Seriously, Rebecca." The rain was making spots on Mary's coat. People moved briskly all around us, unconcerned. "What's wrong?"

He could have written things down. He could have told other people about me. It would be the worst possible thing.

"You're scared?" she asked.

I managed to nod.

"You didn't do anything wrong. It will be okay, I promise."

I reminded myself to breathe. There would not be any evidence, because Mr. McFadden had not loved me. He was not that kind of guy. I would never fall for the kind of guy who lusts after teenagers.

I would never fall for the kind of guy who keeps a dream journal.

Mary was hugging me, pressing my face into her scarf, which smelled like cigarettes and vanilla.

"You have nothing to worry about," she added.

She wasn't exactly telling the truth, but it was such an appealing lie.

"Maybe we should talk about something else," said Mary as we merged into traffic. "I think it would be good for you."

"Okay." Taking advantage of the offer, I asked, "Do you love Jeffrey as much as you loved Nadine?"

Mary made a small sound, like I had shot a rubber band at her cheek. But I didn't take back the question. She clearly felt obligated to distract me from the present; we might as well discuss the past.

"It's complicated," she sighed. "I'll never love anyone

like I loved Nadine, but I do a better job loving Jeffrey. He brings out the best in me, whereas I treated Nadine like dirt."

I considered this.

"You have to give me some credit," she went on. "You don't really know him. I admit his family is kind of insufferable, but they have always been nice to me. Even though I'm sure I'm not who they imagined for their son." She arched her back over the steering wheel, tapping on the brakes as we approached the bridge. "Besides, look at our family."

Our family obviously wasn't perfect. But we were nicer to be around than the Clines, weren't we?

"He plays golf for a living," I said, like she might not have noticed.

She shrugged. "He's good at it. It pays. People applaud." She reached up to unravel her topknot. Her hair cascaded, wild and kinked.

"People applaud very, very quietly," I said.

Mary laughed until I was almost proud of myself. "So you're not gay?" I asked.

"When I was your age, I thought I was."

"Why?" What I meant was: How is it possible to be wrong about something like that?

"Because I was in love with my best friend, who was

decidedly not a boy. At first I thought I loved her without wanting to touch her. But as it turned out, touching her was good. Better than it had been with boys because, you know, I loved her. And suddenly we had this new way of getting to know each other. Almost like we had just met. It was perfect at first and I thought, if this is what it means to be gay . . . fine. I didn't care if I never liked a boy again."

"So you *used* to be gay?" I asked, incredulous.

"I used to be in love with Nadine," she said. "We broke up. The next time I fell in love it was with a man. It's only happened twice."

We were almost home, and the last thing I wanted was to return to our cold museum of a house. I struggled to think of a response. Finally, as we were turning up Elliott Avenue, I asked, "What about Nadine?"

"Nadine is gay. She would be the first to tell you that."

Mary stared laconically at the road, adjusting the steering wheel with the tips of her fingers. Then she slowed the car to a crawl. I looked at her hopefully.

"I'm going to see Nadine today," she said. "I was planning to drop you off and then head over there. But would you like to come with me?" My sister looked sincere, almost vulnerable. "I'm nervous," she added. "You would be doing me a favor."

I thought of the alternative: more private panic. More cold sweat. More of my mother's petulant silence.

"Yes, please," I answered.

Satisfied, Mary pulled an awkward U-turn. The most surprising part was my excitement, stemming from something so simple and strange: more time with my sister.

CHAPTER 30

WE CROSSED THE STEEL BRIDGE AND MERGED ONTO Highway 30 toward Sauvie Island, where Nadine lived alone in her grandmother's old farmhouse. Mary got slightly choked up on the subject of Nadine's grandmother, whom she kept calling "Grandma P." I didn't know how she could possibly cry over a relative that wasn't even ours.

But then Mary told me how bad things had gotten for Nadine after the prom. Her excessively religious parents—having heard about the slow dance to Mazzy Star, having pried the word *gay* from Nadine's lips— practically threw her out of the house. It was Grandma P who gave Nadine enough money to move to New York. Enough money, even, to bring Mary along.

Driving across the bridge to the island, Mary fell silent. Her nervousness was palpable. I couldn't imagine how it would feel to see a former best friend after so many years, let alone a former best-friend-turned-lover, turned partner-in-dramatic-exodus, turned roommate-in–New York City. I tried to imagine driving to Mr. McFadden's house, ten years from now.

Strangely, the fantasy was appealing, and I slipped into it. Maybe he would invite me over for coffee, just to chat about the industry. "I'm not surprised in the least," he would say in reference to my wildly successful career.

The road we were on was narrow, but empty, curving broadly around tree orchards and fields of grazing horses. The rain had stopped and pale sunlight bled through a crack in the clouds. Mary was chewing on her bottom lip, slowing down to read a street sign.

"It's been a while," she apologized, making a sharp right.

This road soon turned to gravel. We bumped up to a clapboard house with wooden shingles and green shutters, like something from a picture book.

Mary killed the engine but sat still, white-knuckling the steering wheel. "Do I look okay?" She turned to me, her face taut with anxiety but otherwise the same as always. I nodded. We got out of the car.

I don't know what I was expecting, but when Nadine threw open the front door, something about her face shocked me. She looked ghostly and dazed, but also extremely familiar. She had wide-set eyes and a long, fragile nose. I felt like I had seen her every day of my life.

"Hey," she said softly, trembling as she wrapped her thin arms around Mary's shoulders.

Mary was uncharacteristically silent.

"You brought Rebecca." Nadine smiled and hugged me too, making minimal contact. "Come inside. It's so cold."

We followed her through a living room of futons and knit blankets and into a kitchen. Nadine wore her hair in a braid so long it grazed the small of her back. She was about six feet tall and as skinny as possible. My sister wasn't exactly short, but next to Nadine she appeared compact and hearty, capable of weathering a storm.

Nadine offered us tea. Just to be polite, Mary pretended to consider it.

"I'm kidding." Nadine smiled slightly. "I know better than to offer you tea." She punched a button on the coffeemaker and urged us to sit at a circular wooden table.

"So," began Nadine. "Are you still painting?" She had a funny, detached way of talking—a little bit like a movie voice-over exposing the thoughts of a disturbed heroine.

"Yeah," said Mary bluntly. "I mean, not lately. Jeffrey and I have been staying with his parents in Lake Oswego. I'm dying to get home, but it's so much more convenient to plan the wedding locally."

I blinked at her. She sounded exactly like our mother.

"I have a great setup in Santa Cruz, a whole studio to myself. And I'm pretty well established within the art fair circuit."

Nadine just nodded.

Groaning, Mary collapsed upon her forearms. "Listen to me. *Art fair circuit*. I sound like—"

"No." Nadine put a hand on Mary's shoulder and quickly withdrew it. "That all sounds great. I'm just nervous. I don't know what to say."

Mary looked desperately toward the coffeemaker still dripping and hissing. "What about you?" she asked. "What are you doing?"

Nadine reached across the table to fiddle with a saltshaker. "I'm a manager at The Rectory Café." She nodded toward the window to indicate a restaurant nearby. "Not exactly ambitious."

"Still don't know what you want to be when you grow up?" asked Mary.

Nadine frowned.

Mary winced. "Sorry."

"No." Nadine shook her head earnestly. "Don't apologize."

It was getting hard to believe that these people had once shared an apartment, let alone a bed. The coffeemaker drew a final tortured breath and then fell silent. I jumped up from my chair, like I might make myself useful.

"Sit," commanded Nadine. She located three mismatched mugs and a carton of cream. The coffee at least gave us something to do with our hands.

"So," said Nadine, creeping toward new territory. "How's the mother-in-law?"

I thought it was weird of her to ask about Mrs. Cline, and not about Jeffrey.

"Not my number one fan," answered Mary.

"No?"

My sister shook her head. "She thinks I'm dramatic and self-involved."

"You are."

They met each other's eyes over their mugs. I think my jaw might have dropped; I couldn't believe Nadine had said that so frankly. But if anything, Mary seemed amused. Or relieved.

"God." Nadine shifted in her seat to stare at me. "You're so beautiful."

"I know!" said Mary, like I wasn't even there. "It's ridiculous."

"Your sister has always been jealous of your good looks," Nadine said to me. I couldn't tell if Nadine was good-looking or not. Speech caused her features to twist in unexpected ways.

Mary flipped her hand dismissively. "Not jealous," she said. "Just resigned."

"Are you still acting?" Nadine asked me.

My heart sank. It was the opposite of waking from a bad dream and letting the pleasant pieces of reality fall into place. "I'm taking a break," I said.

Nadine didn't question this. She just nodded, like it was perfectly natural to take a break from the only thing I had ever done.

"Speaking of breaks!" Mary spoke brightly, sounding again like our mother, but now with an edge. "Let's give ourselves one." She moved across the room and threw open cabinet doors at random. Nadine watched, faintly amused. With a masculine grunt Mary jumped for the top shelf and landed with a bottle of amber-colored liquor.

I half expected Nadine to protest. Her kitchen was very neat, and she seemed fairly reserved—not necessarily like she would approve of drinking in the present circumstances. She watched Mary splash nominal amounts of booze into two cups, and tensed a little when Mary reached for a third.

"Don't worry," preempted Mary. "My little sister is no tequila virgin. I once caught her sneaking a bottle from my parents' liquor cabinet at ten in the morning."

Without missing a beat, Nadine said, "I'm surprised there's anything left in that cabinet to steal."

I couldn't help relishing that moment. It was like Mary had drawn a line from the two of them in high school to me, present day, clutching my half shot of tequila in the farmhouse kitchen—where I apparently belonged.

Either the effect of the drinks was immediate, or the alcohol was just an excuse for Mary and Nadine to relax.

"Your fiancé's okay with this?" Nadine slumped down in her chair and eyed Mary mischievously.

"With what?" asked Mary, all innocence.

"Absconding to a remote island. Drinking with an estranged lover."

Mary snorted. "He knows where my loyalties lie."

"Good," said Nadine, like she meant something else.

My sister thrust her tongue against the inside of her cheek, struggling to phrase a question. "Are you . . . partnered?"

Nadine nodded.

"Well?"

"Disaster. I need to break up with her. I just can't seem to do it."

Mary considered this. "Maybe you should leave town."

Nadine's eyes rolled toward the ceiling. She failed to suppress a grin. "Fuck you," she whispered.

The rhythm of their talk reminded me a little of the Essential Five in our prime. But this was different, I realized. Beneath the surface of their conversation lay a thousand other conversations—which they were somehow having simultaneously, and without acknowledgment.

I could have listened to them indefinitely, the twin buzzes of caffeine and tequila bringing the kitchen into sharp focus. But Mary rose from her chair after about an hour. She claimed she had "kidnapped" me, and that she needed to get me home before our mother issued an Amber Alert. Nadine just nodded, recognizing this excuse for what it was.

My sister and I took our time zipping our coats and winding our scarves around our necks. The three of us gathered on the porch to say good-bye.

Their first embrace was insubstantial. Then Mary

yanked Nadine closer. She clung to Nadine's shoulder blades somewhat desperately, like she was trying to memorize the shape of her old friend. Nadine didn't exactly squirm, but there was an element of endurance in the way she stood. Like she recognized Mary's need without harboring the same need herself.

"I'm sorry," mumbled my sister.

"For what?" asked Nadine.

"For making out with Heidi Cho in the parking lot of the Meow Meow."

Nadine half gasped, half chuckled. When they pulled apart, they stared briefly into each other's eyes. I felt intrusive, like I was watching them kiss. For a second I thought they might. But Mary made the decision to turn on her heel, and the weight of their intimacy just kind of dissipated.

In the car, the stereo resumed playing The Smiths. Morrissey was singing about the sea wanting to take him and the knife wanting to cut him. I felt very tired. Mary started driving and five minutes later still hadn't said a word, which for some reason bothered me.

"That was intense," I said.

She half smiled at me. "It was, wasn't it?"

"Do you think she'll come to the wedding?" I asked.

"Nah." Mary checked her rearview mirror as we drove across the bridge, away from the island.

Her indifference pissed me off. I guess I was jealous; the level of closeness between Nadine and Mary wasn't something I had ever shared with anyone. Maybe for half a second with Liane, or with Mr. McFadden while the rain pounded against the roof of his car. Even then, the intimacy had been mostly in my head. Mary could have been loved by Nadine for the rest of her life.

We passed beneath a weather-worn billboard proclaiming SMOKING KILLS LIVES.

"I hate that billboard!" cried Mary. "I can't believe it's still there!"

I stared at her profile.

"You can't kill a life!" she shouted with conviction.

I started laughing.

"That's not how English works," she insisted.

My laughter yielded to a sob. I was feeling somewhat hysterical.

Now Mary stared at me. "What's the matter?" Then, remembering the shambles my life was in: "It's going to be fine, Rebecca. I swear you didn't do anything wrong."

"Do you actually believe that?"

"Of course." As if she had absolutely no memory of me standing in the backyard, going on and on about kissing my teacher.

Blinded by tears and still kind of laughing, I confessed, "I miss him."

"Yeah." Mary's eyes darted to the rearview mirror. "I can imagine."

CHAPTER 31

ON MONDAY MORNING OUR TEACHER BEGAN, "FOR today's activity, you will work in groups of two." Heads swiveled as everyone made eye contact with their preferred partner. I could have sworn I saw Tim shift in my direction. Then our teacher clarified, "*Which* I have taken the liberty of selecting."

I had probably imagined it anyway. Tim's loyalty to Charlie was evident.

An odd number of kids meant I was partnerless, which figured. Lately teachers were having a hard time acknowledging me. Probably they worried if they showed me even the slightest bit of attention, I would attempt to bed them.

I left the classroom to get a drink of water. I took my time walking to the farthest drinking fountain, near the office. I wasn't exactly feeling better, but my constant panic had sort of assumed its own shape. It felt almost separate from me, like a guest. Maybe it would leave someday and maybe it wouldn't.

After taking a long drink, I leaned against a row of lockers, letting the cold of the metal seep through my shirt. The play would have opened this week, and I still had to remind myself that it wasn't going to happen. I still had to stop myself from whispering lines under my breath. I had never cared so much about a role.

Now I realized I would never play Blanche DuBois—not even years from now, on a stage in New York City. Because in my mind, the play included entire scenes Tennessee Williams hadn't written: Stanley yanking on Blanche's sweater in a dark bedroom. Stanley and Blanche fuming in the foyer, attempting to extinguish the truth with a kiss.

Slowly, I made my way back to class. Rounding a corner, I practically crashed into Principal Gladstone.

"Rebecca!" Gladstone threw a hand to his chest, like the shock had affected his heart.

I looked up at him, unable to keep the desperation out of my eyes. The investigation had to be almost over. I would have explained how my entire life hinged on the verdict, if that wasn't exactly what he feared.

"What are you doing out here?" he asked. "Do you have a hall pass?"

"Uh." Was he really going to pretend like it mattered? "I was thirsty."

"Well, get back to class," he said briskly.

I almost reached out to stop him. I almost lost control, like I had with Detective Bunt, and later with the secretary, and most recently with Charlie. But Gladstone shot me an authoritative look over his shoulder, and suddenly I understood: He wasn't looking at me like I was the victim of an unspeakable crime.

He was looking at me like I was a student, late for class.

At home, my parents stood in the kitchen, identical cups of tea abandoned on the counter behind them. Dad handed me my cell phone. "Your laptop is upstairs," he said. "On your desk."

"It's over?" I asked, sliding the phone into my hip pocket. Dad was strangely calm, but my heart was going a million miles an hour.

"Your principal called this morning and asked us to come down to the school. There was no evidence."

I let myself sink into his arms. It's not that I was overjoyed or anything. I knew things were still far from normal. But I felt a massive wave of relief—like someday, maybe, everything would be okay.

"Your teacher resigned," said Dad.

"He did?" I tried to sound nonchalant and not at all devastated.

"The school will assure everyone the evidence was fabricated, but of course, that won't be enough for some people. Mr. McFadden didn't want to cause any more trouble." Dad patted my shoulder blades tentatively. My mother remained slumped against the dishwasher, looking vaguely upset.

"What's wrong?" I asked, feeling an absolute lack of patience for her.

She looked pointedly at a thin file folder on the counter. With a sharp intake of breath, my father said, "Linda. Honestly?"

I grabbed the folder. Quickly, Dad explained, "The school provided us with the only instance they found of your director crossing any student-teacher boundaries."

Inside the folder was a single page printed from my school e-mail account. But the e-mail wasn't from Mr. McFadden. It was from Charlie, dated September, back when things were good between us—at least as good as things ever were. The first paragraph referenced an awkward moment from rehearsal: Mr. McFadden asking Liane not to "gasp with such euphoria." When she had looked confused, he had said kind of tactlessly, "Try to avoid turning the scene into a Herbal Essences commercial."

Liane had blushed, but I hadn't even understood the joke. Charlie had refused to explain at the time, but he had gone home and sent me a link to a clip on YouTube. He had compared the lady's moans to a noise I made involuntarily the first time he slid his hand inside my pants.

For the record, my noise had been of surprise and encouragement. Not euphoria. But Charlie could interpret things however he liked. The e-mail really had nothing to do with Mr. McFadden. It was just a dumb note from my boyfriend, back when he still kind of liked me.

Which apparently both my parents had now read. My mother looked completely disturbed—like it didn't even matter that I hadn't slept with my director, because *this* had happened. I was mad. Humiliated, but mostly mad.

Crumpling the page and throwing it in the trash, I faced my mother. "I can't apologize for this," I said.

Her eyes focused passively on the floor.

"I never thought you would read it." I raised my voice. "I didn't even *write* it."

"That doesn't make me feel any better," she said primly.

This was the same woman who had bragged to her friends about my perfect relationship, and forced me into a perfect yellow dress, and practically begged me to be a better girlfriend—like Charlie's attention was worth so much.

"I didn't even have sex with him!" I shouted. "I've never even had sex with *anyone*!"

My father's cheeks were blazing. I felt sorry for him, but I couldn't stop. "Did you ever think about *not* reading my e-mail? Like when the school said, here's a private letter that this kid sent to your daughter before he ruined her fucking life—did you ever think, *No thanks, that's not exactly something I would like to read*?"

I was closer, physically closer, to my mother than I had been in days. I could feel her heat and smell her sage-scented deodorant. She tilted back her head to stop the flow of tears.

"I hate you!" I screamed so loud I expected the windows to rattle.

My father grabbed my arm. "You may not speak to your mother that way."

I screamed again. I channeled Mary Rivers, the night she ran away from home. Every muscle in my body went tense with defiance. Flaring my nostrils and widening my eyes, I was practically daring him to hit me.

"Apologize to your mother," he commanded. My anger did not infect him. He stood steady and placid—like he understood the worst was over.

"No," I whispered.

He released my arm. "Then go to your room."

What I really wanted was to build a nest of blankets and invest in a week's worth of Rolos and watch the trashiest stuff on television.

The list of things I *didn't* want was much longer. I didn't want to hear the inevitable knock on my bedroom door. I didn't want to do my homework. I didn't want to go to school in the morning, where everyone would be whispering. They would try to explain Mr. McFadden's resignation, insisting *something* must have happened—a kiss, a hug, a risky compliment—and I would be forced to remember that nothing had. Not even once.

Most of all, under no circumstances did I want to see Charlie Lamb ever again.

School would be out for winter break at the end of the week. Mr. McFadden was not coming back. Why should I? Did the general wisdom behind graduating and getting a diploma really apply after the entire school proved its capacity to turn against me?

Besides, there were other high schools in Portland, the

kind with thousands of kids and security guards in every hall and low academic standards and no funding for the arts. In a place like that, nobody would notice a new girl. They would think I had been there the whole time.

For now I climbed into bed, still wearing all my clothes, and fell asleep. It was a weird thing I did sometimes when I couldn't deal with the present circumstances. I would just fall asleep.

Downstairs, my parents were still fighting and the sound pervaded my dreams, but in a meaningless way, like flies buzzing. Sometime after dark, when we would normally be eating dinner, Dad knocked on my bedroom door. I knew it was him. Linda Rivers didn't knock.

I sat up in bed and croaked permission. Dad entered the room—not unbravely: The room smelled like a week's worth of panic—and perched on the edge of my desk. I felt an unlikely surge of affection for him as he crossed his arms and shifted his weight. His hair was whiter than ever. He hadn't abandoned me like he had Mary, all those years ago. In a strange, practically condescending way, I was proud of him.

"Sweetheart," he began. "There's something I have to tell you."

I had this idea that he would say "I'm gay," and it was

such an absurd idea that I giggled out loud. Clearly I needed more sleep.

He looked at me like I was insane. "Why are you laughing?"

I stopped.

"When Gladstone called to tell me the investigation was over, and I went down to the school to pick up your things, well, I was very frustrated." Dad so calmly pronounced his frustration, I had to suppress another smile. "They put you through a lot of hell, based on what? A blind accusation, that's what. So I wanted to make sure the kid would be punished. Suspension, even expulsion, seemed appropriate."

He paused to study my expression. I wondered when I should mention my decision to never go back to school.

"At first they insisted on keeping the kid's identity a secret. Well, I know what that means in this district: money. Incidentally, I have money too, and I am not above seeking revenge when one of my daughters is wronged."

I started to feel excited. If Charlie was the one to really suffer at the end of this, that would be okay with me. Except, I remembered, Charlie's family didn't have any money.

"When I threatened as much, they told me the student's name. Frankly, I was a little shocked, but her family has suggested that the two of you have personal issues—"

"Her?"

My breath caught in my throat. I saw Liane in her tree house, smiling with her lips wrapped around a cigarette. Personal issues. Jesus Christ.

"Tess Dunham," said my father.

My mind went completely blank.

"Who?"

"You remember Tess. Her family invited you to their beach house two summers ago."

"Remember her?" My heart revved. "I see her every day."

I shut my eyes and heard Tess sobbing on the other side of the locked door. Half asleep, I had imagined the face in the doorknob was hers. Two screws for eyes and a keyhole mouth.

"Rebecca, can you explain why Tess would do something like this?" Dad's voice was like an echo, originating a million miles away.

Not possible. It had to be Charlie.

"Tess's parents told the school that you two have *personal issues* best left *unstirred* by disciplinary action." Dad was having a hard time sounding sincere. I knew he probably longed to wring Tess's neck. He had never liked her, what with the I ♥ MY VAGINA T-shirt and all.

"So far, Tess has been asked to write a formal letter of apology to both you and your teacher." Dad seemed to think this was about as helpful as Tess leading us in a sing-along.

"A letter of apology?" I wondered how that would go.

"It's not enough," he asserted. "Rebecca, we are trying to understand why this happened. Of course, Mom and I are relieved to learn that nothing was going on—that you've always been just as safe at your school as we thought. But what Tess did—well, it was a very serious accusation, and it could have had enormous consequences. Your school is going to need as much information as possible."

Dad was straining the muscles around his eyes, so eager for me to supply the missing pieces of the puzzle. Like some small misunderstanding had prompted Tess to accuse me of having sex with our teacher. I pulled her hair, she stole my ice cream, I vandalized her locker, she put an embarrassing photo of me on the Internet. I spread a rumor. She spread a bigger one. At such a perfectly idiotic and teenage sequence of events, the adults could simply roll their eyes.

And the thing was, I understood. It made sense to me. I kept trying to block out that night at the beach because I wanted so badly to consider Tess on the terms we'd agreed to: costars always, friends when necessary. Just two members of the Essential Five.

But Tess didn't possess my talent for pretending.

"I guess she's always been jealous of me," I said. It was the tiniest fraction of the enormous truth. "She's auditioned for every play since sophomore year and I always get the lead." I forced a shrug. My shoulders seemed to weigh a ton.

Dad waited for more.

"I mean . . ." My voice wavered, I guess at the mere idea of exposing him to the truth. Not talking about sex was, like, our number one rule.

"Look," I said with a sigh. "A few weeks ago, Tess was joking around about Mr. McFadden hitting on her."

Dad looked alarmed.

"He totally didn't. She was just being dumb. Anyway, I defended him, because he's always been nice to me and he's, like, a *good* director."

My *good* came out strangely impassioned. Dad winced a little, like he was having trouble erasing whatever image had been haunting him.

"Anyway," I sped up, "Tess knew about Mr. McFadden driving me home a couple of times . . ." I paused for half a second. How *had* she known about him driving me home on Halloween? I had only told Charlie. "So maybe she just jumped to conclusions? I guess she was spying on me when she saw us in the parking lot. Then she just blew the whole thing way out of proportion."

My father was tempted to believe me, I could tell. His shoulders had visibly relaxed. "Gladstone did seem to think she was motivated by concern, at least on some level," he mused.

"How'd he get the truth out of her?" For weeks, I had been watching Charlie's every move, wondering how he could appear so guiltless. I hadn't been watching Tess at all.

"When Detective Bunt found nothing to suggest your director had crossed any lines, she asked Tess to repeat her story. Tess had already mixed up her claims once before. This time she became, well, rather emotional, and confessed she knew nothing beyond what you admitted yourself. The rides home, and your . . . chat with him in the parking lot."

Of course it wasn't Charlie. Charlie Lamb always stuck to his story.

"The school is going to issue a statement assuring everyone the story is false," said Dad. "You don't have to go back before winter break, but when you do return, you'll have nothing to worry about."

Sometimes it shocked me, how little my father understood about the world.

"I'm getting pretty tired," I hinted. "This has been fairly overwhelming."

Dad stood and moved slowly toward the door. I could tell he had something left to say.

"I'm afraid I'm going to have to ask you to forgive your mother."

Propping myself up on my elbows, I blinked at him.

"Perhaps not tonight. But as soon as you're able."

"Isn't she supposed to forgive me?" I asked.

He ran his fingers through his thin hair. "No," he said. "Because you didn't do anything wrong."

It wasn't true. I had done a hell of a lot of things wrong. But still, I thought I understood what he meant.

CHAPTER 32

IN THE MORNING I WENT DOWNSTAIRS WEARING MY blanket like a cape, intending to sneak a bowl of cereal up to my room. I found my mother staring intently at the little television she kept on the kitchen counter. It was playing a commercial for antibacterial wipes.

"What's going on?" I asked.

She shushed me.

The commercial was soon replaced by the intro to the local news—the same station whose meteorology services I had advertised as a child. A woman with spherical hair and a red blazer began, "Charges were never pressed against the Bickford Park teacher accused of *having an affair* with his sixteen-year-old student. Investigators found no evidence to support the claims made by an anonymous third party. The school has released a statement assuring parents that the stories *were* fabricated, and the teacher's record clean. However, Stephen McFadden *has* voluntarily resigned from his role as the performing arts director."

As she spoke, the screen showed footage of our curtain call for *The Seagull.* I was just a blurry figure receiving a white object from my director while the audience roared. Of course, the white object was my taxidermied puffin, but you couldn't really tell. Most likely somebody's parents had provided the station with the video. Only enthused mothers ever brought cameras to our performances.

The screen switched to a shot of a reporter standing outside my school. In the background, Mr. McFadden emerged from the building carrying a box. His cheeks were covered in stubble and he was wearing black jeans.

The reporter shoved a microphone in his face and asked, "Sir, any advice for your fellow teachers vulnerable to false accusations?"

He shook his head and pushed forward.

Aggressively, the reporter edged in front of him. "Do you think you will ever forgive the student who invented the evidence against you?"

I recognized the smirk on Mr. McFadden's lips. Behind his expression simmered something he would not hold back. "I don't think it's my forgiveness she's going to want."

The segment ended. I was still standing in the kitchen with my mother. I pulled the blanket tighter around my shoulders.

"Well," she said, "at least they didn't use your name."

Before I could change my mind I announced, "I want to switch schools."

At first her face hardened: a programmed Mom-response to a ludicrous request. Then she studied me, wrapped in my purple comforter. I was still about three inches shorter than she.

"We'll talk about it," she said quietly.

Forgetting all about my cereal, I shuffled back to bed.

On Thursday afternoon, Liane knocked on the front door. She was wearing her best skinny jeans and had drawn little wings in the corners of her eyelids. I hadn't left the house since Monday and looked about as frightening as you would expect. My hair was in two greasy braids and my faded *Oklahoma!* T-shirt had a hole in the armpit.

"Want to take a drive?" asked Liane, as cool as ever. Her mother's car was parked in our driveway.

What it really came down to—the reason I forgave her so damn quickly—was the look she had flashed me when she thought I was the enemy. With one arm thrown across Charlie's back, Liane had disowned me on nothing but blind faith.

Incidentally, I could really use that kind of loyalty.

Without breathing a word to my parents, I slipped into my sneakers and followed Liane to her mother's car. I hadn't even known she had her license. Memories of a yearlong drama entitled *Mary Loses Her Shit Over the Volkswagen Stick Shift* had so far dissuaded me from asking Dad for driving lessons.

Liane made a left on Hawthorne, heading toward downtown. Neither of us said anything. To find myself in anyone's company—let alone hers—was fairly shocking. Since Monday I had mostly been eating Rolos and watching *Gossip Girl* reruns. I was going to quit watching just as soon as Chuck and Blair admitted their true feelings for each other, or once I regained interest in living my life. Whichever came first.

Of course, the Hawthorne Bridge was up, meaning we had no choice but to join the line of cars on the ramp and wait for some freight ship to pass. Liane took a deep breath.

Her apology started small, with two cracked words. Then it cascaded.

"When we got to school that morning, Charlie was so pale. Like somebody had died. He told us you'd done something really, really bad."

Liane turned to me, but I stared straight ahead at the rows of brake lights. My hands were all cold and clammy.

"After he explained what people were saying, Tim said it probably wasn't true, that someone just had a score to settle with Mr. McFadden. Charlie *leveled* him with this look, like he knew it was true. He looked so upset."

Charlie, I knew, had a whole arsenal of alarming facial expressions.

"He was there early to retake his chem test, so he heard about the accusation first. I guess by the time we got to school, he had made up his mind."

"Made up his mind?" I wondered how much Liane understood about Charlie Lamb's mind.

"Like, that none of us were going to defend you."

I forced a laugh. "Nice boyfriend."

Once I had realized it was Tess and not Charlie who had invented the story, I had wondered why Charlie went along with it so readily. But then I considered his options. How could Charlie rush to my defense when he thought the rumors might actually be true? He couldn't risk the whole school knowing Charlie Lamb had been played.

Liane's eyes were wet, but otherwise she looked as placid as always. "I was pretty mad at you," she said.

I bristled.

"I guess I always knew you liked Charlie. But I just wanted to matter more than him. To you, I mean. I know that's stupid."

I let my head fall back against the seat. It wasn't stupid. But who had ever made smart choices with Charlie's lips pressed against hers? Neither one of us.

"Pretty much immediately, Charlie was just his usual self, going on about how we should, like, form a new thespian troupe. He told me I should have been Blanche all along, which isn't true. You were perfect as Blanche. And I loved playing Stella."

She looked at me for confirmation. I nodded.

"He was so nonchalant about the whole thing, I started to doubt he knew anything for sure. Once it got out that Tess made the whole thing up, I stopped speaking to her."

"Everyone knows?" Information caught fire fast at Bickford Park Alternative School.

"She broke down sobbing in Principal Gladstone's office. The office aides saw. Her parents had to come get her, then your parents showed up, so it was pretty obvious."

I didn't say anything. I was staring down at my bleach-stained sweatpants, wishing I had taken half a minute to put on normal clothes.

"It's such an insane thing to do, to make up a story like that. She ruined everything." Liane spoke evenly, a few tears still clinging to her cheekbones. "It was all so fake—the Essential Five, our supposed *reverence* for the stage. We didn't even know one another. Like, I had no idea Tess was so fucking insane." She laughed kind of desperately.

"Maybe Tess and Charlie should get together," I joked. "They have a lot in common."

Red lights flashed on and off as the line of cars inched forward. Liane reached up to adjust her rearview mirror.

"I have to tell you something." In one breath, before I could change my mind, I confessed, "Tess and I were friends before the Essential Five."

Liane stared at me, arm still raised.

"At the end of ninth grade," I added.

"Seriously?" Liane sounded intrigued, but also wary, as we merged into traffic on the bridge.

I was quiet for a second, searching for the right words. "So halfway through the summer, not last summer but the one before, her family invites me to Seaside for a week." My heart raced, like in the moments before an audition. "And Tess gets this idea that we should lose our virginities? Or, actually," I corrected myself, "just mine. Tess made me think she had lost hers years ago."

Liane rolled her eyes. "Typical."

"So in Seaside we meet these boys, and we go on the bumper cars, and they won't stop bumping me."

Now she kind of choked. "They won't stop bum—"

"Let me finish! So we decide to sneak out and meet the boys on the beach. Tess starts kissing the good-looking one, Jason. And I try to make out with the other one, Connor, but he's a really bad kisser. And I was getting pretty concerned that, like, kissing in general was just terrible."

"It's not."

"Oh, I know," I assured her, and promptly blushed, realizing we were citing the same source: one Charlie Lamb.

"So everyone's drinking Heineken," I continued.

"Blech."

"So I just leave. I go back to the house and get into bed."

"Good plan."

"But I wake up a little while later because Tess has sneaked both guys through her window, and she's sent Connor into my room."

Liane accelerated up Jefferson Street, past Portland State University.

"And he tries—" My voice wavered. It was a hard story to tell. "Like he tries to force me? I keep saying no, and he basically just keeps going." Now my narration was laced with nervous laughter—the kind that revealed exactly how unfunny I thought it all was.

Liane pulled up to a stop sign. "Oh god, Rebecca." We were the only car at the intersection, but she didn't move.

"So I kneed him in the balls."

She half gasped, half laughed.

"I told him to run. Which he did. He crawled out the window. But I guess Tess was, like, not as worldly as we always thought. Because a while later she was pounding on my door, crying. But I had locked it and I just . . . kept it locked."

Liane's expression was impossible to read. "Did she tell him no, like you did?"

"I'm not sure. Maybe something in between."

"What do you mean?"

"Well, like, sleeping with him was her big plan, right? But I heard them through the wall. She was, you know, upset."

"Something in between means no." Liane sounded certain. More certain than I had ever been.

As my stomach tied itself in knots, I struggled not to cry; I was so tired of people crying. But I guess I had thought that maybe Liane would dismiss this story as inconsequential—something that couldn't possibly relate to current events. Something that couldn't possibly be my fault.

"What was I supposed to do?" I asked, sounding desperate. I had never been able to figure it out.

Liane stared vacantly into the intersection.

"I mean, was I supposed to go in there and stop it?"

Again, she said nothing.

"Is that what you would have wanted? If you had been Tess?"

A car pulled up behind us and Liane was forced to step on the gas. We ascended the base of the West Hills, where the houses were all stately and symmetrical.

"I have no idea what she wanted, in the moment," said Liane, "but clearly she needed you afterward."

I pressed the heels of my palms against my eyes. Unlocking the bedroom door had been out of the question. I hadn't even considered it.

"It's not like you deserved what happened," Liane added.

Only I wasn't sure if she meant that night at the beach—Connor's smile growing against my neck—or what came afterward: the accusation, the investigation. Tess's hope that the lie would turn into the truth and everyone would pat her on the back.

"I've still never even had sex," I admitted.

"I know that."

"You do?"

She cringed. "Charlie kind of talked about you a lot."

"Like behind my back?" I shouldn't have been remotely surprised. "What else did he tell you?"

"Well, he told us about Mr. McFadden driving you home on Halloween."

Somehow everyone knew about Halloween without actually knowing the whole story: how we had waited out the storm, together much longer than we needed to be. The curtain had fallen on the rest of the world, for once.

"And he told us you had no friends at the Shooting Stars Arts Camp, or whatever."

I groaned. "Shining Stars Summer Camp for Performing Arts!"

Liane started giggling and the sound was such a massive relief. As we approached Vista Road, she searched for a parking space. "Which summer did you say it was?" she asked.

"Summer before tenth grade."

"We became the Essential Five in the fall."

"Yeah."

Liane backed the car into a space against the curb. Without a word of explanation, she threw open her door and stepped into the street. I followed her to the Vista Bridge.

It was windy up there. We steadied ourselves against the low stone railing. The city was spread out below us: bank towers, dorm towers, church steeples, trains sliding through the streets. The Willamette River hugged downtown and on the east side, our side, boulevards stretched toward the mountains.

"We should probably amend the pact" was my terrible attempt at a joke.

Leaning boldly over the railing, Liane played along. "I, Liane Gallagher of Bickford Park Alternative School, resolve to stop signing pointless pacts that prevent me or prevent my friends from kissing the people we actually want to kiss."

"Kind of wordy," I observed.

"Whatever. I don't want to be a lawyer." Liane leaned farther over the railing until I was compelled to hold on to her shoulders. "How come you never told me you knew Tess before?" she asked.

"How come you never told me you slept with Charlie?"

Liane took my question in stride. It wasn't like Charlie's talents had ever included secret-keeping. "Because I wanted to be friends with you." She stepped back from the railing. "Your turn."

I laughed. "My turn what?"

"Answer my question. Why didn't you tell me you knew Tess before?"

"Because I'm a liar?" I guessed.

"You are," she said, sounding faintly remorseful. "A good one, too."

We watched a MAX train slide through the street beneath us. Sparks danced on the wires.

"I wouldn't do that to you," I said abruptly, looking hard at Liane's profile—at the curls pressed against her temple, the metal hoop through her nostril. "I mean, if you ever . . ." I trailed off.

"Pounded on your door in the middle of the night?" she supplied.

Grateful, I nodded. "I would open it instantly. I know I should have for Tess. But if you ever . . . there's no question."

After a long pause Liane said, "Okay. Good."

I had this urge to tell her something permanent. Like that I had always liked her better than everyone else and always would. But something stopped me, and in another second I realized that a declaration of friendship would be too much like the pact. Liane clearly had nothing but disdain left for the pact.

And I hoped, privately, that she had something else left for me.

I also declined to mention I wasn't coming back to Bickford Park Alternative School. Liane probably suspected as much anyway, and I didn't want to ruin the moment. I could always ruin some other moment, later.

The second I pushed through the front door, Mom accosted me, wielding a spatula. It was pretty common to find her absently carrying utensils from one room to another.

"Where were you?" she demanded. I had only been gone for about an hour.

"I went for a drive with Liane," I explained.

"Not Charlie?"

"No."

"Good," she exhaled. "I don't think you should see that boy again."

"Charlie Lamb?"

"I don't like him." Cautiously, she lifted her gaze to meet mine. "He's not even very handsome."

I suppressed a smile. God, she was completely insane. "You don't think so?"

Mom shook her head. "He should have stood up for

you. What kind of boy doesn't defend his own girlfriend?" She looked shy, worried I wouldn't agree.

"I won't see him again." I kissed Mom on the cheek before pushing past her and heading upstairs.

The promise came easy. Even my mother—formerly Charlie's number one fan—could see how terrible he had been. Tess had only followed me to the staff parking lot, witnessed my pitiful attempt to kiss Mr. McFadden, rushed to the office with her story, and then let Charlie take the lead, like we always did.

With all eyes on him, Charlie had shrugged: *We knew she was a slut, didn't we?* He hadn't played the victim. He hadn't played the loyal boyfriend. Supporting roles were useless.

He had assumed the part of the prosecutor—the guy who knew to pull the right string, to unstitch all the lies and present the audience with the naked truth.

Of course, Charlie had guessed wrong, but it didn't really matter. With Mr. McFadden gone and the play canceled, there was only one performance left on the bill. *The Charlie Lamb Show*, starring Charlie Lamb!

Every goddamn night.

CHAPTER 33

Dear Rebecca,

I am writing this letter because I know my actions affected you negatively. I know this apology will never make up for the pain I caused you but I want you to know how sorry I am that I was wrong about the relationship between you and Mr. McFadden, which did not turn out to be inappropriate.

Principal Gladstone has given me the very fair punishment of 100 hours of unpaid service to Bickford Park Alternative School. I will be doing things such as taking inventory of custodial supplies and helping teachers get organized for the upcoming semester and possibly even assisting the cafeteria staff. I will also not be allowed to participate in any school plays ever again. This is very fair.

One thing I want you to understand is that I truly believed I was doing the right thing by telling the administration what I had seen in the parking lot. I had reason to think the relationship between you and Mr. McFadden was not an appropriate one. From personal experience, I know it can be hard to tell for yourself when things have gone too far.

And then, when I informed Principal Gladstone of what I knew to be true, he was very interested in learning more, which is why I said things of which I was not 100% sure.

I am very sorry and I hope you will one day forgive me. I have considered you a good friend for as long as I have known you and I'm not going to stop now.

Regretfully yours,
Tess Dunham

I kind of wanted to laugh. My fingers were poised to rip the letter—actually printed on Bickford Park stationery,

meaning Tess had collaborated with some guidance counselor, or with Principal Gladstone himself—into shreds.

But instead I decided to show it to Mary. I knew how
much my sister liked a good letter.

CHAPTER 34

HALFWAY THROUGH HER REHEARSAL DINNER, MARY pulled me into the bathroom.

"What are we doing?" I asked. She locked the door behind us.

"Bonding." She was a tiny bit tipsy.

"Cool," I said, leaning against the sink. "If you were a major American city, which city would you be?"

Mary blinked at me, and then giggled hysterically. "I just wanted to tell you"—she paused for air—"that Jeffrey and I aren't going home right away, as originally planned. Also, Cincinnati."

"Are you kidding?"

"Of course I'm kidding. Who would want to be Cincinnati?"

I rolled my eyes at my half-drunk sister. "I mean, why aren't you going home? You must be dying to get away from . . ." I waved my hand toward the bathroom door, behind which dined our entire family plus Jeffrey's.

Mary started on some excuse about contractors tearing up their kitchen in Santa Cruz—how Jeffrey was super-attached to a certain mosaic of countertop tiles. It seemed unlikely.

"I thought we could hang out," she confessed. "Before you start school again."

"Dad told you about *Gossip Girl,* didn't he?" I asked.

Mary's eyelashes fluttered with confusion. "What?"

"Never mind," I said. "I want to show you something." From my purse I extracted Tess's letter of apology. I passed it to Mary without comment.

Her lips twisted into a snarl as she read. "'This is very fair'?" she quoted. "Somebody should tear this girl a new one." My sister seemed more mad than amused, which surprised me.

"I don't know." I laughed.

Mary looked at me kind of quizzically. I considered telling her what had happened to Tess at the beach house. It felt cruel to omit that particular piece of information, but it also felt cruel to keep rehashing the whole story. Besides, I liked having my sister completely on my side.

Mary refolded the letter and a flush seeped into her cheeks. "I'm getting *married* tomorrow," she gushed like a little kid excited for Christmas. Then she raised one eyebrow. "Do you want to sneak out for a cigarette?"

The restaurant was in an old garage on North Alberta Street. Neither Linda Rivers nor Darlene Cline had approved the location until Mary convinced them it was "industrial-chic," which somehow won them over.

At the end of a narrow hallway we found a back exit and stepped into an alley lined with milk crates and beer kegs. Mary produced a pack of American Spirits from her shiny beaded clutch.

"I do remember him, by the way."

"Who?" I held the cigarette between my lips while she thumbed up a flame.

"Stephen McFadden. We weren't really friends, but we hung out once or twice. He was nice. And very cute. I can see why you fell for him."

I couldn't think of a single thing to say in response.

Harboring smoke in her lungs, Mary added, "Except I think he's gay."

I had trouble sleeping that night. I was extremely nervous, but not with the kind of panic that had plagued me during the investigation. More like the butterflies I got before performing onstage. Only in a certain way, what I was planning was the opposite of a play.

The wedding ceremony was just a ceremony. Mary looked beautiful in her dress. My father looked equal parts proud and embarrassed walking her down the aisle. She wept through her vows; Jeffrey seemed to take vague, masculine offense at having to repeat the judge's words verbatim. Afterward, everyone clapped and breathed a collective sigh of relief, repeating, "That was perfect. Just perfect."

Once the champagne had been poured, and Jeffrey's best man had revealed awkward and irrelevant details about Jeffrey's childhood, I walked to the microphone. My heart was going a million miles an hour. There was no stage, just a parquet dance floor, hardly elevated at all.

Approximately two hundred people had assembled to watch Mary Rivers become Mary Cline, but as I gave my toast, I looked only at my sister.

"I don't know Jeffrey that well," I began shakily. Nervousness surged at the precise moment it usually vanished. "Not yet, anyway. But I know my sister—at least as well as sisters can ever know each other."

Mary's eyes glistened—but to be fair, she had been crying all day.

"And I know that if she says she will love someone

forever, she will. She's loyal like that." I felt like an idiot. Why was I making her sound like a golden retriever? Why, after following scripts my entire life, did I think I would know exactly what to say?

Mary mouthed something at me. Just the three words that everyone mouths at weddings.

My eyes stung with tears.

"I love you too," I said quickly, resting the microphone in the stand with an amplified clunk. Everyone clapped, like my speech deserved a prize. I rejoined my parents at our table.

"That was sweet of you," observed my mother. "I wonder when they're going to serve the salads."

Apparently it didn't always matter exactly what you said.

CHAPTER 35

OVER WINTER BREAK, A SERIES OF TAXING DISCUSSIONS with my parents ended in the decision that I would not return to Bickford Park Alternative School. They agreed to let me transfer to a similar school across the river, with the same academic standards and student-teacher ratio. Starting in January, I would be a west-sider.

I was happy, if slightly terrified, that the new school's website advertised their performing arts program. I had decided that I wanted to get back onstage as soon as possible. Next year was my last year of high school, and I needed to add as many performances to my résumé as possible before applying to college. I had this idea that I would view my new costars as colleagues. Their friendship, if it even existed, would be secondary to my passion for the stage.

Of course, I had told myself that before.

On the last day of the year, I met Mary and Jeffrey at a Thai restaurant on Hawthorne Boulevard. Jeffrey didn't say a lot during dinner, but he seemed amused enough listening to Mary and me banter like sisters. On my way home, I stopped at the Lucky Stars Mart for Rolos.

And, of course, he couldn't have been *trying* to run into me. It wasn't like I went to the Lucky Stars Mart at every available moment. The chances were actually very slim that we would go at the same time.

But also, he obviously wasn't trying to avoid me either.

I recognized him from behind. He was standing at the counter paying for a gallon of wiper fluid. My heart raced—from excitement or fear, from love or attraction, or just because he was the only person on earth I was forbidden to see. And I was definitely seeing him.

I moved slowly toward the candy aisle, giving him plenty of time to turn and notice me. I was sure that he had, but when I got in line behind him, he just kept punching numbers into the debit machine.

Was this the extent of his plan? Was he going to ignore me? I felt suddenly like the entire course of my life depended on this moment. Like his inattention might actually break my heart in some permanent way. It didn't even make sense.

Turning on his heel, Mr. McFadden faced me. "I am moving to Tacoma," he announced, like we were in the middle of a conversation. "That's in Washington."

"I know where Tacoma is," I said.

"I am going to be"—he winced dramatically—"the choir director."

"I didn't know you could sing." I blushed. Why would I know whether he could or could not sing? Why would I know anything about him? He was my teacher.

"For the record . . ." He looked around nervously, like the old man behind the counter might actually care what we were saying.

There were questions I thought he might answer. Like what if I had been older and he had been younger? Or if I had been smarter and he had been straight? Or maybe, if he had to pick a student with whom to have a completely made-up affair, wouldn't he have picked me?

Of course, he didn't answer any of those. "You were the best Blanche DuBois I have ever seen," he finished.

And then he pushed through the doors. Cold air rushed in to replace him. For a second I stood frozen, imagining a scene ten years from now: Mr. McFadden in New York City, waiting in line beneath a marquee flashing—

"Can I help you?" The shopkeeper looked concerned. I still hadn't paid for the candy in my hand.

"Yeah." I smiled like a crazy person, and delivered Blanche DuBois's final line: "I've always depended on the kindness of strangers."

ACKNOWLEDGMENTS

I would like to thank my agent, Susan Ginsburg, for her encouragement and expertise, and for always knowing what to do; my wonderful editor, Namrata Tripathi, for lending her insight and sense of humor to this story; and Stacy Testa of Writers House, for working so tirelessly, and answering all my questions, all the time.

I am also grateful to my parents, Robert and Ellen Adrian, and to my parents-in-law, Lori Finsterwald and Peter Schillinger, for their love and support.